"Hear this word of truth. I have judged the heart. . .
and his soul stands as a witness for him."

"Hear this word of truth. I have judged the heart ...
and his soul stands as a witness for him."

God's
Assassin

A DIARY OF JUSTICE, MERCY, AND REDEMPTION

TO: JOAN
If you READ
MY Book, You
Might WANT TO
START ON THE
BOTTOM OF
PAGE 8.
SincEREly,
GEORGE

God's Assassin
© Copyright 2004 by G. S. Naas

Inquiries should be addressed to Golden Publishing Company, Inc., P.O. Box 150425, Lakewood, CO 80215

Printed in the United States of America
Library of Congress cataloging in progress

ISBN 0-9707142-2X

Dedicated to Sara and Joshua Bloom

In the dead of night the Eternal came to me in dreams telling me what to write down in this book. He showed me wondrous things that will be, and of places and kings and beings I never knew existed.

— G. S. Naas

Horus, warrior god of lower Egypt, from the tomb of
King Djet, 2980 B.C.

Dear Diary,

Today is February 19, 1999 and I performed another task in the 20th Century for the King of the Universe. The Lord of the Hosts does not ask—He touches my heart and I obey.

He commanded that I should seek out the murderer Leroy Dissel. The blood of five children cried out from the earth to the Lord thy God for justice. Great was the complaint of their innocent blood: Oh, Eternal, happy were we in our mothers' wombs and how joyous our parents were at our births. Did we offend thee, Oh God, in an ancient past to deserve such a fate? Is it not true that the taker of our lives was despised by you at the moment of his cursed conception? Yet you let him live! Does he not plot at this very moment to add to his terrible total before the sun reaches its apex!

Dust we were and dust we now are—and we are no more than fading memories in the hearts of those who loved us. Do you love us, Lord? If you do, then cover us with the blood of our murderer and keep shut to us the gates of oblivion so that we may some day live again.

And so He who created himself pronounced a death sentence to be bestowed on Leroy—a total death sentence, not just from the earth but from all reality forever—to a place of such loneliness that even a grain of sand would cry out for mercy.

The Eternal, however, leaves it up to my imagination as to how and when to carry it out.

Chapter 1

I live in a duplex that I rent from Mrs. Bloom, a 55-year-old widow. She has a seven-year-old granddaughter Sara. Sara asked me to have a tea party with her. She had received a plastic tea set for doing well in school. I watched her pour her cup of pretend tea and listened to her sweet voice say, "Here is some tea for you, and here is some for me." As I drank my cup of pretend tea, I came up with the idea of how I would allow Leroy to see me: I would become Death in the form of an innocent child—whatever I imagine, that I could become—so I physically became that. So I will become a boy child, for after all, LeRoy favored little boys.

Where better for a homicidal maniac to meet what he perceives to be an innocent seven-year-old little boy than a dusty country road on an unseasonably warm February afternoon. I was walking along humming, "It's Written in the Stars" from *Aida* (I love that song—it reminds me of my homeland) when Leroy pulled up next to me in his 1977 faded and rusted light green Datsun pickup truck. Until that moment I had never seen his fat ruddy-complexioned face, complete with a phony smile and two yellow, rotting front teeth. As I gazed into his hazel brown eyes, for a passing moment I thought that those eyes were asking for understanding of the wretched soul that he possessed for the 46 years of his life.

As I wandered over to the passenger side door of his truck I noticed a box of donuts open on the seat of the truck. He thought he was enticing me to get into the truck with him because he offered me a donut and a can of pop. He asked me what I was chuckling about as I sat down and closed the door. I

said, "Nothing really." However, I had really been thinking about how his gut would never finish digesting the donuts he had been feeding himself. I asked him what time it was. He said, "See the clock on the dashboard? It's 10:27." I decided then that his death sentence would be carried out at 10:56.

Should I crush his head? Break his neck? No, that's too easy. We had been driving about three-quarters of a mile when he pulled off the road behind some lilac bushes so that his truck could not be seen from the road. He turned off the engine and then reached over and put his hand on my left leg and started rubbing it. He said I had better be nice to him or he would hurt me.

Something amazing happened then. Leroy took his hand off my leg and looked straight ahead and said, "Get out of the truck, kid, and go home." I thought that Leroy must have had a change of heart—what a guy. I said to him, "I think I will stay, and I will kill you. What do you think of that?"

In astonishment he said, quickly regaining his composure, "You got it wrong kid—I'm going to kill you! I'll choke the life out of you. What do you think of that, you little bastard?" I decided to act afraid as I looked at the clock. The time was now 10:32.

I had a brilliant idea. Leroy had broken the hearts of four families, so what better way for him to leave this world but with a broken heart. God created humans in a way where their heart and organs are protected from external forces—not from internal ones. I dropped my can of pop on the floor of the truck and lunged at him with the speed of a cobra and the strength of a lion and shoved my hand into his mouth and down his throat. All the time he was gagging and kicking, he grabbed my arm with both hands in a vain attempt to get my hand out of his mouth. His eyes now had the same look of terror in them that he had seen in the eyes of his victims. I looked at those eyes and

said, "Hmmm. Must be something you ate."

I pulled my hand out of his mouth and sat there amused as he coughed his guts out. He gripped the steering wheel with both hands. He was sweating profusely and took his right hand and rubbed his watering eyes. I took hold of his hair with my left hand and slammed his head into the steering wheel so hard that the wheel broke, along with his nose. Blood poured from his broken nose. I pinned his arms behind him with my left arm and started slapping his face with my right hand. He blurted out from that bloody mouth of his, which was now minus those two rotting front teeth. They were now lying on the floor of the truck. Now, speaking with a lisp, he said, "What are you, man—some kind of super dwarf?"

I pushed his cheeks together with my hand and put my face up to his and said, "I'm Death, you asshole, and I'm going to kill you very slowly—the way you murdered those little children." He said, "I have tried to stop killing over and over—and I can't. I begged Jesus to help me."

I played with his long, straight hair with my fingers. I then looked into his red eyes and said, "So you asked Jesus for forgiveness, huh?" He mumbled, "Yes." "Well, Leroy, I don't work for him. Besides, Jesus didn't help your victims now did he, when you murdered them? Where was he when you carried out your vile acts? He claims he especially loves little children, and yet I suppose he watched while you brought each of them incredible pain and suffering. So don't hold your breath waiting for him to help you. I don't think he's going to show up. If he were here, though, I would still kill you, but maybe he would cry over your dead body. I promise you this, though—the pain will be excruciating as I coax out your timid and evil soul and send it on its way to oblivion."

I wiped away the tears welling up in his eyes and decided to let him have a false ray of hope. I rubbed my chin with my right

thumb as if I were thinking. I then said, "Wait a minute. I believe that you really are sorry. So I'm going to give you a chance to live. I may let you go, Leroy, if you can beat me in a game of tic-tac-toe." Leroy loved that idea, he played tic-tac-toe all the time—even by himself. It is the only thing the dumb ass was good at. But then he really only liked to play it against kids—sometimes before he'd murder them. While shaking all over, he said, meekly, "Thank you."

The lying prick actually thought he could bullshit me by acting repentant. "I believe you, Leroy—I don't think you will ever murder anyone again either." He told me there was some paper and a ball point pen in the glove compartment. I looked at that ugly, lying face of his and told him, "No, no, no, my friend. We are going to use your pen knife—you know, the one you have in your shirt pocket—and the truck's cigarette lighter." He said, nervously, "What are you going to do, man—cut the game into the upholstery?" This was great fun and exciting—the way a black widow spider must feel as it crosses its web to devour a fly that is stuck and cannot escape. I said, "Watch closely, Leroy." I ripped open his shirt with my right hand. I saw on his chest there was a tattoo. It was a skull with a rose in its mouth. My left hand still had his arms pinned behind him. I then took his penknife out of his pocket, and as he screamed in pain, I cut two vertical lines and then two horizontal lines in his chest. Blood ran down his chest and collected around his navel and soon filled it up. The overflow proceeded down to his thighs. He started yelling, "Oh, God; Oh God."

I pushed in the lighter to heat it up, and then I said, "I'll make the first move." I took the lighter and shoved it into his flesh where I thought the center square would be. He brought up his knees and slammed them into the steering column. He begged me to stop. I didn't stop. I said, "You didn't stop when you used the lighter on your last victim—little five-year-old

Mary Lee of the bright eyes, blonde hair and sweet smile. You heard her screaming in agony. You raped her and buried her under a pile of cow shit in a farmer's field where she lies this very day." I then told him it was his turn, but he did not want to take his turn. He was breathing ten times faster than normal.

I said, "I will make your move for you with your pen knife. It's nice and sharp. Of course, you knew that already—you used it to cut the throat of seven-year-old Felix—a precocious and kind little boy whose parents are now mental wrecks with faith in nothing, and each day for them is a living nightmare." I cut an "X" into the middle box to the left of my "O." His flesh was soft—not muscular at all. His screams were music to my ears. Leroy twitched back and forth as I sliced him. I ran my index finger over the "X" and looked at his blood on my finger. Then I ran my finger over his lips. I stared at him and said, "My turn."

I heated up the cigarette lighter again, and he begged me again to stop. I looked at him and rolled my eyes to and fro as if I were thinking about his plea. "I know what I could do, Leroy. Instead of burning another 'O' in your chest, I could shove the lighter up your ass the way you shoved a toilet plunger up the rectum of four-year-old Amber. Remember, you dragged her out of her front yard and took her to a landfill, after hours, of course—after all, you didn't want anyone to see you—but the Eternal was watching. You felt very powerful, didn't you, stud? Little Amber was at your mercy—her life or death was in your hands. You did think about it. Perhaps for just a moment the conscience of even a no-good son-of-a-bitch like you got the best of you. You got over it, though, didn't you? You always fell back on the line of reasoning that you were treated bad as a child yourself, so, shit, you just can't help yourself—when, in your own words, that 'feeling' comes over you. Low and behold! There was a solution for your problem only a foot away. Remember how Amber lay there looking at you with that inno-

cent face. She had no idea an evil son-of-bitch like you existed. When you were done, you had worked up quite a sweat. You have quite a sweat right now—hope you're not coming down with the flu. She wasn't dead, so you strangled her. Silly me! I let the lighter cool back down." I reheated it. I took the lighter and shoved it into the middle square at the bottom, burning some of the hair on his chest. I said, "Your turn, stud."

He said, "Please just kill me and get it over with." I said, "Surely you jest. We haven't completed the game yet." I cut another "X" into the upper left-hand corner. With a voice choking back laughter, I announced to Leroy that my next move would be to burn an "O" into the top middle box, which I did. I cut a line straight down the center boxes. I said, "Well glory be—I won! I won! Leroy, this is fantastic! I never win at games."

Leroy was bleeding quite a lot. I offered to piss on his chest to wash off some of the blood, but he didn't want me to. I said, "Why not? Remember the two kids, four-month-old Nita and three-year-old Manuel, that you suffocated with a pillow while they slept in their beds. You pissed on their little dead bodies, so I figured you must love piss, think of it as a golden shower."

Leroy somehow came up with the courage to look at me and said, "You are no better than me. Why do you have the right to murder me?" I pulled his head back by his hair and said, "I'll tell you why, Leroy. I don't murder—I kill in the name of Justice. I have a celestial double 07 rating—and what I am going to extract from you is justice. Watch the clock, Leroy; it is 10:55. When it changes to 10:56, you will die."

He said, "Please give me time to pray to God." I told him, "God doesn't listen to murdering assholes. Your name has already been erased from the night sky." The clock changed to 10:56. He struggled to get away, but to no avail. I ripped out his tongue with my right hand. I stared at him and proclaimed, "What is the matter, Leroy? Cat got your tongue?" Technically,

that could be conceded as being correct. He went into convulsions, so I decided to end his misery. I shoved my hand back into his mouth and dislodged a bridge he had on his lower teeth. The bridge went with my hand down his throat. The good news is that I don't think he will need to see a dentist ever again. His left foot kicked the fuse panel below and left of the steering wheel so hard that fuses flew all over the cab of the truck. Warm vomit came up from his stomach like a drain slowly overflowing and coated my hand as my hand ripped through his flesh. I pushed his lungs apart and took hold of his beating heart. I let his heart, which was beginning to flutter, push back and forth between my thumb and index finger for a few seconds, and then I crushed his heart. Leroy quit kicking.

His soul had taken its leave from his body and was now in the presence of the Eternal. At first Leroy's soul will think he has been forgiven by the Eternal because the Eternal and Leroy's victims will be no more than one foot away from him. With each passing minute the distance from the Eternal and Leroy will double. Leroy will cry out for mercy, but the Eternal will turn his back on him and the holy light that surrounds the Eternal and his glorious paradise will begin to grow ever dimmer as the distance grows between Leroy and the Eternal. Soon the light to Leroy will appear as only a pinpoint of light—as a distant star to the naked eye. Then the light will disappear altogether and Leroy will be alone forever in the total darkness of space. This is the ultimate hell. All was silent except for someone throwing up gravel as they drove down the road 30 feet from us.

I extracted my hand from his mouth and then I sat in the truck for a while, Dear Diary, looking at his corpse. I was thinking what that asshole had done. I reached for the door handle and realized my right hand was still covered with blood and vomit. I wiped my hand off on the seat of the truck and then used Leroy's shirt to clean between my fingers. He had a bottle

of water on the floor; I used it to finish washing off the last of Leroy. I then ran my hand through my hair and thought what a pleasure it was killing Leroy. I love being Justice and Death.

I got out of the truck and started walking home—only to turn around and go back to the truck. I had remembered that Leroy took pictures of all of his victims with an instant camera. He would then send the pictures to the bereaving parents. He considered it a little joke. He always had the camera in the truck. I had left him leaning with his head toward the back of the seat, and his mouth was open and his eyes were staring at the roof of the truck. I carefully undid his belt and pulled his pants down; I then pushed his right hand into his shorts. It made him look like he was playing with himself. What a great pose. I really should have gotten the Pulitzer Prize for this picture. Maybe his mother can collect the prize, because I'll send her the picture, with the caption: "Woman, behold thy son." I then put the camera in his other hand. I looked over at the Rocky Mountains. There were dark clouds brewing. Maybe the warm weather was over for a while. Hopefully, the police will find Leroy's corpse before the snow flies. I went home. It was a good day. Actually, in the last 26,000 years I have had thousands of good days.

Chapter II

When I got back to my duplex I got to thinking about my life and where I came from. I have been having a foreboding feeling lately about the coming Millennium. So, Dear Diary, I have decided to put it down in words. I was born in the small village of Critus on the banks of what would become the Omo River in the great Rift Valley of Ethiopia. I came from my mother Lillith's

womb when the dog star was in the embrace of the southern cross and the draconian king ruled the night sky. The month and year in which I was born did not exist then, but the lunar god knows the time of my birth. Thoth, the god who records the souls of humans, won some of the light from the Goddess of the Moon and used it to add five days to the year. Years before that were only 360 days long, thus my birth did not come in the previous year or the next.

My mother loved me very much. She called me her little prince from the North. My mother was beautiful. She had long red hair and emerald eyes. When I was very young I would stand up and lean back in a reed chair, and my mother would sit down in the chair and I would lean over and hug her neck and talk with her. From an early age she would tell me of the wondrous things she would do by the light of the full moon. She would visit humans in their dreams. She would bring them pleasure or terror, depending on her mood.

My father was mortal—not immortal like my mother. My mother loved him. My father sat on his lazy ass while my mother and I worked in the fields harvesting wild wheat and barley. Mother would bake flat bread to trade to the humans. No matter how hard Mother and I worked it was never good enough for father. He would beat her with a stick and pimp her out to humans that came into the valley.

One day when his belly was bloated with beer and he was sitting by the river, he called me to his side. I hated him. I can still feel the rocks under my feet as I walked over to him. I would think how mother and I worked in the dusty fields, but I said nothing to the asshole in complaint, although I did not fear him. He told me to bring him a stick to beat both mother and me with for some supposed sin he had dreamed up in his head. I said, "Yes, Father." I pretended to go for a stick, but instead I went back to our house and went inside and picked up the birthing

stone my mother had squatted over when she gave birth to me. It still was stained with dried blood that blotted out the carving of Nan, my mother's favorite fertility goddess. As I left I glanced at my poor mother working in the fields, cutting the stalks of wild grain with a wooden scythe.

I took the stone and as I came up behind father I smashed him in the head. He let out a moan and rolled over on his left side. Blood poured from his forehead and blinded him. He reached out for me in vain. I knew he thought maybe this was an accident and not done on purpose. I felt a feeling of exhilaration come over me as I smashed his head with the stone over and over again. I saw that some of his brains were pushing out through a large crack in his skull. I said, "Father, should I get that stick now? I could use it to poke your brains back in."

I knew he was dead. I then put his body in the Omo and watched him float away. I was 10 years old. It was the first really good day of my life. I went to our hut and Mother said, "Have you seen your father?" I lied, and innocently, said, "No, Mother. I wonder where he could be?" After a few weeks Mother seemed to accept the fact that Father was gone and appeared relieved. Mother seemed to take to being a whore. She would be so tired at night that she told me she could not go whoring in the dreams of men. She just wanted to sleep. Besides, she couldn't trade her services for goods from the thoughts of humans. The whoring and the trading had to be in the flesh. It was a much easier way to bring necessary items into our household.

Mother was good at her profession. She soon bore my brother Seth. Seth's father was a relic of the early times, and he had migrated to Ethiopia from the land of Nod, the place where my mother, Lillith, was created and the burial place of my mother's first husband, Adam. Seth killed his father, too, when he was eight, only he used a spear. Then he dismembered his body. I

guess it ran in the family. He brought his father's head home to show Mom. She screamed and slapped him. He dropped his father's head on the floor of our hut. Enraged, he lunged at our mother, but I came up behind him and hit him in the back of the head. He turned and ran out the door. Mother yelled at me to get the head of her dead husband out of her home. I picked it up and took it outside and buried it.

Seth got over his rage and then he went around bragging that he had killed my father, too. He knew that I knew the truth, but I think he began to believe his own lie. His reputation made many humans fear him, even though he was only a kid.

We eventually moved to the land of Kemt, which was named after the black soil brought by the Nile in its annual flood. Much later the country's name was changed to Egypt. The black soil was perfect for farming, so Mother thought that there would be more wealthy customers there for her trade. We settled in what would become Elephantine, one of the earliest towns in Egypt.

I guess it was when I was about 15 that I realized that we were not like everyone else. I remember that one night I decided to sleep out under the stars and the full moon. I lay down on the ground and used a rock for a pillow. I put my left arm up over my head, and as I did, a viper sunk its fangs into my forearm with such force that he could not extract them. I had seen others die from cobra bites, but somehow I knew that I would not die. I stood up with the snake wiggling and still firmly stuck in my arm. I held my arm up to my head so I could see him better in the moonlight. The snake was beautiful. With my free arm I ran my hand over the skin of his body. He felt cold. I sniffed of his skin. It held the smell of death. I looked at his eyes and realized he was not a "he"; he was a "she," and she feared for the lives of those she held in her body. I then took hold of her head and moved it back and forth till I could get her fangs out of my

arm. I don't know why, but I decided to bite the viper. After all, she bit me first. Like a cat, I bit her right behind her head and bit off her head and crunched it into oblivion. I cut up the snake's body with a stone knife and slowly ate each piece, including all of her offspring. I then lay down and went to sleep, very satisfied with myself—but dreaming of snakes all night long.

My brother and I had abilities and powers other people did not have and could not even imagine. By merely thinking we could do something, we could do it. These supernatural abilities were either a gift from the Eternal or from our mother. We never knew where it came from, but we were grateful we had it because it made us superior to everyone on the earth. We were able to walk through large rocks or become part of the rocks and people would walk by and not even know we were there. We could outrun lions and had vision better than hawks. Our strength was boundless. We could become anything we imagined. If a crocodile attacked us while we swam in the Nile, we would change our forms into two hippopotamuses and frighten them away or stomp them to death.

Seth made the greatest discovery when he found, after losing a game of Senet, that he could go back in time and change the outcome. We practiced this a lot. We found out that there were limitations to going back in time, though. We could not go back before our births. We also discovered we could not change someone's fate. We could not give someone their life back if they had died. If we tried to prevent someone's death, we instantly returned to the present. We also discovered that in going back in time our previous self would merge with our present self. Humans would be born, live out their lives, and die, but my brother and I would not die. No matter how old we were, we always looked like we were 45-50 years old.

Our mother did die, though, when I was 27. Her last sons

were triplets, and it was a breach birth. So Seth and I used our stone knives to cut her belly open and remove our brothers—and with that she died, cursing us. Seth and I looked at each other and had the same thought. Our stone knives possessed the power to destroy immortals. Our brothers were all still-born. I personally put my mother's body in the Nile River so that she could join my father. My brother and I lived by the Nile for untold centuries. We lived a solitary life. We never harmed any humans except evil sons of bitches, but the humans feared us anyway. They all stayed on their side of the Nile to the east.

Chapter III

There was a large outcropping of limestone that had appeared after the annual flood of the Nile had been especially violent one year. In this, the year 13127 B.C. (using the modern method of counting the years), Egypt did not have a king, but the Ethiopians came with a large army and a king named Mina. They subdued all of the people in upper and lower Egypt of the Nile delta. They conquered all of the land to the west to the pillars of Hercules and east to the Glass Sea and north to the falls of Atlantis. There was no Mediterranean Sea for the Nile to flow into, and there would not be until 8206 B.C. when the natural sea wall that ran from the coast of Spain to Morocco would collapse from a colossal earthquake that would take along with it the entire dry Mediterranean Basin. The Atlantic Ocean poured in at a speed of 150 miles per hour. The roar of the water filling the void lasted for 40 days and nights. Then it was over. The water had filled the basin and the Hellespont and the Black Sea.

For the people that survived, the new Mediterranean would always be known as "our sea." But for now the river extended through lush tropical forests north 400 miles to the falls, where the water fell 2500 feet.

Seth and I, in an effort to placate their leader Mina, agreed to carve his face on the outcropping of limestone. We were not fond of the asshole. He ordered the people to worship him as the living god. He would sit on a large wooden chair held in the air by six of his guards and watch while babies were sacrificed to the crocodiles. Women and men would beg him for mercy, but he would put those two fat lips of his together and turn his head away from them with a smug look on his face. Mina did not feed all of the children to the crocodiles. No, he would go out during the day and would pick one out for lunch. The asshole was a cannibal.

He did not like our work on the carving so he ordered us killed. He had originally offered us wives if our work pleased him. Seth and I did not take well to his command to his guards to kill us, so after slaughtering the majority of his guards, we drowned the rest of them, who had not escaped, in the Nile River. We took their two generals, both sons of Mina, and holding them by their legs, swung them at the would-be Sphinx and smashed their heads on the rock again and again until they were just about decapitated. As for their leader and father Mina, we dragged him over to the now bloodied Sphinx and let him look at our handy work on his two sons. He covered his hands with their blood and then reached out to us. We shoved him to the ground and he crawled over to me and grabbed my leg and begged for mercy. I looked down at him and thought about all those kids he barbecued. He was especially fond of their livers.

Mina was an average Ethiopian, five feet tall and fat and stunk like hell. Seth chuckled and said Mina's wives would probably thank us for killing him. It must have been untold misery

having this pig on top of them. He, realizing in that puny brain of his that he was next, offered us anything we wanted if we would spare his life. We sat in silence, Seth and I, by the fire looking at each other. Mina thought we were reconsidering whether to kill him or not. Seth left for a while, and when he came back he had a stick about eight feet long and maybe three inches in diameter. I thought Seth is a genius—this is poetic justice. Seth sat down with the stick and started to sharpen one end with his stone knife and all the while never taking his eyes off of the king.

Mina sat on the opposite side of the fire looking through the smoke and the flame. It dawned on him all of a sudden as to what the stick was for, and he became inconsolable and tears running down his face created little rivers through his make up. He pulled off his wig, exposing his bald head. I told him not to worry and that I would talk to my brother on his behalf. I said I would really like his nice leopard skin that he was wearing. He immediately untied the back paws which were held together with strips of leather and handed it to me. Seth said to Mina, "Why don't you give me your skirt? I like the gold at the top and bottom." Mina took it off and now was stark naked. He was unaware that we could read his thoughts. He was thinking that he could outwit us and kill us if he could get away.

Seth looked at me and said, "I guess it's about time." I said, "I think so, Seth." Mina panicked and tried to escape. We let him run to the other side of the would-be Sphinx He lay as flat as he could in the reeds and low water We pretended to not be able to find him. Seth shouted out to him that we would not hurt him and that we would become his subordinates and he could still be king if he showed himself. We knew where the asshole was all along, so it was kind of irritating when a small Egyptian boy who was our neighbor yelled, "He is hiding over here!" Mina got up and took off in headlong flight for the Nile. We

couldn't let him go because it would spoil our entertainment for the night. Seth went splashing through the water and tackled him and then dragged him out of the reeds by his legs.

We got him back by the fire where he sat shivering. We let him calm down for a few minutes. Then I grabbed him and bent him over a large rock. I said, "If you are the living god, I'm sure you will stop Seth from impaling you on this stick." He again cried and begged for mercy. I held him there while Seth came over with the stick. It was a comical scene as Mina kept moving that big butt of his around trying to keep his butt away from that stick. Seth shoved the sharp end of the stick up his ass while I pushed his body down. Diary Dear, it takes a lot of muscle to impale a fat prick on a pole. Mina let out a mournful moan and clawed at the rock with his long fingernails. With one last push, Seth shoved the stick all the way up to where it came through his neck and pushed his head back. His eyes now had the blank stare of death—no longer the confident look of a king.

We then cooked him over an open fire as if we were cooking a lamb on a spit. Mina put off a sweet odor as his flesh cooked. By the time his beard was ablaze Seth and I noticed all of our Egyptian neighbors had formed a circle around us to worship us. I told them to get up and not to worship us as gods for there is only one King of the Universe—Amun.

Seth then grabbed one end of the stick and I took the other end and we went to the Nile, followed by our curious neighbors, and we waded past the papyrus reeds to the shallow water far enough to provide room service for the crocodiles, a fitting end for the Ethiopian.

One final note about his majesty, King Mina. A few days after we had dispatched him, I was lying down by the Nile River in the early morning. I had been sunning myself. I opened my eyes and looked at a lotus flower that was in the shade. It was interesting how the sun's rays were shining on it. The rays made

an unusual pattern. I turned my head and saw that the rays of the sun were shining through the holes that were now in Mina's torso. The crocodiles had eaten out his guts, leaving only part of his torso. His torso was stuck in the mud with the now empty part of his stomach in the mud and facing east, accepting the sun's rays. I got up and picked up his torso and slung it back out into the Nile and watched it float away.

Our fame spread far and wide, but with the passing of years our story underwent many changes by Egyptian word of mouth. We were no longer thought of as brothers, but as mortal enemies—then as gods of Egypt. I like to think that perhaps there was a seed of truth in the latter. We, just like the story of Atlantis, became legend since the witnesses had all died out except for Seth and me.

Chapter IV

Seth and I began to argue about small things. If I brushed him while trying to get by, he would become enraged and would accuse me of doing it on purpose. He was becoming paranoid and an egomaniac. He relished the attention he received from our neighbors. The humans were in awe of him. He soon began to think of himself as a god, and the Egyptians thought he was, too. He woke me up early one morning and said, "Come, brother, and see what the Egyptians have created." They had carved the statue of a man with the head of a hippopotamus. Seth smiled and looked at me and said, "Behold the likeness, brother. Is that beautiful body and powerful arms not just like me?" I said, "The likeness of the statue and you are so close, it's aston-

ishing, brother. All except the head." I could not hold back the laughter as I looked at him. I said, "I'm going back to bed now." I had not been asleep for more than 15 minutes when a giant male hippo crashed into our house and tried to trample me to death. As I rolled out of the way, I slashed one of its legs with my stone knife. Later when Seth came back to join me for our evening meal, I noticed there was a bloody bandage on his right leg. From then on I was wary of him.

Evil came to the land in the form of King Khufu. Sometimes, though, evil can be a genius and goodness can appear as stupid and dull. So it was with Khufu. It seemed that he was building his pyramid as a monument to himself and a final resting place for all time, but the real purpose of the pyramid was to be a place of refuge for King Khufu, his royal family, and all those who had displeased the Eternal and will flee from his wrath on the terrible day of reckoning that will surely come. The pyramid was ingeniously designed to hold 144,000 people.

Once the pyramid was sealed by the spirit of his chief magician Didi, all the angels in Heaven could not prevail against it. Safe the inhabitants would be until the void of blackness returned and all that was would have never been. Driven by Khufu to build this eternal refuge, many died miserable deaths. He pimped out his own daughter to raise needed cash for his pyramid. She gave so many of his workers a deadly disease that he had her put to death. He knew better, though, than to screw with Seth and me.

The oppression lasted for years as they labored first to carve out the basin for an artificial lake 60 feet deep with causeways to bring water from the Nile. Then the large blocks were carved from the mountains of shadows and brought on ships up the causeways to the lake. The water level had been raised to a level of eight feet from the lake bottom. Rows after rows of blocks

were brought to the lake and put in position and then when one level was finished the water level was raised another eight feet to accommodate the next level of blocks.

After the first six rows of the pyramid were finished they built, using cedars from Lebanon, a square, tall box which they would use as an elevator to raise the blocks to the appropriate height with water pressure as the hoisting device. The blocks were slid on the wooden floor of the box, water would be pumped in under the wooden floor using a very unique water pressure method, and slowly up the elevator floor the block would go to the waiting workers on the pyramid. Only Khufu's pyramid was built this way. He put to death his chief architect and destroyed all the plans.

After twenty years of suffering by the people, Khufu's pyramid was finished and his priests blessed the lake and ordered the water to be sent back to the Nile through a twenty-mile-long causeway with ever decreasing elevations. The land back then did not look anything like it does now There were trees and swamps everywhere. The elevation of the Nile was about 40 feet higher then. As centuries passed, the kings of Egypt would come and go leaving monuments to themselves. The age of hunger came in like a desert wind and the pyramids were abandoned. The ground eroded and the desert reclaimed its land from the kings of Egypt.

Centuries passed and then one night with the waning moon, as I lay on my mat, I heard a noise and raised my head and looked at the door to our home. The door swung open and I thought it might be Seth returning. No one came in. I started to get up but found I was unable to move. I looked again and there in the doorway stood Thoth. He was the messenger for the one who created himself. It was Thoth who numbered the stars for the Eternal, and he possessed the power of divine speech. When Thoth spoke, all but Amun trembled. I asked him, "Oh, Great

Thoth, what is it that you want from me? Have I transgressed against the Eternal?" He spoke to me in my mind. Thoth said, "He whose name is hidden from man commands me to tell you to go to Bab Edu-Dhru and Numeira and kill everyone who tries to escape." With fear in my voice, I said, "I will obey, master, but shall I take my brother Seth with me?" After hesitating for a moment, Thoth spoke again and said, "Yes. You are to go to Bab Edu-Dhru alone. Tell Seth to go to Numeira."

Bab Edu-Dhru was a walled city, but with walls on only three sides since the fourth side was built into a steep mountain. Any attack by raiding bands of Caananites would always be futile unless they could conquer the city quickly because the only natural springs were inside the city's walls and the attackers would run out of water. The Dead Sea was undrinkable due to the salt content. On that fateful day I stood outside the city's main gate as the first rays of the morning sun awakened the desert. A cold wind that had its birth in Holy Ilium caused the waves of the blood-red Dead Sea to slap at the shore line.

A man, his wife and two daughters hurried by me. I took pity on them and let them escape. None of them looked up as they passed by me. I could hear the sounds of the youngest daughter's heart beating in my ears. She lost a sandal but did not stop to pick it up. She was afraid her eyes would meet mine. They ran for the caves of Zoar to escape the bitter wind and the carnage that was about to come. I saw the yellow mountain that was part of Bab Edu-Dhru become a cascading wall of fire engulfing Bab Edu-Dhru—and it was so. At the same time the same fate befell Numeira, a few miles to the south—I saw it in my mind's eye. Everyone, from the very young to the old and infirm, and everything else that drew a breath in Bab Edu-Dhru and Numeira was destroyed.

Chapter V

After all of these centuries I'm starting to feel pity for some of these humans. It must be the pull of the stars that draws out my dual nature. I hear my landlady crying and begging God tonight to save her grandson as she lies on her bed on the other side of my bedroom wall in her half of the duplex. Her grandson Joshua, Sara's brother, has a fatal genetic disease and he will die on December 31, 1999 at 11:58 p.m., never to see the new century. Part of me says too bad if he has to die, because he might grow up to be a first-class prick, so it would not be any loss. But then again the stars intervene and I start thinking he is a cute little kid with pretty blue eyes and the innocent smile God gives all babies.

As far as baby Joshua is concerned maybe I could save his life. I'm not exactly in the "physician-heal-thyself-first" business; however, and if God wants him to live, He would cure the kid himself. I am in the killing business, not the healing business. I will have to give it more thought. If I find a way to cure Joshua, will God be enraged and release my brother and send him to kill me for interceding in the fate of one so little? Would it be a price that I would be willing to pay? Should I run back through time to escape punishment from the King of the Universe? I will have to ponder this. Joshua's name is written in the stars along with his life span; however, the Eternal has been known to change his mind. Maybe he decreed that young Joshua should never reach adulthood. If I should help Joshua, will the Eternal take notice—or perhaps he will pay it no mind.

After paying homage to Amun, the Eternal, in the form of a small stone statue that I have had for 26,000 years, the real Rock of Ages, I was ready to call it a night, but I just heard a

very interesting sound: the noise of a cicada bug. They are prevalent in the south but not here.

What I am hearing is coming from the other side of this wall and it is the sound the people of the dark make when they pull photons from humans. They are aliens to this universe. When the Eternal brought forth light, He miscalculated just how enormous the explosion would be and its consequences. The explosion punched holes in the walls of this universe and they are still having holes from that one original explosion being blown into them this very day. It will go on forever—an unfortunate byproduct was that it gave the people of the dark a way into this universe—and not just them but other evil beings, demons who cloud the minds of men with evil thoughts and make humans do vile deeds in the eyes of the Eternal. In their universe they were imprisoned, but here they are free to roam at will just like the people of the dark.

The people of the dark's universe used to be three-dimensional, like ours. But other universes collapsed on it and crushed it to be only two-dimensional. At the same time it pushed negative energy into this universe, causing it to expand forever. The people of the dark were crushed, along with their universe, and became two-dimensional. When they came into our universe they were able to become three-dimensional again, but they have the physical ability to revert back to their two-dimensional state whenever they want to.

In their world they were cannibals, preying on each other. But here they brought a ravenous appetite for light and an evil disposition. The Egyptians were the first to recognize them. At first the Egyptians thought the people of the dark were from the land of the dead. The door from their world to ours is dead center of Khufu's pyramid. When the Egyptians flooded the artificial lake so that they could lay the foundation blocks of the pyramid, Seth and I would see the people of the dark swimming

under the water waiting for the night. Once King Khufu realized they were not sent by Anubis, he paid Seth and me a bounty for each one we killed. Business was really good. The dike holding in the water of the artificial lake broke one day, sending a wall of water towards the now-completed sphinx, cutting into the base of the sphinx and stacking up many of the people of the dark around it, as if they were fish now thrown up on dry land. We captured and killed over 200 people of the dark that day.

When the water of the artificial lake was restored, Seth and I swam down to the center block of the pyramid one day and entered their world to see what it was like. The whole place was made up of right angles. We were able to deduce this because we were in their universe, and at the same time we could see into our own. We walked right up to Khufu, but he could not see us. We found ourselves walking around him in what seemed like circles but were really right angles that kept expanding. We discovered that the right angles were in the same proportion as Khufu's pyramid in our universe. We surmised that if we could look at both universes at a distance the pyramid would look as one sitting on another with their bases together, making it look like a diamond.

We did not stay long, for whereas the people of the dark hid in the shadows out of fear of us, we soon discovered that we were starting to lose our shapes and become two-dimensional. So we started backing up until we came back through the threshold to our own universe. The right-angle world of the people of the dark had made us temporarily lose our bearings. The blocks of the pyramids sitting side by side seemed like a maze to us. Seth suggested that we should forget the angles and travel in a straight line, looking neither left nor right. We did this and soon reached the outer wall of the pyramid.

As the pyramid went up, block after block, it caused the people of the dark mass confusion. There were eight million

ways for them to turn in an effort to find their way out. The Egyptians, therefore, unwittingly had come up with a way to stem the tide of the people of the dark coming into this world. When they come into our world they cannot comprehend up and down very well, and it seems they don't learn very fast, considering how long they have been around. In packs, though, they are lethal and have decimated a village of 400 people in one night—that was in 431 BC in Thurii, Italy. The towns-people all disappeared in one night. Since the people of the dark had the gall to attempt to kill me while I was sleeping in Thurii that night, I searched every cave up and down the Adriatic coast line and killed almost all of the people of the dark that took part in the Thurii massacre. Only their leader got away. He has been looking for me for centuries. I hope he gets lucky and finds me one day. This one tonight, though, must really be stupid to have picked a house in which I reside. He will survive this night only if I'm in a good mood—and I'm not. I will creep through this wall, and investigate.

Dear Diary, I went ever so slowly through the bedroom wall. Someone had done an excellent job on the walls when this duplex was built. You don't find this kind of craftsmanship nowadays. The builders used double sheets of three-quarter-inch wall board so that the walls would be very sturdy. Somebody named Anthony had drawn a heart on one of the two-by-four studs that said "Anthony loves Mabel—July 10, 1956." Maybe they had a good life. Maybe they still do for that matter.

As I emerged from the wall I saw the dark man busy at work taking light from my landlady, Mrs. Bloom's body while she slept exhausted from tears and prayers. As he took the rays of light he put them in a small bag to take back to his tribe. I've never been able to figure out how he captured the rays of light. It is a problem that only Stephen Hawking might be able to solve. Only the reflected light from humans is of value.

The people of the dark are all between four to five feet tall with black eyes and wrinkled and slightly gray transparent skin. The dark men do the work. They bring back the light photons to be shared by the rest of their tribe as food. Well, I guess everyone has to eat. But Mrs. Bloom has suffered enough for one night. Besides, if she loses enough photons she will become weaker and weaker until she is bed ridden, which means I would have to move. So I'm going to kill him.

I came up right behind him. He was silhouetted from the darkness of the room by the light coming in through the window from a street light reflecting off of Mrs. Bloom and the red reflection from her alarm clock which just happened to read 10:56 p.m. I touched his shoulder and he froze and slowly turned his head 180 degrees so that it was now opposite of the way he walked. He stared with those two pitch black eyes at me and his mouth quivered with fear. I grabbed him by his skinny neck and put my face to where it was touching his and whispered, "You have made a fatal mistake tonight, my friend. You will never see your world or your family again." I held him there for a few minutes in silence, and said, "On second thought, if you promise to go by the name of Yorick for the rest of your life, I will let you try to escape." In his squeaky voice he said "Yorick?" I said, "Yes, Yorick."

He agreed. I released my grip so that he would have a chance to run. After all, it's the chase that is exhilarating, not the finish. Kind of like fishing—taking the fish off the hook is anticlimactic. It's when you first feel a fish take the bait and get hooked and run that's fun. Hmmm. Maybe I'm a fisher of men— evil men and evil beings. Only I kill them and then throw them back—forgiveness is not part of my philosophy. My dark man headed for the small space between the door and the door jamb, as if he were getting ready to slide into third base. I just went through the door. He pulled the same routine at the front door

and headed up the street to an old cemetery. The people of the dark are fast, but I'm faster—and meaner. I let him think he was getting away.

The dark man went between the iron bars of the closed gates and under the door of a crypt that had the name "Donato, 1934" over the door. It was the resting place of Geraldine Donato, the pride and joy of Emilio and Sophia Donato—and their only child. She was struck by a car and died instantly on March 20, 1934. She had only lived 31 years, 11 months, 12 hours and 14 minutes. Geraldine had deserved better. Robert Hanson Walker had gotten better. He was the asshole who hit her. He was drunk when he struck and killed her, but he apologized in court to her parents and had to pay a fine of $500 and lose his license for one year. It would have been worse but Geraldine was an Italian and in 1934 she was just another Wop in the eyes of many, including the judge. Geraldine's parents took every dollar they had to build this small mausoleum for her. They had it built out of granite nine feet by six feet and eight feet tall, with a pointed roof and a small window and with a bench where they could come and visit Geraldine. Plus it had enough room for three caskets. But only Geraldine's casket was there.

Emilio and Sophia went to visit relatives in Rome, Italy in March of 1938. They had hoped that they would be able to return to the United States, but World War II kept them there. Unfortunately, they were arrested by German troops outside of the town of Spoleto where they had gone to seek refuge. On January 5, 1944, the German S.S. took Emilio and Sophia to a small clearing at the base of the Corno Mountain and made them get down on their knees and then gave them a chance to hug each other and then shot them in the backs of their heads. The S.S. said they were American spies. Emilio and Sophia died in each other's arms with their last thoughts being about poor Geraldine and who would keep putting the fresh flowers on her

casket each week. I felt sorrow for Geraldine as I entered her tomb. I knew where my dark man had gone. The lid of Geraldine's casket had shrunk with the passing of time, allowing a space of a quarter of an inch between the lid and the casket. My quarry was keeping poor Geraldine company. I surmised that he would not attempt to run. He would stay silent, hoping he had fooled me.

So I sat down on the dust-covered bench that Sophia sat on all those years ago. There was a clipping from a church bulletin that Sophia had left here to read over and over when she would visit. It told about Geraldine's life and how she attended mass every Sunday and that she was well liked by everyone in the church. It was written in the stars that she was not to die until May 28, 1999 of very old age, so she should have still been alive today with a few months of life left. Somebody must have screwed up. I guess the clipping made her mama feel better Too bad that was all her mother was left with. Though I enjoy dispatching evil sons of bitches, I'm still capable of feeling sorrow for someone suffering an unjust death. On Geraldine's casket lay six mummified roses—the last ones from her mama.

I all of a sudden felt intense rage for my quarry. I stuck my left hand right through the casket lid as if it were water and grabbed my dark man by his head and held him there while I opened the lid with my right hand and pulled him out. I looked at poor Geraldine wearing the blue dress that her mother had bought for her all those years ago so she "would look nice." In her skeletal left hand was a picture of Geraldine and some guy who was her fiancé. I told her, "Sorry you got screwed out of your life, kid." On the back of the picture was a caption: Geraldine and Frank on the day of their engagement. I put the picture back in her hand and closed the coffin lid.

I took hold of my quarry by his neck with my left hand and then with my right hand I started turning his head around as if

I were loosening the lid on a jar. He lasted for quite a few turns. The puny blood vessels in his neck started to bulge right before his head came off. I let go of his body and it lay on the floor of the tomb twisting and shaking while the dark fluid that passed for blood in him ran out of his headless corpse. I held his head in the palm of my hand and lectured him, "Alas, poor Yorick, I knew him well." Now I wonder, did Shakespeare steal that line from me or did I steal it from him?

I took his corpse out of the tomb and laid it in an old abandoned casket in the work area of the cemetery. I then walked away from the casket, turned and made a perfect three-point shot into the casket with his head. Maybe I should try out for the NBA. I took one last look at his body and surmised that the morning sun would reduce him to nothing more than a gray stain on the wood of the casket. I was about to go home, but I stopped and picked up some plastic daisies left by the cemetery office and took them and put them on Geraldine's coffin. It turned out that it wasn't only a good day, but the night wasn't bad either.

Chapter VI

Dear Diary, tonight I was sitting in a glider rocker in my room rocking to and fro and listening to music from Broadway shows. I heard baby Joshua in his crib. He was lying on his back waving his arms wildly in excitement as he watched a mobile of seven stars slowly turning over his head. He who the stars say is the last of the scion of ancient, mighty David deserves a better fate. He who created himself gave David a better fate. Why then

does he allow such an innocent to die?

The Eternal looked upon the son of Jessie with the loving eyes of a father I think the last of David's bloodline deserves better. Little Joshua is not guilty of sending Bathsheba's husband to his death. David was the one who put Uriah in the front of the battle, knowing that he would surely die. David could not get enough of Bathsheba, so he would have done or forsaken anyone or anything to keep her for his exclusive use. David did this all in sight of the Eternal. He could not wait for the joyous news that Bathsheba's husband was dead. After all, David had already impregnated Uriah's wife.

When the news came, David cleansed himself in piousness the same way hypocrites of the twentieth century do. Perhaps he was the father of the most hollow words known to man: "Please forgive me; I'm so sorry." I guess the Eternal bought the lie. I'm sorry he did, for I had envisioned being given the command to pay David a visit. I would have ripped out his liver in front of his subjects and then walked among them showing it off. I would have held it up to the sun god and squeezed it. David's royal blood would have run down my arm. It would have been a really good day. Alas, it was not to be. It is ironic that whereas I would have loved to dispatch David, I now am thinking that perhaps I should try to save his offspring.

I finally went to bed It was too warm, so I opened the window in my bedroom to let in the cool air. I lay there on the bed with just a white sheet over me. Through the window I glimpsed my friend, the North Star. I thought about how my mother and I would sit up on the balcony of our two-story house. On this one occasion we looked down and watched Seth at play in the garden by our house. The cool breeze from the north would toss her long black hair to and fro. Mother's hair would change color much like a chameleon can change the color of its skin. I learned if her hair was black it meant she had something on her mind.

With her penetrating emerald eyes she looked at me and took hold of both of my hands and said, "Behold how your brother plays. He plays at killing and each day his vanity grows, and so does his strength. Be careful, my precious son, for some day you may have to destroy your brother or be destroyed. You two are not from the same bloodline." She gave me an amulet which I wear to this very day—the amulet of the heart.

Dear Diary, I will write later of Seth and how to this very day he sits in the darkness and the rage in him doubles with each hour. The only sound he has heard in 3200 years is the sound he makes sharpening his stone knife. Anyone who has eyes to see and reads this better pray he never escapes.

I closed my eyes and listened to the radio, which was now playing old rock and roll songs. The show tunes had gone off. The radio played a song I really liked: Buddy Holly's "True Love's Ways." I drifted off to sleep, dreaming, only to wake up a short time later thinking: Why is the radio still playing "True Love's Ways"? The light of the moon was shining into the bedroom, and I noticed in the semi-darkness the sheet that I had over me looked like it had splotches all over it. I turned on the lamp by the bed and discovered the white sheet now had a flower pattern all over it—a pattern of black daisies. I looked at the mirror above the dresser across the room and saw that it was completely fogged over.

I got out of bed and went over to the mirror to investigate. I picked up a handkerchief to wipe off the mirror and found to my surprise that the fog was on the other side of the glass. Suddenly a finger on the other side of the mirror began to draw the sign of the double helix. The finger then wrote: "I can cure Joshua. Are you interested?" I breathed on my side of the glass and wrote: "Maybe." Two skeletal hands wiped clear the mirror's surface, and I stood and looked at the vacant eye sockets of Geraldine of the blue dress. She said in a voice that I heard only

in my mind, "I want you to help me." I said, "I can't help you, Geraldine." I had written "Maybe" just to see what she would say. "You made a fatal mistake in life. You became so engrossed with your work that you turned your back on your creator. You forgot you were only a creation and not the creator. Your faith was only in the science of your profession. When fate intervened and cut your life short, God had lost all faith in you, to his sorrow." She said, "I have known that since 2:51 p.m. on March 20, 1934. I have watched you at work, Assassin, and I want to strike a bargain with you."

I told her, "I have already said I can't help you—and there is nothing you can help me with" I started to turn around and go back to bed, but Geraldine beat on the mirror and said, "Please wait—and listen. I watched my modern contemporaries at work. The cure for that little boy is staring them in the face. They just don't see it." "Okay," I said. "Now what do you want from me, Geraldine?"

She said, "I want my life back."

"How do you propose I do that?"

"Go back to 1934 and save my life from the car accident."

"Can't do it, kid," I said. "I cannot give someone their life back."

She answered, "Of course, you can. The Eternal's math rules the universe. If necessary, you could let some evil person die in my place. That way the numbers will work out for the Eternal and he will never know."

I decided to play along with her. "Who do you suggest I let die in place of you?"

Geraldine thought for a moment and said, "I don't know, but I'm sure you can work it out."

I replied, "If I start screwing around with fate, we will wind up with the domino effect. You are the one with the Ph.D. degree. Don't you get it? By the way, there is another problem.

If this were to work, the Eternal may know and become enraged with me for tampering with fate. If that were to happen then maybe you would still be stuck here forever and maybe I would be killed and baby Joshua would die anyway."

She said, "The Eternal would not know if you went first to the kingdom of Amun and stirred the water in the well of fate; even the Eternal would have to wait until the ripples in the pool were gone to see his humanity. There are anomalies like that from time to time caused by the shifting of space, making time slow down or speed up and causing humanity to relive moments in their lives and making them complain that it is déjà vu, so he would not equate it with you. By then you could have changed my fate, because stirring the water in the well of fate is like erasing the blackboard of life and then writing everything anew. You won't instantly come back to the present this time."

"So, Geraldine, what would we do about the domino effect?"

Geraldine, becoming frustrated, shoved her skull up to the mirror and said, "Don't give me any of that crap about a fly getting stepped on before it can mate changing all of reality forever. You know that is bull, Assassin." In a plaintive tone, she said, "Besides the Eternal changes reality whenever he wants—time does not exist for him. We are dealing with humans, you jerk, so find someone who doesn't have a family or any relatives."

I looked at her and said, "We also have another little problem. I cannot stir the water in the well of fate with just anything. I need the ankh of Amun, which is either in or close by the dead tree of life. It is now guarded in the catacombs of the ancient city of Ur by three of the meanest demons ever to inhabit the earth. I don't think they will part with it very easily, but assuming I could get it, Geraldine, I would have to pass by the carving of Amun where the boundaries of time and space converge—the dwelling place of the Alpha and Omega of all that exists. I don't

know if I can do that, Geraldine, and you sure as hell don't know it either. And what if I could not come back. All would be lost."

She said, matter of factly, "Let's say it works as I have planned. What do you say, Assassin?"

"I say this: I will think about it."

I asked her, "If I should do as you ask, Geraldine, I'm curious—would you want to live your life the same?"

She said, "No, I would not marry Frank. I know he loved me. I was pressured by my parents to become engaged to him. My mother was always reminding me that I was 31 and my chances of finding a husband were running out. When I died I thought I would instantly be with the Lord. I sat on my casket at my memorial service and looked down on my dead body. Father Anthony gave a nice eulogy for me. I saw that Frank was truly heart-broken. I also saw my best friend Margaret Ann trying to console him. Most of the people there at the service just showed up out of respect to my parents—but not Miss Labaski. She had always encouraged me in her 10th grade biology class. She told me that I could make a difference in the world. I went over and kissed her. I think she must have felt something because she rubbed her check. My parents were devastated. My mother cried every day for weeks. I started to think after awhile: Why am I still here? Isn't God going to take me to heaven? I considered that maybe Jesus is a fraud. I would see people die and be buried and they were not here. So why was I? They were no better than I. To stop myself from going mad, I would watch my friends at work. The day came when my parents went to Italy, never to return I scoured the earth but never found them. Years went by and finally you came along and I dreamed up this idea. I hope you will help me."

I said, "Okay, Geraldine. Now then, how are you going to cure baby Joshua for me—if I uphold my end of the bargain?

Maybe I would come back to the present only to have a 96-year-old woman tell me to go screw myself."

She looked at me as if she still had eyes in those vacant sockets and said, "Well, you could kill me Assassin, but I doubt that would suffice. So I have a fail-safe system in which we can trust each other. Time is going to run out for that little boy who for some unknown reason you care for, so you better decide in a hurry. Will it be the casket of baby Joshua or the carved door of Amun that you touch?"

She then walked back to her casket, climbed in and turned her face from me so that I only saw her profile; she took hold of the casket lid and lay down and pulled it shut. I looked again and in the mirror I saw only my reflection. As I turned to go back to bed I stepped on a long stemmed rose. I picked it up and tried to smell its long departed fragrance. I thought, hmmm, Geraldine has a flair for the dramatic. I crushed the rose in my hand and decided I would consider her proposition.

Chapter VII

I woke up with Thelma Bloom knocking on my door. She invited me to have dinner with her and Sara and Joshua. I accepted. She asked if 6 p.m. would be good. I told her that it would be fine since I had only a couple of errands to run and would be back in plenty of time.

I went to Antiquities of the East. It was a company that bought and sold artifacts. I needed some cash, and whereas I could easily walk into a vault at a bank and take what I wanted, that would make me no better than a common thief. I had

done business with this antique establishment before. The owner, Toby Graham, was a decent man with a good heart. He had an eye for real artifacts and was willing to pay a good price for what I had to sell. He was a talker who liked to tell others of his joys, his love of Jesus, and especially his woes. He suspected that his wife, who was 22 years his junior, was sleeping with his partner. He loved his wife, and didn't have the nerve to confront her because he was afraid she would leave him. He told me that he had found a book of matches from a local motel in his home. He also opened his partner's credit card statement, thinking it was his own. I knew he was lying about his thinking it was his own credit card statement. However, the very same motel that was on the book of matches was listed on the transactions. So he was sure his wife and his partner had been there screwing. He looked at me with tears in his eyes and said, "If I were not a Christian, I would kill William, my partner." I told him I was sorry for his troubles.

He asked me what I had to sell this time. I told him I had two small crocodile figures covered in gold. He looked at them and said, "Good Lord, these are from the time of the Fourth Dynasty almost 4400 years ago. Where did you get them?" I lied and told him that while traveling in the East I acquired them from a street vendor whose son had found a hidden tomb outside the ancient city of Thebes. I asked him if he knew the mythology associated with the crocodile figures. He said he did not. I told him that if these crocodiles were put into the bath water of his wife's lover that when her lover got into the tub it would create a spell over him and he would never again think of his wife. He told me that his partner liked to have him come over to his house and sit in a hot tub and drink a beer. They would then discuss their week's business—and this was the day they were planning to do just that. He told me he would drop one of the figures into the tub. I told him he should try using both of

them but to make sure his partner was in the tub alone because he didn't want the spell to work on him too. He knew the crocodiles wouldn't be harmed. He paid me for them. I wished him luck and left.

On the way back to my house I went back by Geraldine's tomb. I opened her casket for the second time in less than a week. The picture of her fiancé had slipped down by the side of the casket. I picked it up and looked at it very intensely. The guy in the picture looked like a decent man. I can't kill him. Maybe Father Anthony would be a good candidate.

I had been studying the picture and had not noticed a would-be cop and chief of security, a man about 60 with a gut protruding over his belt about six inches, was looking at me through the iron bars on the door. He said to me, "You can't be in there."

I looked at him and said, "I'm a friend of the family."

He said to me in an authoritarian voice, "I've been working here for 35 years and no one has ever been here to visit the deceased. In fact, we don't even have a key to the Donato crypt. So how did you get in?"

I said, "Obviously, I have a key."

In an irritated tone he said, "Then how come the door is still locked? You can't lock it from the inside. I think someone let you in and locked it again. I'm calling the police." He went over to his electric cart and started to dial his cell phone.

I looked at Geraldine and said, as I closed the lid, "I'm still thinking about your proposal." The cemetery guard was still trying to get his cell phone to work when I walked by him, only this time I made sure he did not see me. He can tell his friends of the mysterious man who all of a sudden was not there. Humans love tales of the supernatural. They use their religion as a way to block out all that they cannot understand.

Thelma invited me into her half of the duplex. As soon as I

came in the odor of lamb filled my nostrils. Too bad! I did not like lamb 10,000 years ago and I don't like it today. I decided that I would eat some of it to be polite. I sat down at the mahogany dinner table next to Sara. Joshua was in one of those baby infant seats that can rock to and fro. On the mantle in the living room was a picture of Thelma's late husband Peter. He had the misfortune to die in a war a long time ago, taking three rounds in the chest that were meant for his friend. His friend Caroll now never knows a peaceful night's sleep in his apartment in Topeka, Kansas. He wakes at night and thinks he sees the people he killed in battle plus his friend Peter sitting on his bed. He hears his buddy Peter whispering to him, "Come and join us. It will be like old times." So he tries to drink himself to sleep.

Next to Peter's picture is the picture of Sara and Joshua's parents. They used to live with Thelma but decided one day that they couldn't handle being parents, so now they live in a crack house in Bayonne, New Jersey, smoking dope and having perverted sex in the hope that it will somehow make their lives worthwhile.

Thelma put the food on the table and asked me if I heard the terrible news on the radio. I told her no I had not. She said the police just this afternoon found the partially eaten body of a local man. It seems he was killed by two six-foot long crocodiles that somehow had gotten into his back yard and into his hot tub. She said the crocodiles are still on the loose. She went on to tell me the police were at a loss to explain where the crocodiles came from and how they could have gotten into the hot tub without the victim seeing them coming. As Thelma babbled on, I sarcastically thought to myself: That's too bad. I must have gotten that spell wrong, after all of these years.

During the reign of King Neb-Ka one of his subjects, Aba-Aner, came and prostrated himself before the king. He lamented to the king that his wife had a lover who she saw weekly. He was

in much distress. He sought the kings' advice. The king offered to have her and her lover put to death because the king loved his loyal servant. This offer by the king was even more distressing to Aba-Aner because he loved his wife and did not want her to die. The king said that he would consult his priests for their advice and that Aba-Aner should come back the next morning. He did. It was then that the king gave his trusted servant the wax figures of the crocodiles. Aba-Aner waited until the two lovers were together in the shallow waters of the Nile, and then he secretly put the wax figures into the water. The crocodiles instantly grew and sprang to life and attacked his wife's lover—who immediately tried to save only himself. Aba-Aner jumped into the water, knowing that the crocodiles would ignore him and his wife and kill only the wife's lover. As far as Aba-Aner's wife was concerned, she believed that her husband had saved her life, caring not for himself. As they sat on the bank she begged Aba-Aner for forgiveness and vowed she would never again make love with anyone other than her husband.

The wax figures were handed down in secret by Aba-Aner to his son and then to his grandson. I bought them from him. Toby used them, so I'm not responsible for his partner's death; he should have gotten out of that tub quicker. Well, I guess my friend's wife will be on the lookout for another lover. Perhaps I should go to Toby's store and tell him to pay another visit to his late friend's house. He should check inside the pump on the hot tub. He will find his gold encrusted crocodiles there. He might need their services again some day.

Thelma asked me what I thought of faith healers. She said one would be in town tonight and wondered if I would go with her. I agreed to go. As we made our way to the convention center that Reverend Dennis had rented for the occasion, I thought about Reverend Dennis. He had actually been given a death sentence by the Eternal two years ago, but I did not have to act on

it. In my heart I felt that there was no rush in executing Dennis. Lo and Behold! Reverend Dennis had performed that act all by himself. Dennis, whose ugly face was plastered nightly on the religious t.v. channels, had laid in sin with one of his junior male ministers. I guess he must have forgotten that part about "man shall not lie with man"—especially since he loves to quote the scriptures. The bad news for Dennis was that when his sexual contact with his lover was completed, Dennis had Aids-laced semen mixing with his blood. The good news was that he was able to take out immoral bankruptcy, so in his eyes he is blameless. I guess God disagreed. The Eternal did not pass a death sentence on Dennis for his sexual perversions. No, Dennis was ordered to be put to death for something far worse: Reverend Dennis offered false hopes to desperate people. He claimed he could cure them of their afflictions. All he could really do was make them part with their money and their faith.

Thelma, Sara, Joshua and I went into the convention center and took our seats. Reverend Dennis had not come on stage yet. He had his fellow minister, Reverend Roland, warming up the crowd by supposedly casting out demons. Roland started on a rant about demon possession. Sara kept squirming in her seat and swinging her legs back and forth, trying to hit the back of the chair in front of her with her feet. Two of Dennis's stooges went out into the audience for their stooge, who was supposedly possessed, to bring him up front for Roland to work on. Roland was about to get more than he bargained for.

Before Dennis's men could get over to their cohort, a family in the front row stood up and brought their son up to Roland. He was taken aback because Roland knew this family was not his "set-up" family. No, this family's son was the real thing. I, all of a sudden, found this very amusing. Roland, a religious con man in his early forties, held the microphone up to his red mustache and said softly to the mom, "Mother, how do you know

your son is demon possessed?" The woman related her tale of woe. She said, "Our son Robert has not been the same since we have returned from New York. He is either his old happy self or he becomes mean and hateful and has tortured our family cat to death. My husband took him to a psychologist, and the psychologist tried to blame us for child abuse."

I thought the little boy looked like the kid who was on the old "Lost in Space" t.v. show of the sixties. Roland did not know what to do so he ad-libbed his routine. He put his hand on the little boy's head and yelled out, "Demon, in the name of Jesus, I command you to come out of this child!" Dear Diary, I decided to give Roland a little help. I put in Roland's mind the ancient Egyptian prayer that really would bring out the demon. Roland recited what I had thought, and soon the little boy Robert began to shake and foam at the mouth. Robert began to speak, saying, "Who calls forth Sacade, the keeper of the pink obelisk?" Roland did not know what to say, so I helped him a little more with a couple of thoughts. Roland found himself reciting words that he did not understand—but Sacade did understand them. Sacade, the demon, flew out of young Robert as a mist, causing the audience to gasp. It entered Roland, who stood there motionless for a moment and then said, "Praise Jesus!" The people in the audience stood and clapped. Roland, now visually shaken, walked off the stage waving to the crowd. Robert and his family went back to their seats. Both of Robert's parents were crying.

As a band began to play in anticipation of Reverend Dennis, I remembered how Sacade had been imprisoned in a pink obelisk in Thebes in about 1200 B.C. The obelisk eventually wound up in New York City, and I suppose young Robert either touched it on the day of the new moon or the waning crescent of the moon. Well, Robert is okay now, but I'm afraid Roland will never be the same. Life will become a living hell for him. I wish all it took

for young Joshua to become well would be reciting an ancient Egyptian chant.

Dennis came out with his arms up in the air, and he began to sing along with the chorus. He even did a little dance, unaware that his pal Roland was now backstage vomiting all over his dressing room. Dennis was a lot like Roland in looks, only he had salt and pepper hair to go with a five foot, seven inch, 150 pound frame. He was immaculately dressed in a $2000 suit. Well, he could afford it. Like his pal Roland, Dennis went into a rant for about an hour. He blabbed on about "seed faith" and how God does not like stingy people. All the time he preached, his ushers worked the crowd for money.

Finally, he asked for anyone who had a medical problem to please come forward and be saved in the name of Jesus. People began to line up. Thelma stood up and took young Joshua down to get in line. Sara ran after her, so I followed Sara. I listened to the people as they waited in line. They truly had misfortune visit them. One of Dennis's ushers walked along the line of people and made suggestions as to how much money each person in line should put in the donation plate. When the usher got to me I hit the bottom of the plate with my hand, and the plate and the money went all over the floor. I acted embarrassed and apologized. Sara started laughing as the usher scurried about trying to pick up the money. I looked over at Dennis, and he had a frown on his face. I guess he thought maybe his boys would not recover every last nickel on the floor.

We were fifth in line to see Dennis and to get his "healing hands" placed on young Joshua. Dennis relied on slight of hand and the power of persuasion to convince the first three people in line that they were healed. The first one was an old black woman in her eighties. The pain she had in her back was real. Dennis's cure was not. After he went through his usual "Praise Jesus" routine, followed by telling her she could now walk with-

out pain, Dennis told her to get up. She was in horrible agony as she stood up and slowly walked three feet toward the lying hypocrite. He put his hand on her head and pushed her over backwards. She lay on the floor, passed out from the pain she had just endured. Dennis did another one of his little dances. The rage in me grew. I will make it a point to visit his mansion the day he dies. As he lies in his bed with his organs shutting down forever, perhaps I will drag him out of his bed and tell him to cure himself.

Dennis made short work of the next two people in line. The second was a woman in her early thirties who had a brain tumor. Her doctor had told her it was malignant. Dennis slapped his hands against her ears and said, "You are cured, my dear." He took even less time with the next person. This was an old man with Alzheimer's disease. Dennis put his face up to the man's and blew into his face. The old man fell over. I thought, "No wonder; I know where Dennis's mouth has been, so I wouldn't want his breath on me."

Dennis did not see any more people. We were all ushered behind a curtain where his cohorts gave us pamphlets on the power of prayer. We were also asked to give one more "seed faith" offering. Thelma was dejected. As we walked home, she said to me, "He did not even look at Joshua." I told her God did not need Reverend Dennis's help and to never give up hope.

Chapter VIII

After a week of contemplating what I would do about Geraldine's offer, I put it out of my mind. As I slept, I dreamed that I was back in Egypt. I looked up at the night sky, and it was empty of stars. There was only a blood-red moon. I sat down on the hot sand on the top of a hill. To the east I could see headlights from cars on the highway that follows the Nile. I thought about the people in those cars and that they were probably happy and content because they never knew what was only 700 yards from them. I somehow had a shovel with me. I saw a scorpion running over the sand right by my feet. I took the shovel and thrust the blade into the sand. It cut the scorpion in half; it also struck granite. I started to dig down at a frantic pace, thinking what have I done to my brother? I unearthed six steps leading to a door on the north side of his tomb. But was it the right door? I cleared away the sand on the east and west sides of the tomb, exposing two more sets of six steps each. Both led to doors—one on the east and one on the west. I had unearthed the prison tomb of my brother Seth. I had tricked him all of those centuries ago into walking into his own prison.

He had become the incarnation of evil and wanted to rule the world, so I had joined with Ramses II against my brother. Seth had fallen in love with the beautiful red-headed princess, Dakulah, the granddaughter of Ramses. I told Seth that Dakulah, his love, was waiting for him in the unfinished tomb of Ramses. I said, "Let me take you to her, my brother. But first let us drink wine to celebrate the union that will be consummated this night." I cajoled him and filled him with wine. We then took flight, as birds of prey flying south and then west, to what would be the tomb of Seth at the home of the hawk. We walked

down the six steps—but which steps—north, east or west? I had forgotten. Seth entered the dimly-lit tomb first. We walked down a passageway that was more of a room than a hall leading to the antechamber. Seth walked in first looking for Dakulah. I said, "I leave you now, brother, to your beautiful wife." Drunk with wine, he staggered forth, calling to his love. Holding a torch high, he looked around the room. On one wall he saw a carving of Amun. He spun around and saw that there was a carving of Amun on all of the walls and the ceiling and the floor. He knew in an instant what this meant. He turned, pulled his stone knife and ran straight at me. I was standing in the doorway watching him. I pulled loose a large beam of cedar and a great stone, also bearing the engraved image of Amun, came down and sealed the door in the tomb between him and me. He hit the door with all his might, and the noise echoed throughout the valley and all the way to Abu Simbel. The door held. Not even Seth can pass by the image of Amun without his permission. He was not alone, for his red-headed princess was with him.

We could not take the chance of letting Dakulah in on the plot. If she knew and betrayed us, then it would have been an all-out fight to the death between Seth and me. There is no power on earth, except me, that can kill him—and I'm not sure about whether I would do it. I'm sure at first that he sat on the throne seat of Ramses with Dakulah sitting next to him in the queen's seat. He told her how he would kill me for my treachery, but slowly, so I would suffer. As the days and nights went by, his queen became weak from lack of food and water. Hate and hate alone was all Seth needed to sustain him forever. But neither love nor hate was capable of sustaining his princess. He took his stone knife and cut the palm of his hand with it and held his hand up to the mouth of his beloved and said, "Drink. This will provide nourishment for you." She became sick at the taste of his blood and vomited all over his arm. The next day she had

gone mad. She walked around in circles and laughed at him. Dakulah called him the king of fools. Enraged, he grabbed her and cut her throat and then offered up her dead body to Amun as an offering to free him from his tomb. As the days went by, his prison smelled of rotting flesh, and finally the last lamp went out. He was now alone in the dark. He still is, and he is on the other side of this wall waiting for me with knuckles turning white as he grips the stone knife—the one I gave him when he turned 15.

I contemplated which door to touch. One would open to a small hole which I could peer through without fear of Seth getting out. The other door is the entrance through which he had entered the tomb. If I touch it with my hand, it will fall into dust and he will be free. The last door, if I touch it, will instantly imprison me in his tomb with him. In my dreams, I reasoned which door was the one I could touch and view my brother. I remembered that Ramses had designed the tomb so that the setting sun's rays could penetrate the tomb through the small opening. Confident with this belief, I touched the door on the west. As my hand felt the stone, I remembered that it was not the setting sun's rays that would provide light to see into the tomb—it was the full moon rising in the east. In my dream I became filled with fear and foreboding as the door fell into sand at my feet. I ran back about 20 feet from the tomb. I pulled my stone knife and stared at the black opening of the door frame. I waited in silence for what seemed an eternity, but then, ever so perceptibly, out of the darkness I could make out the form of my brother. As he got closer I could see that his face was not the same as it was in times past. I then realized that he had fashioned from the mummified remains of his lover the mask of a dragon. Standing no more than eight feet from me, he said, "I missed you, my brother—but I never once forgot about you. It was you and you alone who imprisoned me. You blocked the thoughts of

those around me so that I could be deceived."

I said, "You imprisoned yourself. If you were not evil you could have passed by Amun." With the scream of a banshee, he flew through the night sky and knocked me down an embankment. I sprang to my feet and slashed his arm as he lunged at me. We then circled each other, two arms stretched out, as if we were two scorpions doing battle to the death. The difference was, he was still wearing the clothing of an Egyptian prince, while I was dressed in a short-sleeved shirt, blue jeans, and Nikes, 20th Century clothing. We lunged at each other. I took hold of his hand which held the knife, but he pulled out of my grasp and sliced open my left eye, blinding it. I took off in flight as a one-eyed hawk flying through the night sky. I then woke up from my dream with my left eye killing me, but I knew in my heart that some day it would not be a dream.

Chapter IX

Dear Diary, I didn't have any new assignments so I traversed the land to and fro like a hawk circling in the sky looking for prey. I wound up as the sun was setting outside of a small Mexican restaurant off Interstate 15 in Utah that was about to close for the day. Their sign enticed me to try their food. The sign said, "We serve the best Mexican food in Utah." The place was a real shit hole—a cinder block building maybe 1400 square feet painted white with a screen door that had enough holes in it to stop only flies over four inches in diameter. I went in and sat down in a booth. The owner thought he had classed up the place with the crummy black naugahyde booths and white tables that had seen better days 15 years ago. He had a juke box in one

corner of the restaurant that you could play from any satellite box located at each table. It was plain to see that this guy must have never updated the songs. I was flipping through the card selection trying to find a song I might like when the waitress came over to get my order. I ordered the "Jack Special" (it came with some "deep fried" pork) with a large pop.

The waitress was a small woman, pregnant and haggard from helping her husband Jack run this joke of a restaurant. In fact, Jack had been reading the riot act to Penny (the waitress) right as I came in. Tears had welled up in her eyes as she took my order because she was thinking about how Mr. Jack was blaming her for the fact that the restaurant was not making any money. She considered herself lucky to have married the asshole. She would see a strawberry blond with a plain face and a nose she thought was very unattractive when she looked in the mirror. She would let herself be browbeat and put down every day at the restaurant. Jack was great at telling her what she was doing wrong in the restaurant. She believed it must have been her fault; it couldn't possibly be the fault of Mr. Stud—after all he told her daily that he was a genius. When she brought the food, I convinced her that she should go home and that I would square it with her husband. She put on her old black sweater, smiled at me and then left.

I got up and went into the kitchen where Jack was busy cleaning the grill. He assumed that I was Penny since he only had heard me come into the kitchen and had not turned around to look. He said, "Get your ass over here and take out the trash." Jack was a big man maybe 6 feet 4 inches, 250 pounds with matching barbed wire tattoos on his biceps and slightly balding on the back of his head, which made him self-conscious since he was only 35 and didn't think he should be going bald. I told him, "Penny went home, shithead, so you take out the trash or I'll shove it up your ass."

He turned and said, "What did you say?"

I said, "You heard me." With my last comment he went berserk and lunged at me. I guess he was unimpressed with my appearance and figured he could kick my ass. I grabbed him by his belt with one hand and by his thinning hair with my other hand and threw him out of the kitchen and bounced him off the wall by the entrance door. Forty-year-old plaster came raining down on him. He now had a cut over his right eye, and blood ran into it.

He rubbed his eye and yelled, "What's the matter with you, man?"

I said, "I don't think I like your Mexican food, Jack. It is probably a little too spicy, so I'm canceling the order—and I may cancel you—because you lied, Jacky-wacky; you don't have the best Mexican food in Utah." I kicked him in his nuts. He got up, bent over and moaning. I put my foot up against his butt and slammed him head first into the jukebox. It started playing as I threw him all over his restaurant. I sang along with the juke box, "Take out the papers and the trash, Jack, or you don't get no spending cash."

In a barely audible voice he said, "You're crazy, man." He tried to crawl over and push a hold-up button to summon the police, but I dragged him back and said, "No, no, no, my friend." I stood him up on his feet and then shoved a broom into his chest and said, "Now clean up this room." He swung the broom at me. I ducked and caught him square in his gut with a right hook that doubled him up. I put his sorry ass over my shoulder and promptly body-slammed him on to the top of a table in one of the booths. I picked up my glass of pop and stood over him drinking it.

I said to him, "Like a drink?" I poured it on him. There wasn't much left in the glass except for a few ice cubes. I stuffed $20 in his shirt pocket to pay for that rotten food, and put my

index finger on the tip of his nose and told him to be nice to Penny and that I would know if he was not. I informed him if he continued to treat her badly I would come back and hold him by his feet and deep-fry his head and he would truly be the "Jack Special." As I left, the table he was lying on collapsed and he landed on the floor. Some of the change in one of his pockets came out and rolled on the floor. I thought it was probably tips that he took from his wife. He lay there whimpering like a little kid. Guess those barbed wire tattoos didn't make him tough after all. Maybe he needed a couple more of them. As I went down the road I analyzed myself as to why I did what I did to that jack-off and decided it was a reaction brought about by the way my father had treated my mother all of those thousands of years ago. My mother was always at the beck and call of the ass-hole, even though he was just a mortal. The more I think about it, I would enjoy killing my old man all over again.

I thought about Geraldine's proposal. I decided to become a bird of prey, I glided upon the warm air currents in the canyons of southern Utah. I considered what might happen to me and what I knew would happen to little Joshua if I did nothing. I thought about my life. It had certainly been long and pretty good, so if it were to end—too bad. Then again, maybe I would succeed. If that were the case, then I would have saved Joshua and at the same time tricked the Eternal and rescued poor, unfortunate Geraldine.

I paused for a while and sat in the top of a pine tree. The wind from the north caused the tree to bend towards the south. I watched a coyote run down a small rabbit. The coyote sank its teeth into the rabbit's neck and shook it back and forth. At least the coyote killed for food, whereas humans kill other humans for a variety of reasons, but rarely for food. But they would think they were superior to the coyote. He then sat down next to his dead prey to devour his dinner. I got to thinking, I never

did eat any of Jack's Mexican food. So I decided to steal the rabbit. I flew from the tree branch and, after gaining altitude, I then dove straight at the coyote. He never saw me coming. I put out my talons and grabbed the rabbit before the coyote could react. I took the rabbit up to a large branch where I ate most of it, much to the disgust of the coyote. I dropped to him what was left of the rabbit when I was finished. It should tide him over until he can catch another.

I came back home to see Geraldine. I had made my decision. I went to her tomb and wrote "Okay" in the dust on the floor. As I made my way back home, I again thought about why I was doing this: going against Amun the Eternal. Perhaps he would not care about my going to the ancient city of Ur. He might care about my collecting the ankh and taking it to the well of fate, or he could just find it amusing if he knows. Maybe I'm bored with my existence. Maybe I want to challenge the Eternal. I can't be that concerned with baby Joshua. Hell, I've seen thousands of children die in my lifetime. I remember eating an apple and watching hundreds of young corpses being burned during the plague of Avignon in 1520. The Rhone River was filled with the dead. I did not feel any sympathy for the people there. It must be the challenge that Geraldine has offered to me. I started to offer up an ancient prayer of protection to Thoth, but I did not. I must hope he did not pick up on my thought. The Eternal may not watch all of his universe all of the time, but there are others that do: Angels and demons alike.

Chapter X

I once more took flight, as a falcon flying through the night and flew until once more I had come to what remains of the ancient city of Ur in southern Iraq. Ancient Ur has been left to nomads, archeologists and the demons of the Syrian desert. This, the home of Abraham, has been fought over for thousands of years. First came foot soldiers and then chariots—then tanks and now humvees. It is just a pile of rocks now. Archeologists have excavated the place, but they missed what is only 140 feet below the digs. They might want to keep missing it. It is cold here and overcast. I sat down on a block of stone that some poor son of a bitch pried from the grasp of the Zagros mountains centuries ago. The wind from the north brought a mild sandstorm with it. The wind also brought the cries from the demons of the desert. They told me to go home or I would surely die.

As the sun stretched its last rays from the desert from the west I made my way down an embankment to the east of the city to a long forgotten riverbed. There is a small mound that the archeologists paid no attention to. It was all that remained of the temple of Matt, the goddess of truth. The desert sands and the occasional floods had covered it up. In the fading light, I dug into the side of the mound with my bare hands. I cleared out an area of about three feet square and two feet deep. A rainstorm had drenched Baghdad a few weeks earlier and had done me a favor and sent a wall of water down the riverbed. This time the water took away layers of desert sand and soon would have revealed a door to the catacombs.

I took my hand and cleared away an inscription on the door. Written in an ancient form of the Assyrian language was the message, "Woe unto he who enters herein." I crawled through the rock and stood up. I had brought a small Egyptian

lamp with me. The oil in the lamp would burn slowly and by the time it would run out I would have what I came for and would be gone.

I lit the lamp, which put out an amazing amount of light for such a small flame. I was standing in an ante chamber between what was the door I came through and the door to the catacombs. To the left and right of me on the walls were cubbyholes that held the skulls of the ancient priests of Ur. There were seven rows of seven skulls in each row on each of the north and south walls. The lamp picked up a glint of gold coming from the last row of the north wall. There were six skulls side by side but room for a seventh. In place of the seventh skull was a gold ring. It was about six inches in diameter. Inscribed in Assyrian were the words "Prince of the North." So it was meant for me.

Well, screw them. Whatever is on the other side of this door will play hell getting my head. I was beginning to get pissed off. I took my fist and slammed it into the stone door and watched it crumble. What lay in front of me was more of a labyrinth than catacombs. There were three paths I could take—left, center or right. I had to choose which path—maybe all of them led to the same place. The ceiling was only about eight feet high and the whole place was carved out of solid stone. On each of the entrances were carvings of what I would encounter if I went that direction.

On the wall leading to the left path was the carving of a griffin. Oh, no—a griffin! It was a creation that went awry— humans in the 20th Century were not the first to fool around with DNA—the Atlantians had done it 15,000 years earlier. This thing was more of a monster than a true demon. Its cell structure was such that it could regenerate forever unless it was decapitated. It had the head and wings of an eagle and the body of a lion. Maybe this would be a good time to turn around and go back. I was under the impression that they had all been killed

on the island of Samos about 7000 years ago. The griffin might be here just to guard the greatest horde of gold in all the world— the golden ingots of Belshazzar. I reasoned that if that were the case the griffin would not bother me. After all, I could explain to it that I wasn't here for the gold as I ran like hell.

I was looking at the wall that led straight ahead when I saw something coming toward me. I guessed I wouldn't have to find out what lay ahead, for whatever it was would be on me within 30 seconds. I pulled my stone knife, ready to do battle with whatever this was. It was floating in the air and it lit up the walls of the labyrinth as it passed. As it got closer, I could see that it was just rays of light spreading out in different directions and the rays were all connected to a pure white light center. It was very pretty. The rays of light would change colors from red to yellow to blue to green to violet to purple, then back to red again. I didn't know why I had pulled my knife. I couldn't stab rays of light, so I put my knife back into its sheath. It floated around me in a circle and then it stopped behind me. I did not turn around immediately, but I could see the light reflections on the ancient walls of the labyrinth.

What happened next made my blood run cold. I felt a hand slip into my hand. It was a hand that I had felt before. I was not afraid, but I was strangely melancholy. I started to go take on the griffin, but I knew I had to turn around. I slowly turned and looked into the beautiful face of my sweet mother. All of a sudden there was light all around us. I felt great, as if all my troubles were now gone. I blurted out, "Mama," and hugged her tightly. She took her hand and put it up to my cheek and wiped away my tears that had welled up in my eyes. Mother said, "I am here to save you, my son."

I asked her how she got there. She looked at me with that soft smile of hers and said, "I beguiled Anubis himself to let me pass from the land of the dead."

I wanted to believe her. All of a sudden I no longer cared about Joshua or Geraldine. I only cared about this moment. Mother sat down on a stone bench and I lay down on the stone bench with my head in my mother's lap as I used to do all of those centuries ago when I was young and we lived in Ethiopia—we would have heart-to-heart talks. I looked up at her as she brushed back her hair like she used to do. I started to beg her for forgiveness for the way I treated her on the last day of her life. I said, "I'm sorry, Mama; I did not know what else to do when you were in labor. You were not able to give birth to my brothers, so I listened to Seth. He never loved you like I did, Mother. It was his idea to cut your belly open." I realized that I was starting to pass the blame as a child would do.

Mother put her finger on my lips and, in her sweet voice, told me to speak of it no more. "You must not go against the will of the Eternal, my son," she said.

"I would gladly die this moment if I could journey with you back to the land of the dead and spend eternity with you, Mama."

"Your destiny can eventually be that, my son, but you must abandon this quest. If Thoth knows, he may not remain silent. It might be that he is only going along with you for his own entertainment. If this is true, and you should succeed in getting the ankh of Amun and you make it to the well of fate, he could turn on you."

"Is there any way you can stay with me, Mama? The hell with little Joshua. And Geraldine can go screw herself."

She hugged me and said, "I cannot stay long, my son, for soon I will be missed. So you must go back now, my son."

I said, "Remember, Mama, how happy we were when we lived by the Omo. Even when we worked in the fields, it was good because you and I would talk about everything."

"Remember, the world was young and innocent, and so

were you, my son—and maybe I was, too. Your father was the only man I ever really loved."

"Yes, and I killed him, Mother."

She looked at me with those beautiful green eyes and said, "I forgive you for dispatching him to the land of the dead."

"Do you ever see him, Mother?"

Mother looked deep into my eyes and said, "No, my little prince. He could not pass the test. His heart was evil. I saw it eaten by Ammit, the crocodile-headed creature, who guards the scales of justice. Once your father's heart was devoured, he was sent into oblivion."

"How about Seth's father?"

"He suffers in the land of the dead, my son. He dwells in a cesspool of excrement, struggling every second to keep his head above it. He survives on the hope that his son, your half-brother, will someday escape his confinement and set him free and the two of them might be able to prevail against the Eternal and the universe."

"Could that ever be, Mother?"

She said, "I don't know, my son. For that is not foretold in the stars."

I felt comforted. Mother kept stroking my hair. I dozed off to sleep—the first real sleep that I have had in centuries. When I awoke several hours later I was afraid to open my eyes. I could feel my head still in her lap, but I was afraid she would be gone. I finally opened my eyes. She was still looking down at me with her sweet face. I said, "Mother I will do as you ask. I will leave this place; but first, Mother, if you can, would you get me some flat bread with raisins and dates like you used to fix for me for dinner?"

She smiled at me and said, "I read your thoughts while you slept, my son." She pointed to my right. I turned my head in her lap and saw a dish with her wonderful flat bread on it. I imme-

diately sat up.

She said, "Don't eat this here. Take it with you, my son, and eat the bread when you are out of this god-forsaken place. First, my son, give me your word, sworn on the amulet of the heart that I gave you. Swear that you will not come back once you leave this place."

I looked at her and said, "I swear, Mother." I was starving, so I went ahead and took a bite out of the flat bread.

Mother yelled, "No, no!"

I sank my teeth into dust—not flat bread. In an instant I pulled my stone knife and sunk it deep into her flesh. This was not my mother—it was one of the three demons. Instantly filled with rage, I gutted her from her crotch to her chest. Maggots poured out of her and spilled onto the floor. The demon fell over backwards. It had resumed its true form. It was one ugly sight to behold—pale white skin, protruding ribs, blood-red eyes with yellow pupils, pointed ears and two rows of razor-sharp teeth. The demon's head lay flopped over to its right side, and its tongue, which had a split in the middle of it, pushed out of its mouth.

I thought to myself that the humans think they are kings of the earth and they fight among themselves for supremacy of the planet. In the real food chain humans would rank no better than fourth place. They just don't know it. These three demons down here could have routed even the American army, and their high-tech equipment would not have saved them. I guess I should say these two demons—I don't think this one lying on the labyrinth floor in the dirt will be taking on anyone.

I cleaned off my knife and started to put it away, but then I decided to carry it in my right hand—never knowing when I might need it. I took my lamp and went to the entrance on the right to see what the engraving was on the wall. If this way looked better, then I would go hither. No point in facing the grif-

fin if I did not have to. I wiped away the dust on the stone. Well, I'll be damned, the carving was of Ishtar, the demon goddess of love. Maybe she will try to screw me to death. At least she won't look like that ugly son-of-a-bitch that I just dispatched. Ishtar has been around as long as Seth and I have, and I know that she has some abilities that I do not possess. I looked around—no place on earth is as lonely as this place.

As I walked along this dust-covered path, the walls of granite appeared to be getting closer together. The ceiling seemed to be getting closer also. I can reach up and touch it now. The walls are now only three feet apart, and yet when I hold up my lamp and look back the walls are five to six feet apart, as they were at the entrance. I decided to see what would happen if I tried to go back the way I came. I held up my lamp and walked a few feet the way I had come. The walls this way, too, started getting closer together. I decided to walk through the granite walls, for nothing had ever been withheld from me. I could not go through them. I turned and went ahead again. The walls seemed to stabilize at first, then they started to close in again until I could not squeeze through. The opening between the walls was now only eight inches apart. I was screwed. I leaned up against one of the walls and thought, hell, there's got to be a way out of here. I slammed my fist over and over again into the granite, but the wall held.

I closed my eyes only to open them very quickly when I heard a voice say, "I can let you out if you promise to help me and not kill me." I took my lamp ahead to the opening. I put my arm with the lamp through the opening and the light from the lamp shined upon Ishtar, the love goddess. She was stark naked and beautiful. No wonder so many men in the past gave up their lives for one night with her. She had soft olive-colored skin, dark eyes, and shoulder-length black hair. She had the most beautiful breasts I had ever seen. She took my lamp from my hand and sat

it on a notch on the wall. She then took hold of my hand and rubbed my knuckles.

Ishtar said, "You are bleeding, Assassin." She was right. I was almost in shock. I had never bled, even when the viper bit me all of those centuries ago no blood oozed from the wound. Ishtar said, "You are at my mercy now, Assassin, for this is my home."

I looked through the opening at her and said, "Then kill me now."

With laughter in her voice, she said, "That would not help either of us, would it?"

I said, "I guess not."

She then said, "If I make the walls recede, will you promise not to harm me?"

I was in no position to bargain. I said, "Yes." She put her arms up to each wall and started caressing them with her hands and they began to move apart. I could not take my eyes off of her. I was thinking, maybe I should bed her right here in the dust on the floor. I knew this was her true form.

I walked over to her and she backed up and said, "You promised me no harm."

I looked into those beautiful eyes and said, "You have nothing to fear." I put my hands on her waist and said, "What do you want from me?"

Ishtar pointed with her hand and said, "This will lead you to the eternal garden. If you look hard enough you will find the ankh of Amun there. When you take it in your grasp, the griffin will come out of his lair to destroy you. If, by some chance, you should prevail in battle and slay him, then the path out of here will be clear to you. I want you to free me from this place when you leave." Ishtar patted the walls with her hand and looked at me knowing that I could not refuse her, for she could bring the wall back again.

I said, "You have a bargain. Now let me pass."

Ishtar stepped aside, and I took my lamp and walked ahead until I had come out of the labyrinth to the edge of the cliff. I looked and saw that there were three exits from the labyrinth, so obviously, whichever one I had taken would have led to this same place.

I looked down from the cliff and about 100 feet below was a petrified forest. I was standing now in a large cavern. I looked up at the roof. It looked like it was moving. I realized that it was covered with bats. There was a path that went down the cliff to the edge of the forest. I walked down with trepidation in my heart, knowing the griffin could be on me at any minute. There was a small stream that I waded across. When I got to the other side, there in petrified bushes were the skeletal remains of those who had passed this way centuries ago, and strewed around them were the gold ingots of Belshazzar's treasure—which he had stolen from King Solomon's Ethiopian gold mines. In this one place, there is more gold than the entire known supply for the modern world. Funny, no one has ever come looking for it, especially since its location is written on an obelisk which is stored in the Museum of Natural History in Baghdad.

I started to make my way into the forest when I heard the flapping of a giant pair of wings. The griffin had come out of his lair and flown up to the cavern ceiling and had begun to devour some of the bats. The bats began to fly in all directions to escape. The griffin gorged himself for a good hour. I hid in the bushes and extinguished my lamp. There was an opening far ahead that let in enough sun light for me to see just how formidable my opponent would be.

The griffin was magnificent. His body was at least twice the size of a normal lion. His wings, though huge, were no threat to me, but that eagle's beak could tear me to pieces. I had already discovered I could be harmed in this place. The griffin did have

the brain of a bird, so I might have a chance. He either did not see me or did not care about me or was waiting for me to get the ankh. I waited until he returned to his lair. Then I relit my lamp for extra light and slowly made my way through the forest.

This place had been a beautiful garden in a long ago past. In all of my travels I had never been to Ur. I had only heard tales of it. All around me were the remains of every kind of fruit tree that had ever sprung from the earth. There was even a fig tree with petrified figs on it. Even the grass beneath my feet was petrified and made a crackling sound as I walked along.

I was scratched up and bleeding when I looked ahead and saw the tree I was looking for. It was a large tree with twelve gigantic branches, all pointed up towards the heavens. The tree was a forlorn sight. It looked as if it had died weeping. I went over to it as if I were drawn to it for some reason other than to steal the ankh. I put my hand on it and began to look for the ankh. I could not find it. I climbed up into the branches, but nothing looked like a cross with a loop on the end. Maybe the ankh had been carved out of it and just left somewhere around here.

As I climbed down, my foot broke off an exposed root. I picked it up and held it up to my lamp. I thought I had found my ankh of Amun, but no loop on the end. Next to it was another large tree that looked like it had been cut down, leaving only a stump. I held my lamp down close to the stump and thought that there was something wrong with it. This tree had a trunk with a diameter of maybe three feet. All of a sudden it struck me as to what was the matter. There were no rings on the exposed stump. Trees have rings for each year of life. It was as if this, and I suppose all of the other trees here in the garden of stone, were created in a single instant. Did the Eternal create this oasis in the middle of chaos as a refuge for himself only to abandon it to the ravages of time? Maybe he became enraged and cursed it. When

my mother's first husband Adam was put here, then perhaps Adam discovered even paradise can be a prison cell if you cannot leave. Maybe Mother planted the thought in Adam's mind that to toil in the ground for your sustenance and face the terrors of the demons of the night would be worth the price to be free.

My mother was the first to be banished from here. Perhaps mother's husband knew all along that he would some day leave with his second wife—or at least be evicted. This garden of death is monumental proof that the Eternal can make a mistake. If he can make one mistake, he can make more. Perhaps my quest is not so impossible after all.

When I had been up in the tree it was like visions of the ancient past would flash in my mind—just glimpses of wondrous scenes. It was as if I could even smell this place as it was then— the air was fresh and clean and the fragrances of a million different types of flowers filled my nostrils. I sensed there was no evil—only peace and contentment had been here. Here there had been no loneliness and no sadness.

I went over and sat back down on my tree stump again and noticed that there was something sticking out from under the fallen tree. It was the skeletal remains of a giant snake. I pulled one of its bones out from under the tree and held it up. I had found my ankh of Amun. It never had been part of the dead tree of life after all. I looked at the snake's skull and said, "Sorry, my friend, but I'm taking this with me. I doubt it is of any use to you any more."

I thought that this could be a lucky day for me, until I heard the tree begin to creak. I looked up and in the highest branch of the tree sat the griffin looking down at me. I took off running and headed back toward the river and the path to Ishtar's realm. I reasoned that she had not been bothered by the griffin for all these centuries because maybe he could not get past the walls

either. I did not make it. The griffin flew directly overhead and kept striking down through the trees trying to finish me off. As I ran I pushed the branches off with one hand while my other hand held the ankh over my head like an umbrella. The griffin managed to take a chunk of my flesh from my hand. For the first time in my life I felt real pain. I thought about crying out to the Eternal for help, but I did not because I would have been discovered being in a place forbidden to me.

I stopped before I came out of the forest because I could see the griffin down on all four feet waiting for me by the stream. He had his wings spread out and his neck was bowed and his eyes were fixed only on me—a classic attack position, but his body was crouched down like a lion would be before it would attack its prey. So I headed in another direction. I could hear the griffin scream. It echoed all through the cavern. I glimpsed Ishtar sitting up on the hill watching the whole thing.

I stayed in the forest but followed the stream. I thought that I was free of the griffin, but then I heard a splash in the stream. The water went everywhere. Some of it came into the woods and hit me. The water hit my wound and mingled with my blood and dripped down on my leg. I kept on the move. For once in my life I was the hunted and not the hunter. This all seemed surreal to me because 140 feet straight up was another world—jets flying overhead, people, cars and cities—none of the humans up there could ever imagine what was going on beneath their feet. I came to a small opening where the original streambed had been centuries ago. I could hear the griffin crashing through the trees and under brush, and each sound was bringing him closer to me. Now my heart was the one that was beating fast. I thought my stone knife probably could kill the griffin, but, hell, there is no way I could get close enough to cut off his head. My stone knife was only eight inches long.

I hid in a thicket between two large trees by the old

streambed. I thought about the first time I ever saw a griffin. It was in Porantium, the capitol city of the country of Atlantis. I guess that was about 13200 B.C., give or take a few years. Now the city is at the bottom of the Mediterranean Sea, south of the Island of Crete—put there by the Eternal. Porantium had a zoo of sorts. This zoo, though, held only the animals that the Atlantians had created in their quest for immortality.

The people were the opposite of the Egyptians. The Egyptians wanted immortality in the next world—the Atlantians wanted it in this one, and they came close to getting it. Their society was amoral, and strangers were not welcome for more than few days. Of course, they did not have many visitors from other countries. People were afraid of them. I went to the zoo and watched the griffins as they were being fed. There were about ten of them behind iron bars. They had their wings clipped when they were young so they could not fly. The griffins would pounce on the raw meat with their paws much like an eagle would do with its talons.

I thought that the griffin would probably come after me the same way. It would not act like a lion. The griffin came crashing out of the wood and across the small ancient meadow right towards me. The son-of-a-bitch probably wanted to have me as a variation of his lunch. He tried to jump into the thicket, but the petrified bushes held him up. He did manage to get one of his paws through the thicket. I drove my knife into his paw. Unfortunately he pulled his paw back so fast that my knife was still stuck in his paw. Now, I thought, I'm really screwed. I reached around to find a rock or anything else I could use as a weapon. There was nothing there. I took off running again. I headed back toward the dead tree of life. The griffin was having problems getting through the underbrush, so he took flight and soon caught up to me. I crawled under the petrified underbrush, thinking once more I had outwitted the griffin. I had not. He

was no more than twenty feet from me. He was being careful because he must have sensed that I could kill him, and for all he knew I had something that could hurt him more than the stone knife did.

Next to me were the remains of the tree of good and evil. In panic my eyes darted to and fro looking for anything that I could use to fend off the griffin. I was struck by a beam of light coming from the side of the tree of good and evil. With my heart in my throat I crawled over to investigate. The light was the sun's rays coming through the small opening to the cavern and hitting the metal shaft of the sword the Eternal had left here thousands of years ago. I prayed that the blade was still sharp. The ancient sword had writing on the blade that I could not decipher. I reasoned that the griffin would try another approach. After all, now he was bleeding. I took the sword and hid behind the tree. There was an opening in the trunk. I sought refuge there. The griffin, though very close, was not having great success in finding me. They can't smell that well. He walked right past me, limping on three paws. I decided then and there that this was the moment I would either live or die.

As he passed, I jumped on his back and grabbed his neck with my wounded left hand. He tried over and over to turn his head to take another chunk out of me. He then rolled over on his side in the dirt trying to throw me off. I gripped the sword as tightly as I could and swung it at the griffin's neck. The blade of the sword struck the griffin's neck about an inch above my left hand and continued on until I had actually sliced into my own left arm. The griffin's head flew off into the thicket, but his body got up on his feet again and began to run around in a circle. I held on to the neck as if it were the reins on a horse. Blood kept pumping out of the neck, covering me. After what seemed an eternity, the griffin staggered and keeled over on his side. I stood next to him, shaking and relieved that I was still alive. I retrieved

the stone knife from the griffin's paw, and then I took the sword to the dead tree of life and stuck the blade in the ground in front of it. I washed myself off in the stream and went back up the hill to get Ishtar so we could get the hell out of this place.

I climbed up the bank to where Ishtar was sitting. She was still stark naked. For some reason, I thought I would find her with clothes on. The view, however, was delightful. She sat staring at me with a smile on her lovely face and her legs in a very inviting position. She said, "Well, Assassin, you did it. Now we are both free. Why don't we share love here before we leave. One more desecration won't hurt this place."

I looked at Ishtar and said, "I gave you my word that I would lead you out of this place. So let's go now."

She said, "Wait, I want you to see something that you missed when you first went down the bank to the garden."

I said, "Okay, tell me what did I miss?"

Ishtar took hold of my chin and turned my head. She said, "Look there!"

I did. I said, "So what?" She said, "Look how the golden ingots are arranged. Don't you think that is a little strange?"

It dawned on me all of a sudden. I said, "The griffin was building a nest. So, Ishtar, how long has he been working on the nest?"

She looked as if she were trying to count the days backward. "I think it has been about four years."

I said, "Then we have to destroy the griffin's eggs before we go or soon there won't be much of a world left. We made our way down to the nest. The griffin had buried four eggs into the soft soil in a location where each day it would receive the rays from the setting sun through the small opening in the rocks. I dug up the eggs and pushed my knife through the ivory-colored, leather-like shells. I cut the shells open and cut up the embryos. After I had destroyed all four eggs I checked to make sure there

were no more. I looked at Ishtar and said, "I guess the griffin was androgynous, being both male and female. I never knew that. Ishtar, you may have just saved the human race! I guess there is some good in you after all."

She retaliated, "Maybe there is some good in you, too."

I took her hand and we followed the small creek around the garden and up an embankment to a small opening in the rocks where the now setting sun's rays were shining through. As we squeezed past the rocks, I decided to look back at the garden for one last time. It had vanished. We had traveled a great distance in the labyrinth and cavern, unbeknown to me. The lights of the city of Baghdad lay before us. I told Ishtar that this is where we part. I kissed her on her forehead and told her there would be plenty of evil men in the city ahead with whom she could ply her trade.

As I turned my back on her, she said, "Good bye and good luck, Assassin. Maybe we will meet again."

I took my prize, the ankh of Amun, and put it in my talons and flew towards the setting sun. Part of my ordeal was over, but a far more deadly quest lay ahead.

Chapter XI

Dear Diary, I went straight to Geraldine's tomb. I tapped on her casket and watched dust fall off of it to the floor. I thought if that would-be cop shows up again I'll cremate the bastard. I should just have minded my own business and I wouldn't be in this mess. I opened the casket and pulled Geraldine up by her shoulders and said, "You better have good news tonight on how

you will guarantee living up to your end of the bargain. If not, see this ankh? I will go back to 1910, not 1934, and I will crush your skull with it and you won't live to see eight." I then shoved her skeleton back down into her coffin.

When I got back to my home I sat down and wrote of my amazing adventure in the Garden of Eden. When the moon is full in a few days, I will descend with much trepidation into what modern man cannot even imagine. The door of Amun in the west was designed to work one way only. I can get in, but the only way out is through the east. And I have to travel all the way to the other side of the well to get to it. As I lay in bed tonight I wondered just what Geraldine had in mind.

I closed my eyes for just a moment. I was very tired. I lay on my back with my right arm dangling off the side of the bed. All of a sudden I felt something grab my wrist as if it were trying to pull me under the bed. With a startled look I quickly opened my eyes and looked into Geraldine's face. She was prostrate and hovering about ten inches over my body. She reached out with her skeletal hand and ran her index finger over my lips. She said, "Ye of such little faith." Then she told me, "Here is what you are to do, Assassin. I am going to leave you one half of the answer to a genetic puzzle that can save the life of the little one. Take it with you when you go back to 1934. If you don't, you won't find it when you come back because all of reality will have changed. Remember it is only one half of the answer. You would be wasting valuable time running all over the country trying to get some brilliant geneticist to figure it out without the other half. You will need to get the first half of the answer from my brown notebook. You see, Assassin, just by pure chance I worked on the problem of Tay-Sachs back then. I could not solve the problem then, but with what I have seen in the past few years, I now have the answer. I keep it on top of my dresser in my bedroom.

"You know, Assassin, I was way ahead of my time. My contemporaries could not begin to comprehend my work. Of course, since I was a woman, my work would have been the subject of scorn anyway. Maybe when you give me back my life I can solve other genetic problems. Take my notebook with you when you return to the present. When we meet again I will be an old lady. I like to think that when you show me my work I will still be in a good mental state where I can decipher it for you."

I said, "Well, what if you can't?"

She then said, "Some Ph.D. in genetics can claim credit for my research after telling you how to save Joshua. Be kind to me, Assassin, and help me with my faith. You are always saying people like Joshua do not deserve the fate that they receive. I did not deserve my fate!"

I said, "That's it? This is your guarantee! How do you propose giving me one half of the answer. What do you want me to do, you dumb bitch—take it down in shorthand? Besides, you can give me anything and I would not know the difference until it is too late. So that's no guarantee!"

Geraldine then came up with the knockout punch. She floated under the bed and came up beside me and said, "That's the only guarantee you are going to get, Assassin. But answer me this: If you don't like the bargain, what are you going to do with the ankh? The ancient garden is gone forever. There will be no going back to it through time. The Eternal will eventually know the ankh is missing, and guess who he is going to think took it. Go to save all of us. You have to leave it in the well of fate where all things exist. So, Assassin, I believe you will live up to our agreement."

I got pissed and thoughtlessly grabbed my clock radio and threw it through her formless body. The radio slammed into the wall, causing young Joshua to cry at the noise and wake up

Thelma Bloom.

Thelma came over and knocked on my door. I told her I dropped something and that I was sorry for the disturbance. When I went back to my bedroom, ingrained into the mirror was a rectangle about four inches square. The answer consisted of a chromosome strain followed by a chemical formula and an equation in four parts. I ran my hand over the surface of the mirror and wondered how Geraldine had engraved it into the glass.

I thought she had left until she whispered into my ear, "Do you know why I got hit by that car and killed? I had something on my mind and so I was careless and not paying attention. Otherwise I would have seen that drunken slob run the red light. What was on my mind, Assassin, was a part of the missing answer, which if you don't have you will not be able to solve the problem. I had not written it down in my notebook. I was going to, but I died before I could. So don't plan on screwing me once you retrieve the first part of the answer by taking the two parts to the head of microbiology at Harvard University. He won't be able to figure it out. Your only hope is to save me and have me tell you what I was thinking. Once you save my life from the accident, all will be changed and by then you will have already killed someone in my place—so I will be safe from your wrath, if you were planning on betraying me. Goodbye, Assassin. Good luck and good hunting."

She disappeared into the mirror. I took my stone knife and cut out the answer. Where the lines of convergence become one at the valley of the twin mountains, I will find the untouched false door of Amun. But at least right now I went back to bed, after picking up my radio.

Once more I had the misfortune of dreaming . This time I was in Seth's tomb. There was a faint glow in the tomb. The place was enormous—much bigger than I remembered it. I hid behind a statue of Ptah, the god of Memphis. I saw my brother

sitting on his throne, only his left arm was stretched out and his left hand was around the neck of the King of the People of the Dark. Seth had managed to capture the King of the Dark and was holding him ransom. The ransom was brought to him by other people of the dark and was light rays they had stolen from humans.

Seth had not been in the dark for centuries after all. Standing before him were kings of the demons of the night, presidents, prime ministers and despots, and they were guarding a cage that contained a beast that was part man and part leopard. The leopard's teeth were out of proportion to its mouth. It was looking around and I was afraid it would see me and give me away since it could speak. I backed up and fell into an abyss, but before I hit the bottom, which was filled with crocodiles, I managed to break my fall and hold firm to the side of the abyss. I managed to climb up hand over hand. As I got to the top of the abyss I looked up to see my brother and his demon allies looking down at me. The king of the people of the dark begged Seth to let him kill me. I let go and fell back down and was devoured by the crocodiles. I then dreamed of my mother.

I woke up. I had rolled over on the ankh that I had left on my bed. I turned on the lamp next to my bed and sat up. I picked up the ankh. It was interesting how the bones were fused together. Someone or something had stomped on it while it was still alive. The serpent will bruise thy heel and humans will strike at its head. Maybe the snake's bones have been there all of these centuries because the Eternal was waiting for me to pick them up. I put the ankh down on the floor and turned off the lamp. I looked out the window at the night sky, and for anyone who has eyes to see, the announcement of the end of days is there like a celestial violet neon sign. I have glanced at it before, but tonight I stared at it in astonishment. The Eternal has changed the date. I now know it will be sooner, but I don't know the exact date. I

thought: Is he fed up with his creation? I must ponder this. I wonder if I have tricked the King of the Universe or am I unwittingly doing his bidding on my quest? Why doesn't he tell me or kill me? Does he have a master plan that must be played out?

Chapter XII

Dear Diary, it was a good day! I know what I have to do, and I'm glad to be away from Geraldine. It is nice to be back in my homeland. The Egyptian desert will always be my special place. I sat alone at the top of Khufu's pyramid and remembered when these stones were new. There were no vapor trails from jets overhead then. Now these stones are weather beaten by the 4500 years of desert wind.

I climbed down and took the tourist's tour. In the crowd was a little kid—a girl named MacKynzie—maybe seven years old. She kept staring at me as if she knew what I was. It is an insight the Eternal sometimes gives to the young. She was still staring at me when I decided to take a right turn through the stones to Khufu's true resting place—and the resting place of Didi, his magician. I had been at the back of a line of tourists, so only MacKynzie saw me go through the stones. I'm sure she will never forget it. The pupils in her eyes dilated. She started to cry out to her parents, but I put my finger to my lips and whispered, "Shhh."

Khufu's true resting place was lit with sunlight from small shafts about four inches in diameter leading to the outside, and my friend, the North Star, shines directly on his sarcophagus at night. His resting place was made out of pure crystal, and he lay

there sealed in his sarcophagus looking exactly as he did on the day he died. His flesh was still soft, and his black hair was combed to one side. The priests of Egypt had filled his crystal coffin with manna from heaven itself, so he was perfectly preserved.

Dear Diary, I feel sick and full of remorse in this lonely place. Even though Khufu was an evil man and a tyrant, I would be willing to talk to him since he is from the old days. If, just for a moment, I had the glory of the Eternal, I would put my hand on his head and say, "With these eyes, see again; and with this nose, breathe in the breath of life again; and with this mouth, speak to me again." Then I thought: Maybe the Eternal is lonely, too, but he can withstand the onslaught of loneliness and acts as a buffer between all that does not exist and all that does. I looked back down at Khufu and thought, "Even though he could prevail against all of his enemies, he could not defeat blood poisoning from abscessed teeth." He died believing his life was too short—an injustice—even though he had reigned for 27 years. He felt justice only existed for himself and his family and friends. It is the same today

It is interesting how the human race never changes. The humans' weapons of war and their technology have improved greatly, but the one constant is the human heart. Only a very few humans have kind and giving hearts, and they go their way in life living in obscurity, doing good works that go unrewarded. That will always be the case, but the evil ones, from the priests of Khufu to the religious assholes of today, are awash in riches. Perhaps on the day of reckoning the Eternal will allow me to kill them all. I would enjoy it immensely.

I stayed in Khufu's tomb for another hour, reliving the old days again and again in my mind. As I started to leave, I picked up a pot that once held bread that had rotted away a long time ago. The pot was made by Khufu's grandson. It was made out of

love for his grandfather. Everything else in this chamber of solitude were offerings shaped by fear and duty to the mighty king. It is the simple things in life that represent real love and faithfulness. I put the pot back down and picked up a small gold statue of Amun that was hooked to a gold necklace. I took it with me, and as I did I said, "Khufu, old friend, you never did settle our account on the true number of the people of the dark that we dispatched for you. Your tally sheet was incorrect. Of course, you knew it was incorrect, so now I say that this necklace is payment in full."

I rejoined the tour, which was just ending. MacKynzie was a few yards behind her parents. I put the necklace around her neck, and she happily kept rubbing the small statue of Amun with her fingers. Then she ran to join her parents. I put a thought in their minds that they had bought the necklace for her. That way they will let her keep the necklace, because, like the amulet of the heart, the statue of Amun has magical powers also—and, from what I saw in the stars, MacKynzie will need all the help she can get in her lifetime.

The End is coming. There will come that terrible day when the moon will appear ten times larger than it now looks as a full moon on an autumn night. Little veins of red will slowly make their way across the lunar surface. This time, though, it will be at midday and the sky will be black. The streets will be deserted. A stifling hot and relentless wind will envelope the cities, and locusts will destroy the Earth's food supply. It will be the day that some will have found God and at the same time others will betray the Eternal. There will be gnashing of teeth. Governments will plead for calm. So-called experts will appear on television channels trying to explain away all that has happened. Religious hypocrites will flood the sanctuaries of their churches and pray in earnest for the first time in their lives. Parents will desert their children. Murder and theft will be the order of the day through-

out the world. Panic will reign and a gray haired MacKynzie will franticly look through her dresser for her necklace. She will keep telling herself, "I know it is here somewhere. I must find it!" She will then see something glowing under some of her keepsakes in her dresser. She will look at the glowing, golden statue of Amun. Quickly, she will put it on, knowing that the necklace will be her pass back into Khufu's pyramid, while others beat on the stone door begging for entrance—she will be safe from the death raining down on earth.

I went over and visited my old friend the Sphinx. The Sphinx was not Egyptian—at least not at first. Mina was not an Egyptian. After the work that Seth and I did trying to carve Mina's face on the Sphinx, there it sat with only children playing around it from 13127 BC to 8310 BC. After we had dispatched Mina, Egypt's first king, there would not be another king of Egypt until about 4400 BC. The place was pretty much deserted.

In 8310 BC the Atlantians read in the stars that their civilization was coming to an end. They had become obsessed with creating monsters in the hopes that somehow their research could elevate them to the rank of gods and immortality. They now knew the Eternal had turned away from them, for their sins were too great to be forgiven—but they did not know how their end would come. In despair the Atlantians completed the Sphinx as a warning to the human race forever more. Their Sphinx was their monument of terror.

No one bothered the Sphinx, with its remarkable human face, until King Khafre, wanting to outdo his father, King Khufu, had the face changed to look more like him. It was actually an amazing job of sculpturing by the artist. The original face had been engraved into the granite since it was so hard to chisel. This time the stone was cut away, making it a true sculpture. Khafre liked the work of his artists very much. As time went by, though,

he thought about their work more and more. One night he finally got up about 2 a.m. and had his guards go and bring the artists before him. He told them he had had a dream that, unfortunately, they all had to be put to death. Otherwise, other kings would try to hire them to create monuments to themselves, and this the gods of Egypt would not allow. The artists begged for mercy, but the king said, "I'm sorry but even I cannot go against the gods of Egypt."

I thought to myself what an egotistical, lying son of a bitch he was.

My thoughts returned to the present. It was amusing listening to two morons talking about how they were sure the secrets of the universe were buried under the right paw of the Sphinx. There is nothing under the right paw except what is left of Mina's sons. I guess I'm dragging my feet now—not wanting to face what I came here for. Well, not exactly here—400 miles southwest. I will go there with the rising sun in two days. Until then I will go and visit Seth's tomb, and it won't be a dream this time. It is in the direction that I will be traveling. I will look through the window at my brother and see what he has to say. He and I are both blessed and cursed, and in some strange way, I still care for him.

Chapter XIII

Dear Diary, I had not been back to the dwelling place of my brother since I had betrayed him. I had been everywhere else in the world many times. I guess that is why I still envisioned Seth's tomb and the lay of the land to be the same as it was 3200 years

ago. Much has changed since then. Lake Nasser came within six miles of his tomb. Lucky for the humans no one excavated the area with a bulldozer and caved in one of the walls of his prison when they were building the Aswan Dam. Ramses II had built this tomb in an inconspicuous place in the wall of a small gully. The Egyptians called the gully a wadi. I called it Ramses Wadi. I climbed about twenty feet down a cliff into the gully.

I had remembered it being deeper, and it may have been all of those years ago. There had been small stone steps leading up to the entrance. I walked about a half a league when I noticed crushed granite stones lying about. I climbed up about twelve feet and discovered a small hole hidden behind two pieces of broken granite. The steps were gone—a victim of the ages. I crawled in and found myself in the antechamber of Ramses' tomb. Water had flooded the room in the past and filled about two thirds of the hall with dirt and debris. I had brought along a flashlight with me which I used to explore the room. It seemed that tomb robbers had taken everything of value many years ago.

There was not much there—only enough to fool Seth. But the one place they did not break into was the next chamber. It bore the engraving of Seth's cartouche on the door. The carving of Amun was on the other side of it. It was still easily recognizable. I slid down a dirt bank and carefully walked to the wall. The only sound that would break the silence was that of the desert wind that found its way past the rock, into the chamber. I ran my hand over Seth's engraving. I felt a lot of different emotions going through my mind. I shined the light on the wall and found a crack that was about three feet long and maybe two feet wide in its middle. It must have been created by water pressure. The crack must not have gone through the engraving of Amun because if it had Seth would have escaped.

I next did something very foolish. I put my hand into the

opening and shined my flashlight into the room. It, too, was filled with a lot of debris, but one corner was relatively dirt free. I thought that is because the viewing window acted as a drain for the water. I shined the light into that corner. At first I thought that there was a pile of rope in the corner of the room. However as I moved the light around I realized it was not a rope but a snake. It raised its head and turned toward the light. I froze. I had found my brother.

With the strength of a lion and the speed of a cobra Seth lunged at me. I pulled my arm out of the opening and, as I did, I dropped the light on to Seth's side of the wall. It shined straight up. I fell backwards and heard a clicking sound. I looked into the illuminated opening and saw Seth's stone knife trying to thrust through the opening. I instinctively pulled my knife out, but I don't know if I could have used it on him. I know he could not get out or he would have been all over me. I lay back on the dirt bank and just kept staring at that hole in the wall.

Out of the gloom came the voice of a child. He sung in ancient Egyptian a song that he used to sing, and one that I hated: "I went to the Nile to get a drink of water, to get a drink of water. A snake swam by me as I got a drink of water. A crocodile ate the snake as I got a drink of water. A hippopotamus crushed the crocodile as I got a drink of water."

I covered my ears and yelled "Shut up!" As I did, I realized I was speaking in English, so I repeated it in Coptic. I waited for a reply that did not come. Instead, all I heard was his soft, evil laughter. I turned and began to crawl back up the bank to get out of this place when I heard Seth say, "Don't leave me Horus."

I slid back down the bank and looked at the hole in the wall. "What do you want?"

"Well we have 3,200 years to catch up on. Do you know how I kept my sanity–sitting in the dark in the silence? The first few days of my imprisonment I watched Dakulah, the one true

love of my life, slowly die of hunger and thirst. I held her in my arms until the end. I put her in a corner of the tomb and covered her with a royal tunic befitting her noble rank. You murdered an innocent when you left Dakulah here with me, my loving brother. Would you like to show me the ruling from Amun granting you the authority to carry out your crime? Do you have any idea, my brother, how hard it is to live day and night in a tomb for thousands of years. The first ten years were not too bad. I saw the light of the rising moon. It was the only good part of my day—or I should say, night. After a few more years, the sand covered the entire tomb and with that there was only blackness. My thoughts went back and forth from feeling intense despair to absolute rage. I would fantasize facing you one on one. I always won in those dreams. I killed you, Horus, every time. Only the method would vary in my thoughts.

"I also considered every day that there must be a way out of my prison tomb. There was not a way out, though, because you did an excellent job with the engraving of Amun. As the years went by, I wondered how the world was changing outside. I even wondered whether you were still alive. I thought maybe you were dead because otherwise you would have surely freed me. I had not done anything that warranted the punishment that you had bestowed on me. We are, after all, brothers. Cain was more merciful to Abel than you were to me. You knew that I would not die. How could you do this to me? Do you think I would have done this to you?"

I said, "Seth," but before I could go on, he kept talking. "Horus, I thought maybe you wanted to rule the world by yourself. I would run through my mind our memories of close to 23,000 years. I could never come up with anything that would make you do this. Would our mother have approved of this? Floods would come every so often and I would spend days and weeks with water up to my neck. Didn't any of this ever cross

your mind? Did you lie in bed at night and laugh at how your treachery had brought me down?"

I thought about what he had said and then replied, "You would have ruled the earth in terror and in fear and everyone would have to bow down to you, if I had not stopped you. Maybe it got to your ego, Seth, when you led Ramses' armies to victories over the Babylonians and Ramses kept all the glory for himself. I tried to tell you, Seth. Remember, when you came home that day, drenched in blood that was caked with the desert sand, I told you Ramses would never honor you. That is why I have never fought a war for any country. There have been hundreds of wars, and each one was a war of justice in the eyes of someone. You thought the war you waged for Ramses was just—but it wasn't. Ramses then did the unthinkable in your eyes. He wanted Dakulah for himself—the beautiful princess with the red hair and soft white skin and an innocent smile—all a rarity in Egypt. So you started to go a little nuts."

"Yes, Dakulah was like you said, Horus, but I had the misfortune to watch her slowly rot away and saw her beautiful white flesh fall away from her bones. I began to hate with the ferocity of a desert sand storm. I could have murdered tens of thousands in an effort to become king, but I did not. I've killed no one in thirty-two centuries. Would you like me to recite your accomplishments of murder and mayhem?"

I interrupted Seth and reminded him of something he had forgotten. I said, "It is true that you haven't killed in centuries, but Ramses joined me in what was treachery in your eyes because you joined with the Jewish slaves in a revolt that killed many of the young children of Egypt, including the son of Ramses."

Seth did not counter what I said, but instead provoked me by saying, "I don't blame you entirely though, Horus. You were Mom's favorite—the favorite of an ancient demon and a

whore—what an honor!"

I lunged at the opening in the wall, enraged and with stone knife in hand. Our hands met in the middle of the opening—knife pressing against knife. The flashlight still shined straight up, illuminating Seth's face. He did not look any different. His white scraggly hair was shoulder length, his eyes were almost black but surrounded by white rings caused by the darkness. It obviously had not affected his eyesight though. He had his jaw locked, and his teeth looked as if they had been ground down from being ground together. Both of us pushed our knives together as hard as we could. I heard a cracking sound and saw that my right elbow was putting so much pressure on the wall that I was afraid the crack in the wall would become enlarged. I withdrew my knife and arm from the opening.

I realized then that Seth had tried to goad me into taking down the wall to get at him. The last thing I wanted was for that wall to come down. "I think I will leave you now, Seth, to the darkness and to your dreams. I have places to go to and fro. Enjoy your life my brother."

Seth then said in a conciliatory tone, "Wait! I withdraw my statement." This was the Egyptian equivalent of an apology. Seth continued, "What would I have to do to convince you I mean you no harm, my brother? You know yourself the end is coming. Do you really plan to leave me here until then?"

"Seth, I will have to think of this some more. You know where I have to go. I can still tell, Seth, when you read my mind, and I can tell you are blocking some of your thoughts from me. In answer to what you are thinking, Seth, I don't have a good reason for risking my life for a little boy."

Seth said to me, "Why don't you take me with you? You don't know what you will find at the well of fate. The two of us can take on anything!"

I said, "This is a journey I must take alone." I suggest you

hope that I survive. If I do, I will be back in seven days. I will not forsake you again. I give you my word as an Egyptian."

Seth in resignation then told me, "Then I will look forward to our next meeting. To hasten our meeting though, my brother, why don't you just kill Robert Hanson Walker? He is part of the reason for your ordeal. After all, you said yourself that you have to kill someone." Then he said to me, "May the god of the universe keep you safe and soften your heart."

I climbed back out into the daylight. I sat outside of his tomb and I kept thinking that there was something unusual about Seth's prison tomb and our meeting. The way the granite stones were arranged the setting looked staged. It also crossed my mind that, with all of the people scouring Egypt looking for tombs, it's hard to believe no one had found and investigated this one. Seth had been there for all of these centuries, and yet he did not show that much emotion at meeting me. It was as if he were expecting me. I guess if you haven't seen your brother for 3200 years and then you meet him again, it would always be unusual. He's right about one thing, though, I doubt I could keep him imprisoned forever. I thought to myself maybe I had done some great noble deed by coming here. Then again, maybe not. Maybe I came here out of loneliness or curiosity. One thing is for certain, though—Seth now has hope that he did not have 30 minutes ago.

Dear Diary, I waited until the 19th day of Thoth, out of honor of him. I sat on a rock watching the rising sun spread its rays across the desert. When the sun reaches a height of 45 degrees, it will reveal which rock on the hill to the west of me that I should touch. An Egyptian and his wife passed by me. We exchanged greetings and they went on their way. They had taken the back of an old pick up truck and attached it, using two long poles, to the sides of a donkey. It was an interesting form of transportation. I waited until they were out of sight and then

made my way to the one rock that appeared purple in the morning sun. I tried to pull up on the rock, but I was not strong enough. I decided I needed some leverage. I remembered the man and his wife had a piece of steel rod in their cart. I ran them down. After much haggling, I got him to sell me the six-foot-long by two-inch diameter piece of steel for $5 American.

It was a good thing that I had left my lamp by the rock of Amun or I might have spent the rest of the day looking for the right rock again. The sun was high enough now so that all the rocks were the same color. Using my pole as a lever, I pried up the stone. I propped up the rock with my rod and squirmed through the opening and found myself sliding down a set of steps. When I hit the bottom, I stood up just in time to hear my rod give way, and the boulder came slamming back down. I had my lamp with me, so I started to light it, and then I realized that there was light in here, and I had no idea of its origin.

I was standing in front of another door. I put my lamp down and pulled as hard as I could on the door. It started to open. Even I can't walk through the door of the well of fate. The well has been here for all of time, but this door had been built by King Akhenaton and his wife Nefertiti when they ruled this land. He would later pay for his sacrilege at the hands of the priests of Thebes. King Akhenaton, the Egyptian king who had faith in only one god, the Sun God, paid with his life. He was slaughtered in front of this door, which still bears the stains of his blood. It was interesting how some of his blood had run down the door and filled little cracks in the limestone, creating an image of a scorpion.

I squeezed past the door opening and found myself in a cave that did not appear to have been chiseled out by man. This place had always been this way. As I made my way down into the cave, I discovered the place was full of belosaurus, the cave-dwelling, blind scorpions. There were thousands of them on the

floor, the walls and ceiling. They had white bodies with maroon pincers. They were not very big—maybe two inches long. Water droplets kept falling from the ceiling and hitting me on the head, and the water would then run down my face. It was irritating. I kept thinking it was one of those little scorpions landing on my head. I kept making my way down toward the bottom of the cave. I climbed down all day and soon began to notice that the light was failing. I took my lamp and tried to light it, only to discover that I had carelessly let the oil leak out. I decided to lean up against a rock and wait out the coming night.

There was a hole in the cave floor, and in the fading light I could see water glistening in the cave room below me. Was that the well of fate or only the remains of lakes Natron and Maat? Wherever the well of fate was in this holy place, legend says the Eternal filled it up with his tears—tears brought about by the thoughts of yesterday and the knowledge of what tomorrow will bring to his creation. From what I have seen of his creation he might not want to cry any more tears for them. I have a rare perspective on the human race, thanks to longevity. I know the great majority are assholes. Soon they will probably breed themselves out of existence, for the one thing that the intelligent, the rich, the stupid and the poor—especially the poor—all know how to do is to screw. Of course, if they keep waging war, then maybe they can keep the population in check. It is interesting that whereas I have little regard for the human race, I am at this moment sitting in total darkness with scorpions crawling on me and ready to put my existence on the line for a small boy who the world would never miss if he died.

I wonder if Seth had been free all of these centuries, how would the world be? It could be that the world would be better off. I don't know for sure what he would have done. I'm not much better than he is—in fact maybe no better.

I decided to take my frustration out on the scorpions. I

started crushing them. I would crush them and wipe my hands off on the rocks. I sat in total darkness, crushing and wiping. I had to find a new rock. The one I was using was now covered in scorpion blood. I reached out into the blackness and rubbed my hand against another rock to clean off my hands. As I did, the rock moved. I recoiled in fear. Whatever it was brushed by me. I felt for the rock behind me and quietly climbed over it. I drew my stone knife and sat in the blackness waiting for the dawn. The dawn could not come fast enough for me now.

I kept coming back to the same conclusion. I had never gone against the Eternal. This I considered a noble cause. I never killed anyone who was just—only the unjust faced my wrath. Even then it was usually with the mandate from the King of the Universe. Dakulah's death was an accident. If there had been any way to get her out of the tomb and leave Seth in prison, I would have done it. I was sorry about Seth. I had given Seth my word as an Egyptian that I would return. I didn't trust him, though— if our positions were reversed, I would have asked that I wanted the blood of an Egyptian along with his word. I wondered if I had put my hand in the opening of his prison wall would he have sliced my hand and his with his stone knife to seal the bargain— or would he have tried to take my arm off with that cursed knife of his. I created and gave him, unwittingly, that knife when I was only 24.

Diary Dear, all those years ago I had made a journey south to what would become Kenya. The smoke from the sacred volcano of Mount Kenya could be seen for thousands of miles, like billowing clouds on the horizon. My quest was to find the sacred glass crystals that can only be found in the belly of hell. I knew Mount Kenya would vomit up from time to time that which I was seeking. As I made my way there, my heart, at the time was gladdened with the thought that I would make a stone knife for my brother.

I walked across the plains of Kenya. I remember that I came upon a smoldering camp fire and found death. The last of God's first creation of men were laid out on the ground next to each other—a man, his wife and three children. All of them had been skinned while they were still alive. These five were the last of the Neanderthals. Gone was a race of gentle and kind humans. They had been murdered for sport by the offspring of those who were cursed and were then kicked out of that now gone garden of stone. I buried them all in one large grave.

If I survive my ordeal here at the well of fate I will go back and honor their memory at their gravesite, where I interred them so long, long ago. I went hunting for their killer. I didn't have to go far. In a village less than two miles away I came upon perhaps 200 people chanting and dancing while paying homage to their chief. He was acting out before them how he had courageously slain the Neanderthals. He had draped himself in the skin of the Neanderthal's wife. I stood and watched while the rage in me grew. Cowards love to prey on the weak. The crocodile creeps up on the antelope as the antelope drinks at the river, and then the crocodile executes the perfect ambush. The crocodile kills only to eat. It never bothers the lion, though, even if the lion cools himself by the water's edge. The crocodile knows the lion represents death on four feet.

This murderer went after the helpless and kills for fun, and now I was going after him. The people saw me and stopped dancing. One of their warriors came at me with a spear, which I promptly took away and thrust through his heart. The people scattered. The chief of their tribe attempted to run also, but I grabbed him by his throat, and then, taking a vine, tied him by his feet and hoisted him up in a tree. All of his people were hiding in the jungle, looking at me. I looked around for a clay pot. Another one of the fools, now hiding in the jungle, threw another spear at me. I sidestepped it. I then picked it up and threw it

back and heard a scream. I guess it hit its mark. I put the clay pot directly under the head of their murderous leader. I cut his throat and watched his blood run into the pot. He made sort of a gurgling sound in protest, as I recall. The pot was the size of a two-quart pot. I had taken the skin of the female Neanderthal and lined the pot with it. It actually did not take too long before the pot was overflowing. I had done what I could to avenge his victims. I took the pot with me. As I left, behind me I could hear all the weeping and wailing of the people of the village. It made me feel good.

After three more days of walking I got to Mount Kenya. I made my way to one of the rivers of lava, and there I found my glass crystals lying amid the fumes of sulfur. Using a flint rock I would heat and chip my crystals over and over. Then I would temper them in the blood of the unjust. Little by little my stone knives took shape. With each reheating in the lava and the subsequent tempering, the stone knives took on a deep red color.

The cave was now starting to get light. So enough about my stone knives. I strained my eyes to see what I had encountered in the night. At first I could not make out anything, but then I saw a movement out of the corner of my eye. I stared at what was the true scorpion king. It was the last eurypterid—a giant sea scorpion that was also able to survive on land. Perhaps it came out of the well of fate. Maybe it is the well's protector. It measured maybe 14 feet long with pincers big enough to crush a small car. The scorpion's stinger was another six feet or so above his body. If he could get me with his stinger, he wouldn't just sting me—I would be impaled upon it. I thought that maybe he was blind, like his little brothers. I was wrong. As soon as I moved he came toward me. I could not go in any direction, but then I remembered the hole in the floor. I squeezed through it as the scorpion kept trying to reach at me with those pincers of his. I hung on to what was now the ceiling to me, and I looked for a

place to land.

I dropped about ten feet to the floor. Ahead of me was a suspension bridge over a pool of water. I guess I wasn't the first man here—somebody built this bridge. I wonder who. I was making my way across the bridge when it began to shake. I looked back and the scorpion was attempting to cross the bridge, but he was too big and weighed too much. The bridge broke and fell into the water along with the scorpion. I reached out and grabbed one of the support ropes to avoid falling into the water myself. As I hung onto the rope, the ankh fell into the water. I thought for a moment that maybe I should go into the water for it.

Diary Dear, out of nowhere a giant vortex began to swing me and the rope around in a circle. I hung on for dear life. I looked, and below me the water was swirling around faster and faster. Soon the water enveloped the scorpion, and the water began to disappear. First it was just a hole in the middle of the water, but the hole kept expanding, much like the opening of the shutter on a camera. Then the water was gone and so was the vortex. The rope was just hanging still with me at the bottom.

It was as if the cavern was now a giant inverted planetarium. The water had been replaced by stars. I saw the morning star. I hung there looking down for a while and then thought that I had to do something. I watched rocks and scorpions falling down into the abyss. I felt for my life. I have a lot of strength—but I have limits, too. I climbed up the rope and found handholds, much like that on a climbing wall. Hand over hand, I made my way to the opposite side of where the bridge had been. I did not know what lay ahead of me. I climbed through another tunnel. Whatever happened now, I was glad to be rid of the ankh of Amun. I saw in the distance a warm orange/red glow. I hurried a little faster now. I kept staring at the light. It was all encompassing.

Chapter XIV

I was startled to hear the sound of brakes on a car. I looked to my left and saw a 1932 Model A Ford with a very unhappy driver behind the wheel. He yelled at me, "You should watch where you're going, mister. I could have hit you."

I apologized and asked him where I was. I had become mesmerized staring at the morning sun. He said, "You don't know where you are?" I replied that I had gotten off a freight train and wasn't sure.

He then said, "You are in Brighton, Colorado."

I walked towards Denver and then realized that my god-given supernatural abilities may have returned by now. They had. I flew as a bird of prey towards Denver. As I did, I felt buckshot fly by me. Some asshole was trying to shoot me down. It was his lucky day because I was still in a mood of awe. I had just survived something that no one other than Seth and the ghost of Geraldine even knew existed. I got to Denver and picked up a copy of the *Denver Post*. It was dated March 17, 1934. I had bought myself three days. I looked at the clock on the tallest building in downtown Denver, the Daniels and Fisher tower on 16th Street. It read 10:11 a.m. I have until sunrise on the 21st —a little over three days. That is all the time I will have to solve my problems. There will be no extensions.

I was looking forward to meeting Geraldine. I went to her house. She was living there with her parents. It was a nice two-story house, and the city had just put in a new sidewalk. I was careful not to step on it since the cement was still wet. I went up to her front door. Obviously, there was no one home because Geraldine had left a message on her front door to her parents. She had gone to the Granada Theatre to see the latest Hollywood heartthrob, Spencer Tracy, in the movie *20,000*

Years in Sing-Sing. I thought to myself, I'll go to a movie. This time, though, I will have to sneak in. I don't believe the ticket seller will accept money from 65 years in the future.

I went through the theatre wall and found myself in the women's bathroom. Fortunately, no one was there so I made my exit and went in to look for where Geraldine was sitting. I took a seat right behind her. The movie was terrible. I sat there in the darkness studying her. Another thought crossed my mind. When Seth was young he would sometimes blurt out an idea or a suggestion that had an ulterior motive—one he would benefit from. He would think that he was playing a trick on me and that I was too dumb to understand his true meaning. So that brings me to the following: Diary Dear, why did he suggest that I kill Robert Hanson Walker?

Thankfully, the movie came to an end with Spencer Tracy going to the electric chair. I decided to follow Geraldine out of the theatre. As the people left the theatre, I thought about the six young male teenagers in front of me. Within ten years some or all of them would be dead. They will die or be wounded in jungles, deserts, or towns that right now none of them have ever heard of. But this has always been the plight of young men. In my ancient times the young men fought at Buhen, Napata, and Meroe. The young have always paid for someone's glory.

This theatre was what was known as a neighborhood theatre, prevalent up until the 1960's. Geraldine got up to leave. She was a little plump, I guess. Not bad looking, though. I found it interesting that she had told me that people had made fun of her size and weight. She had black hair and a nice complexion. She had a warm smile and a soft voice. She greeted just about everyone she passed on the sidewalk. Geraldine was about 5 feet 3 inches tall, and for some reason, she appeared taller to me as a ghost. Maybe my mind played tricks on me when I had first seen her in her coffin and then later in the mirror and in my bedroom.

I think now I will make her acquaintance. This should be very interesting.

I came up to her as she walked along. I said, "Excuse me, Miss. I'm new around here. I'm looking for the Town Talk Bakery. Could you tell me where to find it?"

Geraldine looked at me and said, "Why, yes. It is located right across the street from where I live."

I exclaimed, "Golly! What a coincidence."

Geraldine then said, haltingly, as if she were reconsidering her thoughts. "You can walk with me if you like. Otherwise, the bakery is at 27th and Decatur Street—only about three blocks from here."

I looked at her and smiled and said, "I would be delighted to walk with you."

She said, "You are wearing unusual clothes. I mean, there is nothing wrong with them. I have just never seen clothes like you have on."

I had to think fast. I had not taken what I was wearing into consideration earlier. I said, "Well, these clothes are all the rage in Europe." I changed the subject by saying, "So what do you do?"

With pride in her voice, Geraldine said, "I am a pathologist. I have a Ph.D. in pathology."

I said, "Gee whiz, that is really impressive!"

She looked at me and said, "What do you do?"

I said, "Well, I'm a monk on sabbatical from the Monastery of Saint Anthony in the Arabian Desert."

Dear Diary, I am familiar with Saint Anthony's Monastery. I had stopped by there in 1799 and executed a murderer who had taken refuge in the caves located in the mountains behind the monastery. He (whose name escapes me now) had joined with Napoleon and then deserted. He had managed to save himself from the guillotine in Marseille, but alas! he then ran into

me. I drowned him in the sacred water in the cave that had saved Saint Anthony from thirst centuries earlier. It beats going to the guillotine—besides, he said he was thirsty.

I said to Geraldine, "I'm so sorry. I should have introduced myself. My name is Father Phillip."

Geraldine smiled at me and said, "I am so pleased to make your acquaintance. I am Geraldine Donato." She laughed and said, "I guess I did things in reverse order, Father. People usually say their name before talking about their occupation."

I said, "Please just call me Phillip. So, Geraldine, tell me about your work. It sounds fascinating. Do you work with test tubes and things like that?"

"Well, kind of," she said, as if she were thinking of a way to put things in simple terms. Geraldine then said, "I am more interested in genetics. I believe that many diseases can be cured through genetics."

I said, "Holy smokes, Geraldine, that is really something."

In a firm voice, she stated, "We don't know how to do it yet. This concept is just a theory."

"Well, I say it is a good theory, Geraldine."

Then in a somewhat somber tone, she said, "There is my house, and there is the bakery."

I said, "Well, thank you, Geraldine." Then she asked me where I was staying. I replied that I had just arrived in Denver and did not yet have a hotel room.

Excitedly, she said, "You can stay with us. Mom and Dad won't mind. Besides, we are Catholic. I know they would be honored to have a priest stay with us. We have a spare bedroom. Where is your suitcase?"

I told her it was in a locker at Union Station. I knew I could lie and say it must have been stolen if I were confronted later. As we climbed the steps to her front door, she said, "Mom and Dad are home now. I left them a note on the door and it is missing

now, so they are home."

As Geraldine and I walked into the living room, Emilio, her father, put down the *Rocky Mountain News* that he had been reading. He stood up to greet me. Geraldine introduced us and Emilio said, "Mama, come quick. We have a visitor—a priest." Sophia looked like a carbon copy of Geraldine, only with gray hair.

Sophia gave me a big hug and then said, "Sit down. Dinner is almost ready." Geraldine followed her mother into the kitchen. I heard her tell her mother that they must talk me into staying. Emilio asked me if I followed baseball. I told him I did some and that I thought the St. Louis Cardinals would have a great year. Emilio looked like he had worked hard all of his life in the meat packing business. He was pretty stocky with black hair and blue eyes. I thought that in ten years he would look at his wife for the last time, but maybe they will know their daughter still lives this time. I thought we are both in the same line of work (so to speak, Dear Diary). We both work in blood. The dinner was very nice. We sat at the table talking and eating lasagna with sausage from Donato Meat Packing and washing it down with Chiantti wine.

Geraldine told me she was engaged to Frank Mazeri, III. "Want to see his picture?" she asked. I told Geraldine I would be honored. She took Frank's picture off the mantel and handed it to me. It was the same picture that had been in her casket. I had put her fiance's picture back in the casket after that cemetery guard discovered me in Geraldine's tomb. I thought: I wonder what would have happened if I had taken that picture with me? Would there have been two of them? I then thought, while smiling and eating: They are a nice family. They deserve better than what they will get in the future. Geraldine said that Frank was in the National Guard and was gone for a week down in Louisiana on army maneuvers.

After dinner Geraldine asked me if I would like to sit on their porch swing. I said that would be very nice. Geraldine sat in the swing playing with her hands and looking down. She said, "Father Phillip, can someone be good and not believe in Jesus?"

"Of course, Geraldine," I said.

She looked shocked and said, "But you are a priest. How can you say that?"

I said, "Well, Geraldine, I have learned in my travels that the Eternal cares only about the human heart. Kindness and charity is what has always mattered. The King of the Universe has faith in you, Geraldine. You keep faith in him and all will be well. What about Jesus? Well, Geraldine, think of him as an emissary. I have studied ancient manuscripts, and even the Egyptians had emissaries. Just because they were around before the Israelites and the Christians, doesn't mean their faith in the Eternal is counterfeit. After all, it's going to take the Christian church another 5000 years before they can claim the longevity record. But, above all, the Egyptians believed in one superior god. They called him Amun. It doesn't really matter, Geraldine, if the Egyptians called him Amun or you call him Jehovah or God. The main thing is just never give up your faith and never be a hypocrite."

Geraldine looked at me and said, "Father Phillip, you are a very unusual priest." Geraldine told me she was hoping to be able to do some additional pathology work at Notre Dame, but since she was a woman she might be turned down. I told her perhaps I could intervene on her behalf. I said I was a friend of a local priest who I was sure would write a letter of recommendation for her. She said she would be grateful. Geraldine showed me to my room, and I told her I would get my suitcase the next day.

I lay in bed, Dear Diary, staring at the ceiling and thinking about Seth. I then had a sobering thought: What if that hole in

the wall in Seth's tomb had not been made by flood water and the ages, but had been made by a man? My mind began to race. What if he can already get out? I thought the hell with it—I can "what if" myself to death.

I got up early and left a note for Geraldine telling her I would be back to take her out to lunch. I saw Emilio go off to work, while Sophia slept in. After a quick trip to the South Platte River, I found an antique dealer in Denver. I sold him a small Egyptian medallion. I now had spending money—all yellow-back $5 bills. People that I passed on the street didn't pay that much attention to my clothes. They did notice my sneakers, though. Since I was here to save Geraldine's life, I turned my attention to who I would kill. I passed a panhandler who was especially obnoxious. For a moment or two I considered ending his life, but then I thought that I didn't know what his future holds. I guess it was his lucky day.

I went to see a Catholic priest in a small run-down Catholic church. I knew he had some pull with the faculty of Notre Dame. I got there just as he was walking into his church. I waited for about five minutes and then went inside to meet him. His secretary asked me if I knew Father Michael. I told her to tell him that we both had a mutual friend. She went into his office and he agreed to see me. He came out of his office, and I shook his hand. I stared into his eyes and told him that I had something very personal to discuss with him. We went into his office, and he closed the door and offered me a seat. He said, "Now what can I do for you, sir?"

I said, "Father, I am here to ask you to do a friend of mine a favor. She wants to do some research at Notre Dame University. She specializes in pathology. I know you have some pull there—lots of friends on the faculty—so you are going to help me out."

With a puzzled look on his face, he said, "I don't under-

stand what you mean. Why would I put in a recommendation when I don't know him or her?"

I said, "Well, Mike—I hope you don't mind my calling you Mike. It's a she, Mike, and she comes highly recommended."

He said, "Recommended by who?"

I said, "Recommended by Betty Jean Thompson."

He stared at me with an open mouth and in shock. I got up and went over and sat on his desk right next to him. I took his fountain pen out of the holder and pushed the pen into his white shirt. I watched the ink spread out and make a big blob on his shirt. I said, "You remember Betty Jean, don't you, Mike?"

He stared at the fountain pen and said, stuttering, "How, how is she doing?"

I breathed a sigh and said, "Not bad for someone at the bottom of the South Platte River. Golly, Mike, I almost forgot! I have something for you—your driver's license. When you killed her and left her in the car and then pushed the car in the river, you mistakenly left your driver's license in the car, too. I thought you might want it back. Never know when a cop might stop you, huh?"

Father Michael was starting to break down. He said, "What do you want? Are you a policeman?"

I said, "No, Mike. I'm here for a recommendation for my friend, remember? You will have to answer later for killing Betty Jean. Now this is who I want a recommendation for, Mikey— Geraldine Donato. Here is a college and work history about her. By the way, Mike, her faith isn't all that strong, so don't get any ideas about taking advantage of Geraldine and then forgiving yourself." I kept patting his cheek. "You understand, Mike, you understand? You don't want me to have to come back and kill you, do you? I would come back, Mike. You see, I don't give a shit about your being a priest."

He said, "Yes, I understand. You made it very plain.

Whoever you are, I want you to know that what happened to Betty Jean was an accident."

I took my foot and shoved him and his chair into the wall. "Don't lie to me—I know the truth," I said. "You were afraid she would ruin your career. It was easy to get her to go with you because she loved you. Then you strangled her. You have always had a problem with women, haven't you, Mike? Of course, there is a bright spot shining through your indiscretions. You only like women, so at least you're not a queer—that's something to be proud of, Mike. Some in your profession seem to have a thing for little boys, don't they? Is that what you call an accident, Mikey—killing Betty Jean? Now you get me that letter of recommendation by the 20th of this month at 2 p.m. You have two days to write it, and it better be really good. Otherwise, you are going to be headline news. I can see it now—asshole priest convicted of murder and sentenced to hang." As I left, I smiled at his secretary and said, "Ma'am, you have a really nice day."

I met up with Geraldine. She was waiting on her front porch for me. I looked at her and said, "Are you hungry?"

She said, "Yes." I asked her where we could go and she recommended Woolworth's Five and Dime in downtown Denver. She said they had a nice lunch counter there. We took the trolley car. It was about a 20-minute ride. The trolley car was not crowded, so we sat side by side, looking out the window at 1934 Denver. She asked me if I had been inside a pyramid, since I worked and lived in Egypt. I told her, "Yes, several times."

She said, "Isn't it interesting how the pyramids were built? Thousand of workers using ropes pulled the blocks up long ramps. Some of the blocks weighed thousands of pounds."

I glanced at her and said, "That's not exactly how the heaviest blocks were put in place. The blocks would be cut out of the limestone in oversize squares. The blocks would then be cut down into a hexagon. The hexagon block would be rolled up the

ramps. Once set in place, the block would be cut down into a cube. This greatly speeded up the moving process of the blocks."

Geraldine said, "Why, I have never heard of that theory before."

I said, "Well, it is not a theory. Why, in Egypt it has been known for thousands of years—you can take my word for it." Geraldine asked me if I had met any of the archeologists who were working in Egypt. I said, looking straight into her eyes, "You mean tomb robbers?"

Geraldine exclaimed, "Oh, that's a terrible thing to call them."

I said, "What I'm calling them is what they are. How would your country like it if the Egyptians came to America and took the body of Abraham Lincoln and transported it back to Egypt to be put on display?"

Geraldine said, "It's not the same thing. The tombs of Egypt are very old, and Lincoln has been dead for only 69 years."

I said, "Time does not diminish the desecration of one's final resting place. The Egyptians believed that the immortality of the king was taken away when his tomb was violated. The stars will remember, and a price might be extracted from the thieves if the offense is great enough. The punishment for tomb robbers who were caught was death by impalement. Sometimes the king himself would pronounce the death sentence. There was never any mercy for these people. The thieves would be taken to the entrance of the tomb that they had attempted to rob. It was there that they would be impaled—very slowly. Their cries would echo off the canyon walls of the Valley of the Kings. Then their dead bodies would be left there as a warning to other tomb robbers."

Geraldine said, "Have you ever been to the tomb of Tutankhamun?"

I said, "Yeah, I've been there."

Geraldine said, "You see I have to disagree with you, Father Phillip. I don't think of it as a desecration but as an advancement of science—the science of archeology."

I said, "I doubt the boy king would agree with you. If you ever get the chance, Geraldine, study the gold mask of King Tutankhamun. You will see dignity and wisdom in that face—and he was only 22. You won't see that in the faces of Carter and Carnarvon, the discoverers of this tomb—their faces had the look of triumph, as if they had just beaten an adversary."

Attempting to keep up her side of the conversation, she said, "I read somewhere that he died when he was 18—not 22—and that was according to Howard Carter."

I told her, "Tutankhamun did not just die—he was murdered by drinking a concoction of blue lilies ground up and put into a glass of wine. He died from the ultimate high. The wine was offered to him by his trusted advisor, Ay, who later became king. He then married the dead king's young wife and then killed her, too. So Carter must have been mistaken. Maybe he doesn't read the sacred writings as well as he thinks."

Geraldine sensed that I was getting annoyed, so she changed the subject slightly. "What do you think of the Tutankhamun curse?"

"Well, Geraldine, that question should really be asked of Howard Carter's benefactor, Lord Carnarvon."

Geraldine said, "I can't ask him—he is dead. He died of an infected mosquito bite. His doctor thought it was pneumonia."

"Yes, he did. He died at 1:55 a.m. on the 5th of April 1923. Maybe he believes in the curse now."

Geraldine stared at me and said, "To be more precise, he probably died of hystoplasmosis. It is a fungus disease that can attack the lungs, throat, spleen and liver; it mimics pneumonia symptoms. It is found in the dust on the floor of Egyptian tombs. By the way, it's common in the United States, too." She said that

as if she had beaten me.

I did not like playing "one-upmanship" on her, so I lightened the conversation. I said, "Well, Geraldine, maybe what really did Carnarvon in was that he played a game of Senet with the god of fate, and the stake of the game was immortality. And, alas, Carnarvon lost."

Geraldine asked, "What kind of a game was Senet?"

I said, "Think of it as an ancient form of Back-Gammon."

Some old bastard sitting across from us put in his opinion. He said, "Well, the Egyptians were all pagans—too bad they did not all get right with God. That's why they're all in Hell, son," giving me an all-knowing stare.

I thought: He called me son. If he only knew who I really was, he would die of fright. If he loves his savior so much, maybe I should do him a favor and let him join him today.

The trolley car finally came to our stop. We got off and went into the Woolworth five and ten. Geraldine had fries and a hamburger and a cherry coke. I munched down a BLT and a lemonade. Geraldine began to tell me about her fiancé, Frank. His family had moved into a home only a block away from her house. She said that she was picking grapes and eating them from an old vine on the fence in front of Frank's house one day. She said she didn't know anyone lived there. She said the house had been empty for a long time and the people who owned it had just moved out one night. They were victims of the depression. Frank had walked up behind her and said, "I'm going to have to charge you, miss, for those grapes." According to Geraldine, she only took one look at Frank and it was love at first sight. With pride in her voice, and using heart-felt words, she said, "Frank told me later he felt the same thing about me."

I said, "Good for you, Geraldine." I said, "So when do you plan to be married?"

What she said next shocked me. She said, "Well, I'm meet-

ing with Father Anthony at our parish on the 20th at 3 o'clock—
only two more days. Frank told me to arrange everything and
just tell him when to be at the church. Isn't that wonderful,
Father Phillip? Frank is so kind and considerate."

I said, "I'm really happy for you both." She asked me if I
would be able to stay and meet him when he returned the next
week. I said that I wished I could but that I had pressing business. I told her I would be thinking of her. She asked me when I
had to leave and I said, "I have a train to catch at 4:15
Thursday." I said, "Geraldine, I have an idea. How about on
Thursday when you go to see Father Anthony, I walk with you.
We will say our "so-longs" outside the church. It will not be
"goodbye" only "so-long." I just know we will meet again in
our lives."

Geraldine reached over and hugged me and replied, "I sure
hope so, Father."

We finished our food, and as we left, a kid was selling news-
papers. He said to me, "Want a newspaper, Mister?" I glanced
at him and said, "Sure, kid." I took the paper, paid him, and
looked at the front page. Well, well, well, I thought to myself. I
made the cover. I had forgotten what I had done in 1934 the last
time I was here. Geraldine saw what I was reading and said,
"Isn't that just awful! Some maniac killed an entire family of five
people in the Oklahoma panhandle."

We stepped back as the trolley car came to pick us up. I
said, "Yes, Geraldine, what is this world coming to? There's just
too much evil nowadays." Note to my diary: Actually, the family of five thought they were vampires and immortal. I convinced
them otherwise. Geraldine had forgotten her purse and ran back
to the lunch counter to get it. The trolley waited for her. I went
ahead and paid for both of us and took a seat in the back of the
trolley. There was no one other than me sitting in the back of the
trolley. I knew from past experiences that my former self from

1934 had merged into my present self. Seth and I had discovered that's how things worked the first time we went back in time. Don't know why it works that way, but it does. I did pull out my stone knife, though, and sure enough, the blade was still stained with the blood of the would-be vampires. I quickly put it away as I saw Geraldine walking down the aisle of the car.

She said, "Thank goodness no one stole my purse."

I said, "Well, that's living proof that not everyone is immoral." When we got back to her house, I told her I thought I would take a nap before dinner. She told me that she was going to visit Frank's mother and that she would be back before dinner.

I waited in my room until Geraldine had left. I then went into her room and there on her dresser was her brown notebook. I leafed through it. I was struck by two things. One was the fact that she had the best penmanship I had ever seen. The second was that I was not qualified to read this stuff. I would have to rely on someone in the future to understand it. Amun had not blessed me with every ability. I thought, "What am I going to say to her in two days at 2:51 p.m.?" I don't think the truth will work. I liked Geraldine. I'm sorry she suffered the fate that she did. Geraldine is an innocent. There is no malice in her and her heart is pure. I just had an interesting thought: It is as if déjà vu is playing a trick on me. I thought all of a sudden I had been here in this room holding her notebook before. I heard Sophia coming up the stairs. I thought I would leave the notebook where I had found it. I didn't need it right then. I made a hasty retreat to my room. I lay down on the bed and thought about who I was going to kill so that Geraldine could live. I thought it would have to be someone her family doesn't know.

I came downstairs in time to see Geraldine and Emilio and Sophia sitting next to the radio. They were listening to the Amos and Andy radio show. Amos and Andy were a couple of white

guys pretending to be two black guys on the radio. They were somewhat amusing. Emilio thought they were hilarious. Sophia looked at me and said, "Dinner is almost ready. The radio show will be over soon." After the show was over we sat down to a very nice spaghetti dinner. I looked at the clock on the mantle and thought: 6:35 p.m. Geraldine is now down to 44 hours and 16 minutes of life left. In the past I had counted the hours down in the life of a human, but that was someone I was going to kill. The countdown was a sport for me, but this time I had to save a life and take one in exactly 44 hours and now 15 minutes. Sophia asked me to say a blessing. I thought it would look a little strange if I did not, so I said, "In the name of the Father, the Son, the Holy Ghost, bless us, Oh, Lord, for these thy gifts, for which we are about to receive through thy bounty, Christ our Lord. Amen."

I looked at Sophia crossing herself with her eyes closed and praying to the Eternal with her head bowed. I also saw that Geraldine was staring at me as if she had discovered my deception. After dinner Geraldine and I went out to the swing again. Emilio and Sophia were back at the radio listening to President Franklin Roosevelt's fireside chat. He was talking about the rise of Fascism in Europe.

As Geraldine and I swung gently back and forth, she said, "Are you really a priest?"

I said, "Why would you ask such a thing?"

She said, "You don't act like one. You don't speak with conviction in your voice. You say things in a matter-of-fact tone—like you did when you spoke the other day of the five people in Oklahoma who were murdered, as if their deaths meant nothing. Priests don't do that—at least the ones I've met."

I told her, "Well, Geraldine, I doubt if you have met any priests from Egypt before."

She said, "That's true. There is something about you,

Father, that I can't quite figure out. It is like we have met before in another time and place."

I said, "That is highly unlikely. I think we would have both remembered." I changed the subject, "So tell me, Geraldine, do you plan to have a family and work at your pathology projects, too? I have encountered couples before who have run into problems when the wife worked."

"Frank and I don't want children. The world is getting over crowded as it is."

" I think you are right, Geraldine."

In an irrational tone she said, "You just did it again."

I said, "Did what?"

"No priest would say that it is a good thing for a couple not to have children. A priest would say that it is against God's will not to procreate. I think Pope Pius XI would not be too happy with you, Father Phillip! I do hope you are a priest, though, because I like your attitude. Have you ever read any of Willa Cather's books?"

"No," I said.

"She is one of my heroes. She is a non-conformist like me!"

"How so, Geraldine?"

"Her characters were strong women. They believed in traditional values, but they believed also in themselves. I love Frank, but I'm going to be my own person. I must say, Father, I'm not a very good Catholic. I believe in science. When I look through a microscope I do not see any of the bacteria praying to God."

"Well, Geraldine, they don't see you praying to the Eternal either. But it doesn't mean God does not exist. You don't want to let your work be all encompassing. Consider when you work that maybe you are fulfilling a celestial plan. After all, some believe the history of the human race and its future is written in the stars. If that is the case, Geraldine's future is written in the

stars, too."

Geraldine smiled and said, "I'm in the stars, huh? Is Frank there with me?"

"He is if you want him to be and he wants it, too." I lied and told Geraldine I had to meet a priest at the Immaculate Conception Cathedral and that I would be back later. As I left, I saw her still swinging. To me, she looked lonely. I hope Frank turns out to be as good a man as she thinks.

I walked for hours looking for some son of a bitch to dispatch. I went to a local bar and had a beer. I thought I might find someone there, but no such luck. I considered going to the state prison in Canyon City, Colorado and killing someone serving a life sentence. He would not be getting out, so I don't think he would be procreating in the future. But I thought better of it.

I went back to Geraldine's house. It was about 10:30. Sophia had left me a note on my bed. She had written that there were some leftovers in the refrigerator if I was hungry. I decided to go to bed. Once again I lay in bed thinking of Seth and that hole in the wall of his tomb. I dreamed he climbed through it and was free and that he sealed up the hole, only with me on the other side. I was now imprisoned. I found the flashlight and crawled around the room looking for a way out.

In my dream I dug into the dirt in a corner of the room, and as I brushed the dirt away, thinking I had dug down to the floor, I uncovered the face of Dakulah. I shined the flashlight on her. She opened her eyes and said, "Are you going to let me die again?"

I scrambled to the far wall. Dakulah got up out of the dirt and crawled over to me. I shined the flashlight on her all the way. She came over and sat down next to me and put her head on my shoulder. I looked at her face—only it was the face of Geraldine. All of a sudden she attacked me with Seth's stone knife. She stabbed me over and over again. I saw my blood pour

from my body. I kept trying to fend her off, but I could not move my arms. I woke up to find I had both of my arms through the slats of the headboard.

Dear Diary, I'm sure sick of these nightmares. I looked at the clock: 7:47. I got up, dressed and went downstairs. Sophia offered me some breakfast. As she cooked it, I read the newspaper. Sophia brought in the food, and as I put the newspaper down, I noticed the date: March 20, 1934. I asked Sophia what was the date. She said, "It is the 20th I think. Yes, I'm sure of it." Somehow I had messed up time. One entire day was now gone! I don't know what happened to it. I picked my brain thinking of every possibility. I guess that is what I get for screwing with the Well of Fate. I now must act fast or I will run out of time.

By the time breakfast was over it was almost 9 a.m. I asked Sophia where Geraldine was. She told me she thought she was at the Denver Library looking up information on some disease. She said that Geraldine might not be back until supper. Well, I knew where she was going to be at 2:51 p.m. I thanked Sophia for the breakfast and decided to head back down town to see Father Michael. I was now running out of time, so I was not going to leisurely take my time finding a replacement for Geraldine. I hoped Father Michael enjoyed his morning— because he was going to a wake the next day, and he was to be the man of the hour. I hurried on my way. As I approached the church, I saw a dozen or so people milling around outside. I walked past them and went over to Father Michael's secretary. She was sitting at her desk crying. I asked what was the matter. Choking back tears, she gave me great news! Father Michael had hung himself from the light fixture in his office. I was shocked. I had glanced at that light fixture when I was in his office. Dear Diary, I didn't think it could hold him. As I offered my condolences to Beth, his secretary, I heard a loud noise. I guess that

light fixture gave way after all.

A cop came out of the now late Father Michael's office and apologized for the racket. He asked me who I was and I told him I was Father Phillip. Beth was in such a state of shock that she did not question my stating that I was a priest. The cop asked me if I wanted to give Father Michael the last rites since no other priest was there yet. I told him of course I would. I asked him to clear the office and I went into Mike's office and closed the door. Mike was draped over his desk with the light fixture lying on top of him, with plaster all over his face, which was face-up to the ceiling. It looked like he wouldn't be bothering any more young women. I closed his bulging eyes with my hand and brushed off the plaster dust from his shirt. He was still wearing the same shirt with the big ink blob on it. I lectured him, "Mike, Mike, Mike, look at yourself. Guilt got to you, huh! I guess the thought of getting sodomized at the Colorado State Penitentiary must have been disagreeable, huh? Well, Mike I hope you left me that letter of recommendation. But if not, I don't want you to worry about it. You did good, Mike."

One of the cops knocked on the door asking if I was done so they could come in and remove the body. I said, "Come on in. I'm through now." I went out of the office and put my hand on Beth's shoulder and told her I would pray for Mike. I did so in silence, "Mike, I pray no one will stand up against you in the presence of the Keeper of the Balance and that you will be able to go forth into a happy place that knows no death and no pain. From time to time I will speak your name so that you may live again." The day was getting off to a really good start. It was now only 10:25—plenty of time to meet up with Geraldine.

Dear Diary, as I walked along, I thought I might as well get Geraldine's journal. As I went into Geraldine's house, I knew this was the last time I would be seeing Sophia and Emilio, who to my surprise was home with Sophia. I sat down on the couch

and talked to Emilio for a short time. He asked me where I was headed. I said, "I'm going to be traveling quite a long way. I will be going back to Egypt." He offered me a glass of wine. I took it and sat there thinking that it was really too bad about Emilio and Sophia.

But I don't decide fate. On second thought, Diary Dear, I guess I'm playing with fate for Geraldine and Joshua. I drank the wine and told Emilio I needed to use the bathroom. I went upstairs and went straight to Geraldine's room. Her journal wasn't there. She must have had it with her. I would have to find her and get it. It was now 12:11 p.m.

I went down to the library and looked for Geraldine. She was not there. I asked a clerk if she had seen a small Italian woman in her early thirties. The clerk said, "Could you mean Geraldine Donato?"

I said, "Yes." She told me that Geraldine might be at a library branch on Federal Boulevard and 34th. I hurried there. I made it to the branch library at 12:31 p.m. I spent five minutes looking all over the place, but Geraldine was not there.

I decided to do a little research myself since I still had some time to spare. I decided to wait at the corner of 29th and Federal. I knew she would be there at 2:51 because that was the corner where she was to die—just one block from her church. There was quite a bit of traffic considering that this was 1934 Denver. There was a tavern a couple of blocks down Federal Boulevard. I decided to see if Robert Hanson Walker was there. After all, he must have got drunk somewhere. He wasn't there. I tried other taverns and bars in the area to no avail. I then went over to the Rustic Tavern on West 29th and Zenobia. It was about two miles away from what would be the scene of the accident. I went into the tavern and ordered a beer. There were only three customers in the place. I saw a 22-year-old kid sitting in a booth drinking by himself. I asked him if he would mind if I

joined him. He said, "Go ahead. It's a free country." I did.

As I took my seat, I noticed a picture of Babe Ruth on the wall. I held out my hand and said, "I'm Phillip—Phillip Ruth."

He said, "You have two first names, huh?"

I said, "Yeh. I never thought of that before. Who might you be, sir?"

He put his beer down and said, "Robert Walker."

"So, Robert, what do you do for a living?"

"Nothing!" he replied. "My family has money. So what do you do, Phil?"

"Well, I work with people. I'm a people kind of guy." The way he looked at me I knew he thought maybe I was a fruit trying to pick him up. I concentrated on his mind. I probed the deep recesses of it. Dear Diary, I was astonished to discover what his mind held. Now I knew why he was drinking alone. He thought he was a loser in a family of highly successful people. The booze soothed, at least temporarily, his inferiority complex. A clock on the wall in the corner now read 2:10 p.m. I was not going to leave until either he left or the clock read 2:40. I would have enough time to find Geraldine because Walker would be finding her.

We talked about cars. He told me that he had a 1928 Buick. He then blurted out in anger that his sister drove a new Packard, but his father would not let him have one—because he wasn't responsible enough. I told him that was terrible for his father to treat him like that. He ordered another beer and told me through his alcoholic breath, "Can't cause a scandal in the family, you know." I sat there listening to him gripe. I kept my beer up to my face. I was thinking how ironic this all was. I had a smile on my face, and I knew he would think I was laughing at him. The glass of beer was a good camouflage.

As he bitched on and on, I would intersperse any breaks in his dialogues with an occasional, "That's too bad" or "You were

wronged. No wonder you are so pissed." Actually, he was a failure in a family of successful people, and I think I know why Seth wanted this obscure drunk killed. He got up and staggered into the men's room to take a leak. I finished my beer and looked at the clock: 2:31. Walker did not come back, so I left to meet Geraldine. I figured he went out a back door. As I left, I heard the bartender tell a customer that the time was really 2:46 because his clock was 15 minutes slow.

I ran as fast as I could down 29th Street. I saw Geraldine waiting for the light to change so she could cross the street. Walker's car was weaving and heading straight for her. I thought of myself as a falcon. I felt my feet leave the ground and my arms become wings. I flew directly at Walker's Buick. I smashed through his driver's side window, causing him to veer off the road and run into a tree. I landed on the seat next to him. He was knocked out cold. I returned to my original form and kicked out the passenger side door. Walker would survive with a scar that would run across his face from below his right eye over to his nose. As I got out of the car, people had congregated around the car. I pushed past them and there was Geraldine standing there with her mouth open, and she was clutching her notebook.

I walked over to her and said, "I must talk to you now." Geraldine asked me why I was in that car. I told her, "It doesn't matter. We have to talk. Change your appointment with Father Anthony." She did.

We went to the pathology laboratory at the Republic Building in Denver where she worked. She kept trying to question me about the car wreck. She said, "No one could walk away unscathed from that wreck." She then looked into my eyes and said, "Who are you? No, I mean what are you?"

I said, "I'm not like you, if that helps any. Geraldine, I'm here to help you live. You were supposed to die today, killed by that car I was riding in."

She said, "You are insane! I want to leave."

I blocked the door and told her to sit down. "Tell me what you were thinking when you were crossing the street."

She thought about that in silence for a few minutes and then said, "I thought about Frank, and then I was thinking about my work."

"What were you thinking about your work?" She said, "It was nothing special. I had cultured a strain of bacteria, and I was thinking I should go check on it. It is right over here—do you want to see?"

I yelled, "Hell, no! What else did you think about?"

She said softly, "I thought about you."

I said, "Me? Me? You never thought about Tay-Sachs disease?"

She said, wide-eyed, "No!" She spoke again, "I was thinking there is something ungodly about you."

I said, "You are right—and you are wrong. The ancient Egyptians would disagree. They wanted to worship me as a god."

Geraldine said, "You must be crazy."

I put my hand on the desk next to her and said, "Watch this." I let my hand slowly sink into the wood. She screamed out in panic. I tried to settle her down. I said, "Relax. I'm trying to prove to you I'm not crazy. Do you know anyone who can do that? Huh?"

Geraldine was about to cry but said, "What do you mean I was supposed to die?"

"Because in another time you did die. Now I'm going to prove it to you. I'm going to tell you something that only you know. You have been having second thoughts about Frank. Last week you met a pathologist from England. You bumped into him in the elevator thirty feet from where we are now sitting. He smiled at you and you thought he was handsome, and you liked

his English accent and gentle manner. You were wearing a brassiere that kept rubbing up on your left shoulder, and it was annoying you because you were trying to keep up a conversation with the guy from England. Do you want me to go on?"

"How do you know these things about me? I only met you a couple of days ago."

I decided to tell her everything. I leaned back in the chair I was sitting in and said, "Your spirit told me. It knew I would have to convince you with something that only you would know. As for your spirit, Geraldine, I met it or I should say you sixty-five years in the future."

She was really getting panicked now so I got her a glass of water. As I got up to get it she bolted for the door, but I beat her to it. She stood there beating on my chest with both fists and yelling, "This is not true. Jesus, please help me!"

I took hold of her hands and said, "It's not as bad as you think. You are going to live now. You will have a long, good life. I want someone who won't be born for another sixty-four years to be allowed to live, too. He is a little boy, Geraldine, and he needs your help to live. I want you to see something." I took out the piece of glass and showed it to her. "What does this mean? Look hard, Geraldine. This formula is engraved into the glass, but the writing is yours isn't it?"

She stared at it and said, "This is just a formula for Hydroxanthine and some genetic nonsense."

"Does it have anything to do with your notebook?"

Her answer was an emphatic "No! What does the little boy of 1999 suffer from?"

I said, "I'm told it is a disease called Tay Sachs."

She said, "He will die then—probably before he is four years old."

"What will the disease do to him?"

"Well, he will begin to have convulsions, deafness, blind-

ness, and finally in the last stage, he will become listless, his brain damage will become critical, and then he will die. There is no treatment for it. There is a theory that it might be caused by an enzyme, but no one knows for sure. The enzyme or lack of it is caused from a defective gene. The symptoms were first discovered by Warren Tay and Bernard Sachs in the 1880's."

"You—I mean your spirit—told me that you could figure out how to cure the disease."

"Why would I have told you that? It would be a lie!"

"You told me that, Geraldine, because you wanted me to give you back your life. I did, and I paid a great price."

Geraldine said, "How could you have spoken to my spirit if I died like you said? I would be with God."

"You were not with God because you do not have enough faith in him. You have no faith now do you?"

"What kind of faith do you have, Phillip, or whatever your name is?"

"The name is Horus."

She said, "You mean like the Egyptian god Horus?"

I said, "One and the same. I was believed, by the Egyptians, to be the god of the kings—that is what they called me. Remember the other day when we were talking about Egypt? Well, Geraldine, I was there at the birth of the Egyptian Empire. I have known personally every king of Egypt and where they are buried."

She said, "That's impossible. You would have to be five thousand years old."

I said, "Hell, I'm a lot older than that." I picked up an industrial razor blade and said, "Watch this." I sliced my forearm. "See, I don't bleed—and watch—my arm will heal itself."

Geraldine then said, "I'm beginning to believe you, I think—or maybe I'm going crazy. You have to be real, though—my parents saw you. So what is your purpose? Why are you

here?"

I told her, "I guess I was created to kill unjust people, but now I want to save a life—not take one."

She said, "Why don't we pray to Jesus?"

I said, "It won't do any good, kid."

"Well, why don't we pray to your Egyptian god Amun?"

I said, "We can't do that either. I guess I can when I return to the future."

"Assuming you can go into the future. What will happen to me? You said you are a killer, and that I lied to you, so will you kill me?"

I thought about what she said and then replied, "No, I won't kill you. I want your word, though, that you will work on a way to cure Tay Sachs from now until you die. I will look you up. Remember me and our bargain. Remember all that has transpired between you and me. I have given you back your life just like I promised your spirit. Before the sun rises I must leave this time and place. This is not a dream, Geraldine, so don't look at it that way. Once I have left, keep the memory of our meeting locked in your heart because to speak out will only make people believe that you should be in a mental hospital. Keep this piece of glass. Never lose it. And with the passing of the years, if you start thinking this is all unreal, look at the glass and you will know it was very real."

Geraldine and I sat in her office looking out the window at the fading light as the sun set on the west side of the Rocky Mountains. She quizzed me about my life. She was convinced that I was who I said I was. "Do you like killing evil people?"

"Sometimes I do. In fact, I do most of the time I guess."

"When you saw me as a spirit, was I nice to you?"

"You were okay, but now you are getting a second chance, so maybe you will stay nice."

"You know about my life, don't you, Horus?"

"I knew about your previous life. I don't know how your life will be this time."

"You know, though, that I live to be an old lady in her nineties."

I said, "I know you are supposed to live that long. Maybe I'll check the cemetery when I return, or maybe I'll look you up in the phone book. Come to think of it, I don't know where you will be living or what country you will be living in for that matter."

She took my hand and said, "I will try to stay in Denver, and I will be waiting for you. My parents have a couple of lots in the cemetery. By then they will be long dead. So I will leave a message for you somehow on one of the tombstones—or I will be there with them. Either way, you will find me and you will find my message. I thought about how you were able to put your hand into the table. Somehow you aligned the atoms in your hand to match the spaces in between the atoms in the table."

I said, "I don't know, Geraldine. I just know it works."

"You said you have killed thousands of people, but I'm curious—did you ever love anyone?"

"No, not the way you mean love. I did care for my mother. It is just as well. If I loved someone then I would have seen her grow old and die. I would then be alone again. I have felt sorrow for people though. Mainly they were Egyptians, but they are all gone now."

We talked late into the night. Geraldine wanted to know everything about my life. I told her about the past, but I was careful not to tell her much about the future. She asked me, "Did you ever meet Jesus?"

I said, "Yes, but in his day he was only a minor prophet. There were many of them in the past. In today's world he has been blown out of all proportion as to who he was and what he did. I will give him this, though: there was no malice in his heart.

If, however, he was the son of the Eternal, someone forgot to tell the Jews. They are still waiting for their messiah. It could be that they could be waiting for two messiahs. Time will tell if either belief is correct."

Geraldine said, "But you believe in Amun."

I said, "That is because I know that Amun is the true king of the universe."

She asked me about all of the gods of Egypt. She said, "How can there be so many gods if you really only believe in Amun, as you say you do?"

I said, "Some of the gods of Egypt have several names."

Geraldine said, "But that doesn't answer my question."

I said, "Okay, think of it this way—the Egyptians have many gods to do their bidding for them. There are gods of the sky, gods of the fields, fertility goddesses, gods for the under-world, and gods for just about anything you can imagine, but you must pray to them in earnest. It's true that you can circum-vent the process and go straight to Amun and just pray to him. In the western world the Catholic church elevates nuns and priests to the rank of saints, so there is no difference—gods and saints are all the same."

Geraldine said, "Not exactly. The people who were named saints by the church really did exist, whereas, Horus, your Egyptian gods were only a myth."

I said, "They are not a myth. Most of the gods of Egypt started out as just regular people, like your nuns and priests."

She said, "I have never heard of that."

I told her that there were many mysteries that the human race didn't know much about, but that they were still true, though suppressed by the churches in the west out of fear that the truth may be known.

Geraldine said, "Horus, what do you mean, two messiahs?"

I said to her, "Some say it is written that one will come to

herald the coming of the second."

She said, "Is that like John the Baptist coming to announce the arrival of Jesus?"

I said, "Once again, the Jews don't think so, and neither do I. I don't see it written in the stars, although it is true some things the Eternal keeps hidden from the human race. Maybe, Geraldine, in your lifetime you may live to see a prophecy fulfilled or denied." Since I wouldn't answer all of her questions about the future, she asked me specifically about the next ten years. I said, "You will have to wait and see. That way it will be a surprise for you, but it will be the most interesting time the human race has ever witnessed."

About 2:30 in the morning Geraldine fell asleep. I sat looking down five stories to the almost deserted 16th Street in Denver waiting for the rising sun. I saw some guy crank out canvas awnings that were attached to various buildings. The awnings had the names of the businesses on them. I heard a night watchman in the hall on the floor we were on. He was making his rounds checking each floor. I knew he was done with our floor because I heard him turning his key into the station clock for this floor. It was his proof to his company that he had been here. He left and all was quiet again. Down below a milk truck made its way down the street. Geraldine turned in her sleep trying to find a more comfortable sleeping position. I started thinking about Seth. Maybe he is right. Perhaps there isn't any difference between him and me. I am going to confront him, though. He thinks he has outwitted me. He will soon learn the truth. Dear Diary, it is now five minutes after five—time for me to go. I got up and leaned over and kissed Geraldine on her forehead. She did not wake up. I quietly left her office and made my way down to the street.

I transformed myself back into a falcon. I began to fly higher and higher over the Denver skyline. I looked to the west at the

snow-capped Rockies. Not far from downtown Denver the city dump burned. Its smoke rose up to meet me and joined with the spring air to fill my nostrils. I flew back one last time to the Republic Building. I perched on the ledge outside of Geraldine's office and I looked through the window at her sleeping form. I thought I will keep my word. I will not harm her. I then took off in flight toward the red glow that to the ancient Egyptians was Amun rising in the east. My heart was gladdened. Perhaps one of the two children of upper and lower Egypt had outwitted the Lord of the Hosts. Once more the sun shown all around me in its glory. This time though I knew exactly where I was: back at the prison home of my brother Seth, the evil one, the god of the Hyksos invaders who were the kings of the fifteenth dynasty of the ancient Egyptian empire. I will go and see 96-year-old Geraldine just as soon as I finish with Seth.

Chapter XV

I went over and pulled up some weeds from a small clump of bushes and fashioned them into a torch around a small branch. I then once more crawled into the antechamber, slid down the bank, and lit my torch and made my way to the hole in the wall. I called to Seth, but there was no answer. I sat down and thought about what I should do. I had sat down in front of Seth's cartouche engraved into the door. I looked at the engraving. When the cartouche was engraved a second time, someone had left off the most important phrasing on it. On the original it had said: "Behind the door is the greatest evil known to man. He who opens it will let loose the final curse on the human race, and

that individual will suffer eternal damnation."

Howard Carter believed it, but someone else did not. It was a fake. I ran my hand over it. I had been played for a sap. Seth was no longer imprisoned. He was free, and I had no idea for how long. I drew my knife and then I kicked in the door. It crumbled into pieces in front of me. I kicked at it one last time and as I did, I lost my balance and fell over backward. Now, lying on my back, I saw a black pig come squealing out of the darkness and head straight for me. The first thing I thought was a black pig was one of the animal forms that Seth used to turn himself into in bygone years. I grabbed the pig by his snout and began to plunge my knife into its body over and over again. It staggered away from me and buckled under its own weight. I plunged my knife in once more—this time right behind its head and into its neck. I waited for it to expire. If it were Seth he would return to his true form. It didn't. It was just a pig and a parting joke that Seth had left for me. I held my torch out to the pig, and as I looked at it I began to laugh. It was pretty funny at that. Well, I guess Seth still has a sense of humor. Since he left this pig for me, maybe he left something else.

I went into his prison tomb. I held up my torch and saw something in the corner. I went over to investigate. It was only my flashlight. The batteries were now long dead. On the wall though, next to the hole, Seth had left me a message. He had dug away some of the dirt down to the floor exposing a shred of cloth that was part of the royal tunic of Dakulah. I picked it up along with a handful of dirt and begged Dakulah for forgiveness. I kept the piece of cloth.

I held up the torch and began to read Seth's message to me. He began: Hail to you, Brother. I have been free since 1996. I have gone to and fro across the desert consolidating my forces, and when the time is right, I will wage the war against the West. After all, when the world was new it was decreed that you and

I would finally do battle to the death and that if I lose then Amun will personally reign in a new and all-powerful Egypt until the end of time. But, Horus, my brother, it was not decreed that I should necessarily lose the fight. In a way, Horus, I'm sorry that someday soon it will come to this. I could have killed you many times. I even sat one night by your bed and put my knife to your throat while you slept, but I spared you. I guess you could say I returned the compliment. Your friend, the spirit of Geraldine, was watching me through your mirror. I guess she conveniently forgot to tell you. You might want to know how I got out, Horus, although I suspect you have figured it out.

In 1922 I lay down on the large pile of dirt as I had done every day for close to 3200 years. I sat up when I heard a racket on the other side of the wall. I thought my deliverance had finally come. I listened to a couple of Egyptians speaking excitedly about what they had found. They began to knock on the wall. I transformed myself into a large serpent and waited. But then they left, only to return the next day. This time, though, they brought with them two Egyptologists, Lord Carnarvon and Howard Carter. They knew what my cartouche represented and became very cautious. I listened through the wall as they discussed what to do. They decided to cut a hole in the wall next to my cartouche. I guess they, too, knew I could not escape as long as the Amun engraving was still intact on all of the walls, ceiling and floor. Once the jackhammer had broken through, Carnarvon shined a light into the tomb. I transformed myself into a black pig. He shined his light on me. I was waiting for my chance. One of their workers laughed at seeing the pig and tried to wiggle his head and shoulders into the opening. I heard Carter yell, "No! Get back!" I guess it was just my nature. I was on Amed, the tomb worker, in an instant. I cut off his head, and saw his body fall back out of the hole and land at Howard Carter's feet. I threw Amed's head back through the hole. Howard Carter

caught it. I heard him tell Carnarvon that they should seal the hole back up and bury this tomb for all time. That is when I came to my senses.

I said, "Wait, wait. I can make both of you rich and famous beyond your wildest dreams."

Carnarvon said, "How?"

I came over to the hole and said, "I know where every king of Egypt is buried. I can lead you to their tombs."

Carter said, "The Valley of Kings is exhausted. You could not help us. We know where they are all buried."

I told him and Carnarvon, as they shined the light into my face, "You don't know where the boy king is buried. I know his tomb is untouched and just waiting for you two to discover it. Your names will be on the lips of every human." I then told them, Horus, that this would be just the beginning—that I would show them the splendor of the Babylonians and the resting place of the Israelite's Ark of the Covenant. They told me that they would think it over and come back with the rising sun. They did. They agreed, as long as I gave them my word that no harm would come to them. I gave them my word as a god of Egypt that no harm would befall them. They also wanted proof of where the tomb of the boy king was buried before they would set me free. I agreed. They showed me a map of the Valley of the Kings. I recognized some of the tombs, but some of the burials were of kings that had died after I had been imprisoned. I reasoned that they should go to the tomb of Ramses VI and dig. I told them there they will find the obscure burial place of Akhenaton and Kiya's offspring, resting in all of his splendor just a couple of hundred feet from the burial place of that traitor Ramses II who conspired with you, my brother, to imprison me.

They found the boy king's tomb and received the riches and glory that I had promised, and then they never came back. I

think Carter thought that I somehow had killed Carnarvon, but you know the truth, Horus. I lost much of my supernatural abilities in this forlorn place. Once Carnarvon was dead, Carter did not want to deal with me again. He sealed up the opening of the tomb.

I then sat in the darkness alone for another 74 years. Once again, though, I was awakened by a noise on the other side of the wall. It was three Egyptian children who had found an opening and had come in to make the antechamber into their own playhouse. I beguiled them to knock down the door. They could not break it down, but their beating on the other side made part of the cartouche of Amun on my side of the door break off and fall to the floor. I walked through the wall and rewarded all three children with death. After all, if the news of an undiscovered tomb had gotten out you would have known before now and I would not have been able to begin to wage a subtle war in preparation for the final battle, which I plan on winning. I was free. I came out of my prison.

I sat down by the opening in the sunlight. I looked at my hands and arms and legs in great detail. After all, I had not seen them for centuries since I had been sitting in the dark. I thought, "I hope my mind is not playing tricks on me and that this was not a dream." I was afraid that I would wake up to find myself back in the damp dark prison—the prison that you put me in. I discovered, though, it really was true. I was no longer in my prison tomb. It crossed my mind that you were somewhere out in the world. I thought maybe you ruled some nation. I had read the minds of the three children that I had dispatched, so I had a fair idea of the new world that I had come into. It was pretty easy to pick up the language. I must say I found Cairo very interesting. I was able to adapt quickly. After all, the new world was really not much different from the old world. This world had the same kind of dumb asses in it, just like the ancient one.

I visited our old haunts. I thought maybe I would bump into you. One thing that I discovered actually astounded me. The archaeologists believe, Horus, that you and I are only a myth. I guess Carter managed to take the secret of my existence to his grave; I wonder if he ever thought about you. Well, they will learn that this myth is a reality. Thoth knows, and the Eternal Amun knows. I guess, Horus, you were the last to know the truth that I was free. That would have dawned on you earlier, Horus, when you first came back to my prison tomb if you had looked down at my wrist when our stone knives were pressed together. I was wearing a Rolex. You concentrated on my eyes and never saw it. Oh, and, Horus, once I found you, guess who gave you all of those nightmares for the past 1290 days. Well, I've got no more room to write, but be assured I'll keep in touch.

Seth was right. I had figured out that he might have been able to get out or at least that he had met Howard Carter because Robert Hanson Walker was a distant blood relative of Carter's niece. My research at the Denver Library had proved that. Seth had given his word that he would not harm them, but he did not say anything about Carter's bloodline and he could not go after Carnarvon's bloodline because once Carnarvon was dead, all vengeance against his family had to cease. I guess he wanted me to do some killing for him.

I knew that there was not any point in looking for Seth. He and I would meet again. Now I was really beginning to wonder if the Eternal had set this whole thing up for his own entertainment. I decided to go back to my 20th Century home.

Dear Diary, well, I'm home now. I paid homage to Amun and cleaned up my kitchen, which I had left dirty. Then I added water to a small bamboo plant I have in my bathroom. Someday I will take the plant back to where it can be with its own kind in the jungle. There is nowhere I can go to be with my own kind other than with Seth. Deserted tombs and stone monuments rep-

resenting a dead civilization are all that is left of my people.

Thelma had invited me into her half of the duplex. She had invited me for dinner. As she put the food on the table, she asked me if I had heard the terrible news on the radio. I told her I had not. Since I had thrown time out of sync, we were now experiencing déjà vu. She said the police just this afternoon had been called to the home of a local man that had been bitten by a crocodile in his hot tub. In fact, there had been two crocodiles, but his business partner had arrived in time to save him. The crocodiles had escaped and the police were looking for them.

Well, well, I thought "My stirring the water in the well of fate has given Toby Graham's adulterous wife back her lover. If his partner keeps loving up Toby's wife, Toby can kill him the next time."

After dinner I went back to my half of the duplex. I listened to music late into the night. I sat there thinking little Joshua acted a little bit withdrawn. Maybe the disease is starting to take its toll. I looked at the mirror and thought how I actually missed seeing Geraldine's spirit in it. It crossed my mind how Seth had said in his parting message that he had been giving me the nightmares that I had been suffering.

Dear Diary, I thought about those nightmares. Maybe Seth tipped his hand in them. If he were to make peace with the people of the dark and could call up the demons of the desert, he would have the makings of one formidable force. Who could I call on? No one! Maybe he has already done it. He has had three and a half years to work on it.

I could not sleep, so I went up to the old cemetery to see what had changed. I was shocked to see that the crypt was still there. I thought: The crypt should not be here because Geraldine did not die in 1934. Maybe the crypt belonged to someone else's family and just looked like the Donato crypt. As I drew close to it, I looked at the name on the top. It was the same, only the year

was different. It no longer read 1934—it read 1947. My heart sank at seeing this. I went inside. The moonlight shown in through the tiny window. This time there were two caskets there. One contained Emilio and the other held Sophia. Geraldine was not there. There was a space for one more casket, but there was not a third casket. Geraldine must still live. I guess Geraldine discovered where her parents had been buried in Italy. She obviously had them disinterred and brought back here after the end of World War II. I'm grateful she had not gone to Italy with Emilio and Sophia. If she had, maybe she would have died with them. This tomb inside was exactly the same as before. I sat down on the bench. It looked exactly like the same bench that Sophia had sat on before. Perhaps Sophia and Emilio had the tomb built before they went to Italy and Geraldine had the date put on it when she brought her parents' bodies back from Italy. I leaned back against the cold granite wall and closed my eyes. I rested for about an hour thinking about Geraldine. As I got up to leave, I saw in the corner on a ledge next to Emilio's casket a folded sheet of paper being held down by a small rock. I opened it up and by the light of the moon I discovered, to my amazement, it was a note from Geraldine to me!

She began: "Dear Horus: I have kept my word, but I don't have a cure for your friend—but I do have a theory. This theory is based on the scientific information available as of 1983. I'm getting pretty old, so I wanted to get this note in our family crypt while I was still mentally alert and still alive. I know you will come looking for me here. You said you would check the cemetery. If I'm still alive, Horus, when you read this, you will find me still living in my parents' old house. If my casket is here, you will find my notebook in my casket. It has my theory written down in it. If I'm still alive, come to my house. My notebook is in my old bedroom with your name on the front. I had your name written in hieroglyphics . Ha, ha, you will probably find

my attempt at Egyptian writing humorous. I hope that you have found only this note because I would love to see you again. Love, Geraldine 6-24-83"

Dear Diary, I put the note in my pocket and went back home. As I walked into my living room I sensed something was not right. I pulled my knife and very carefully checked each room. Everything was okay. Then I went into the bathroom, and my bamboo plant was gone. It did not get up and walk off by itself. I went back through the wall to Mrs. Bloom's half of the duplex. Everyone was asleep. In her kitchen the faucet was dripping water into a cup in the sink. I looked out the kitchen window and saw a falcon flying in circles slowly in the night sky. My brother had come back. I went into baby Joshua's room and sitting beside Joshua in his bed next to his teddy bear was my bamboo plant. It had slipped over on its side and the water that I had put in it earlier had drained out and soaked part of the blanket covering Joshua. I picked up my plant and turned the blanket around so that Joshua would not be lying with a wet blanket over him. I then went back to my bedroom. That obnoxious jerk moved my bamboo plant next to Joshua as a message to me that he can do anything he wants. Well, I have a few tricks, too.

Chapter XVI

Dear Diary, I stayed up all night painting the cartouche of Amun on every wall of the duplex plus the roof and basement floor. I was careful to paint them in such inconspicuous places that Thelma would never notice them. Like the old legend of

garlic keeping Dracula away, the drawing of Amun really will keep Seth at bay. Never know when he might decide to make a return visit. I think I will make another trip to the Denver Library. I've got some more research to do. First, though, I will now go see Geraldine. Her kind and just heart can't beat for much longer.

Dear Diary, it was depressing going to see Geraldine. As I walked up to her house I looked across the street at the building that housed the Town Talk Bakery. The bakery was long gone now—just like the Granada Theatre. The theatre had been transformed into a Pentecostal Christian Church. From the pulpit a preacher offered up sermons that were more believable than the Flash Gordon serials the theatre offered in the thirties. In this neighborhood now, though, there are mainly poor people. They are looking for something that can give meaning to their miserable lives.

For me, it was only yesterday that I was here at Geraldine's home. Sixty-five years had taken its toll on her house. The sidewalk, so fresh and new just a day ago, now had king size cracks in it. The paint on the overhang on the second floor was peeling from old age. I came up to the front door and rang the bell. After what seemed about five minutes a middle aged black woman answered the door. She stared at me with suspicion in her eyes and asked me what I wanted. I told her I was a friend of Geraldine. She said, "Miss Donato doesn't see visitors," and tried to close the door.

I put my hand between the door and the door jam. She slammed the door on my hand. I shoved the door back open and said, "Tell Geraldine that Horus is here to see her."

Geraldine's housekeeper, ashamed that she closed the door on my hand, said, "Please wait here."

I stood at the door and, after ten minutes, I saw a bent-over old woman with a walker slowly coming toward me. Her hair

was solid white now. She looked up at me and said, "I knew you would come back. Come in."

I looked at her and said, "You look well, Geraldine."

She replied, "Don't lie to me. I look terrible." I followed her into the living room and watched her as she painfully sat down in a leather rocker, after first picking up a piece of cloth she had been crocheting. I glanced around the room and saw the picture of Jesus was still on the wall, just like it was when I had dinner with Emilio and Sophia. Geraldine's housekeeper came into the room and told Geraldine that if she needed anything she would be in the kitchen. Geraldine asked me to sit close to her, so I moved the chair I was sitting in to where it was touching hers. She then did something that unnerved me. She took hold of my hand and held it up to her cheek. She looked at me through the thick glasses she was wearing, and said, "I began to think, as the years went by, that you were not real. But I never gave up hope. I would look at that piece of glass and I would think about our last conversation. I never married. Frank was killed in the war. He died just weeks before the war ended on Li Shima in the Pacific. He left Margaret Ann a widow with six children. We had broken up right after you left, so he took up with Margaret Ann. It was partly your fault, Horus. After the conversations you and I had, I looked at life in a different way. I tried to help people and, though I never did develop a strong faith in Jesus, I did find strength in a belief in the Eternal. After my parents died, I turned one of the bedrooms upstairs into a shrine to your god, Amun. I can't get up the stairs any more, so the room stays locked. My notebook is there—not on my dresser. I can't do anything much nowadays. I waited for you and now my life is complete and I wait to die. When will I die, Horus?"

I said to her with sadness in my voice, "Pretty soon, Geraldine. But you won't be back as a spirit. Your faith and kindness have set you free."

"Will you be with me when I die, Horus?"

I told her, "Yes, I will come and hold your hand. I promise."

Geraldine then asked me, "How is the little boy?"

"He is still alive, but getting weaker," I said.

"Horus, I really thought I could solve the problem of his disease. I really, really worked on the problem."

"Geraldine, I'm sure you did the best you could. I can't ask for more than that."

Geraldine lightened the conversation with a question: "Well, Horus, have you killed anybody lately?"

I said, "Nope, but then I've only been back a little while."

Doris, the housekeeper, came into the living room to check on me. I guess she didn't trust me. She really looked pissed when Geraldine told her to take me upstairs and unlock her "secret" room and let me go into it alone. Doris went up the stairs ahead of me and sarcastically said, "There is nothing in that room except some Egyptian nonsense."

As she unlocked the door, I told her, "You may have a change of heart one of these days as to what is nonsense and what isn't! Sleep lightly and enjoy every day because you may find yourself up a creek real soon, kid." I closed the door in her face.

Once inside the room I turned on the light because the curtains were closed. Geraldine had done her best to fix this room up as a temple to Amun. She even had a small statue of Amun. On the bottom of it, it said, "Made in China." I did not realize that the Chinese worshipped Amun, but then maybe they should. I guess Doris must have considered that maybe Geraldine was on to something. Lying in front of the statue of Amun were several lotto tickets. I guess Doris must have thought maybe it would bring her luck. I picked up Geraldine's notebook and flipped through the pages. I figured I would read the whole thing when I got home. I closed the notebook and opened the

door only to see Doris standing there waiting for me. As I walked past her, I said, "Try 22-9-31-5-28-41." She pretended that she did not know what I meant. I went back into the living room to talk to Geraldine, but she had dozed off to sleep. She held her crocheting in her lap. She looked very peaceful. I told Doris, who was busy writing down the numbers that I had recommended, that I would be back to see Geraldine again.

As I left, Doris yelled at me, "What was the last number again?"

I turned and said, "Forty-one, but don't play them on the 26th—that is a very unlucky day. Forty-one, that's how old you are isn't it?"

Doris said, "Yes."

I went by the library. I asked the librarian if she had any books on the political history of Iran, Iraq, Egypt, Syria, Sudan, Libya and Afghanistan. She said, "What time period are you looking for?"

I said, "1996 to the present."

She looked them up on the computer and told me they had several but that I could not check out twelve books all at once. I settled for Egypt, Sudan and Iraq. She asked me for my library card, which I didn't have. I put a thought in her head that made her believe that her card was mine. I then went home to do a lot of reading.

Dear Diary, as I put down the book on my coffee table, I glanced into my bedroom and at my statue of Amun. A thought crossed my mind: The Eternal has another job for me. My deception must have worked for he made no mention of it. I did ask his mercy, however, for young Joshua. I have things to do, places to go, to and fro, so I will dispatch those two murderers in a hurry, who have been given a death sentence by the Eternal.

Chapter XVII

Dear Diary, my mission took me to a ramshackled one-story house on a dead end street on the outskirts of Columbus, Ohio. I thought to myself: This is five missions in a row in the United States. Maybe this country is beginning to have more and more murdering assholes in it. Perhaps the evil ones just believe that they have a better chance of getting away with it here. Americans with their religion don't believe that the Eternal requires an eye for an eye. They are mistaken. I have extracted justice for the Eternal in every country in the world many hundreds of times over. This was the home of Bert and Ethyl Walla.

Dear Diary. Bert and Ethyl now reside wherever the Eternal sent them. Bert was a slob who worked driving a trash truck. He was 47 years old and next Monday would have been his 48th birthday. He didn't make it. He was a scrawny piece of white trash about six feet, 140 pounds, brown eyes with dark brown hair and tattoos all over his arms. Like his pig wife, Bert wasn't fond of taking baths. He smelled like crap. His big problem in life was he couldn't keep his hands off young women. He really only got his kicks in life when he had some poor frightened young woman under his control. He would find them in various places: donut shops, parks, convenience stores, and he would pick up hitchhikers when he got the chance. He took a chance when 16-year-old Brenda Ayler came to his door. It was about 7 o'clock at night. She had come to the wrong house by mistake. She was a good person with a kind and giving heart. She was much loved by her family and her friends. Brenda's parents consoled each other with thoughts that maybe she ran off with a boy friend and would phone soon. Brenda's sister, Nancy, believed that Brenda would come traipsing home soon as if

nothing was wrong. She did not approve of the way that Brenda lived her life. She also was tired of hearing about Brenda's many boyfriends. Nancy was four years older than her sister and was jealous of the way her parents would carry on about Brenda. They called her "daddy's little girl." She would watch Brenda spend every dollar she had on frivolous things—then Brenda would run to her father and ask for a loan—a loan that she would never repay. Nancy also knew that Brenda was basically lazy. She would never help around the house. Nancy was the opposite of her sister. And she had remained chaste. So Nancy could not understand the big panic of Brenda being gone. She watched her mother keep cleaning Brenda's room so that it would be in perfect condition. Her father kept looking at her picture and grieving in his heart. He would relive her life in his mind from when she was born to the day she did not come home. They both prayed to God for help and mercy.

Brenda's killer cared nothing for them or the sorrow and grief he was inflicting on them. He only wanted to satisfy his cruel and evil lust, the same way he had done 24 times before. He would bring his tied-up victims into his house in the dead of night, dragging them by their hair into the living room where his 350-pound pig of a wife was waiting. When Bert was ready to begin his work, he would turn off their portable t.v. set. Ethyl would be sitting on her fat and hemorrhoid–racked butt in a recliner rocker. She sat there watching old t.v. sit-coms and game shows all day and most of the night. Ethyl liked her "shows," but she loved watching Bert at work with his victims. As Bert did his horrific work, Ethyl would sit there laughing and stuffing chocolate-covered cherry bonbons into that fat, pimpled 45-year-old face of hers. Ethyl would get all hot and bothered watching Bert at work. Sometimes she would blurt out, "Don't kill her yet. I want to have some fun with her, too!"

When Bert was done he would strangle his victims.

Sometimes after his victim was dead, he would pick them up and dance around the living room with the corpse while Ethyl applauded with those two fat hands. Bert would take the poor victim down to the basement and throw the body into a hole that he had dug just for that purpose. When he would throw the body in the hole, rats which had been feeding on the rotting corpses would scatter in temporary fear—only to come back when Bert went back up the creaking stairs. Dear Diary, this time Bert had made a colossal mistake. Brenda had not just found favor in the eyes of the Eternal, she was one of his favorite humans.

The Eternal's love is like that which he instilled in humans: a love that overlooks transgressions and forgives when forgiveness might not be warranted. Brenda's morals were something else. She was not the brightest. She would go with anyone anywhere. Brenda had faith in the Eternal—kind of. Brenda liked to have a good time. Men liked to have a good time with Brenda. She possessed a sexy smile and a slender figure, built on a 110-pound frame. She was five feet, two inches tall, and she had a set of breasts that men would die to touch. Of course, they did not have to die to touch them. She offered that free of charge. Still, though, whenever she prayed to the Eternal, he looked at her with the loving eyes of a father. At the same time he dismissed the praise of others. There was just something about the vivacious and happy Brenda, with her auburn hair and blue eyes, that the Eternal cherished. She was in the same category as Ruth, Esther, Rebecca and Rachel—the Eternal's beloved from a long ago past. When he had come back from the far-reaches of the Universe, he looked around for Brenda. Then he peered into that black hole in Bert's basement and saw his beloved. He became enraged. The universe trembled, but the human race took no notice of his wrath. He wiped away Brenda's tears and took her soul to his bosom. He then issued me a one-word command: Kill.

Bert and Ethyl soon found that I was not with Welcome Wagon. They would not become celebrities on the nightly news, followed by endless trials fought over by legal pimps. No, I'm the executioner; their non-revocable sentence had already been handed down. I decided to pay them my surprise visit by coming in through their back door. It led into their kitchen and then into the adjacent living (or in their case, dying) room. Ethyl was sitting in her easy chair with lover boy sitting on the floor leaning up against her fat legs, and he was drinking a beer. He kept complaining to her to quit farting or he was going to move. They were watching an old Lucille Ball "I Love Lucy" show. I had been watching them through the window in the kitchen door and listening. I decided to get into the spirit of the occasion. I kicked in the kitchen door (kicked it down actually) and announced, "Lucy, I'm home." I used my best Desi Arnez impersonation.

Bert stood up and came at me and said, "Who the hell are you?" I shoved him toward the couch. He landed on his back. I told him to stay there. I turned off the t.v. Ethyl sat there looking at me and, incredibly, kept feeding her face. Bert tried to get up off the couch. I pushed him back down and said, "Tonight your soul will be required of thee."

Bert said, "What does that mean?"

I replied, "It means I'm going to kill you." I glanced at Ethyl and said, "You, too." Ethyl yelled at Bert to call the police.

I said, "Go ahead—and while you're at it, tell them what you have in your basement." They both looked shocked.

Ethyl said, "We don't know what you are talking about."

I said, "Would you like to show me?" Bert mumbled that the door leading to the basement stairs was locked and he did not have the key.

I said, "What do you two have in that hole downstairs?"

Ethyl screamed, "Bert, he knows!" Bert lunged at me. I let

him believe that he might prevail in a physical contest—it made it more exciting. He picked up an electric carving knife and swung it at me. I stepped out of the way and backed up toward Ethyl.

She yelled, "I'm coming to help, Hun!" As she tried to get her pathetic body out of the Lazy-Boy rocker, I kicked her in the face, and she and the rocker went over backwards. I let Bert sit down on top of me. I held him by both of his wrists. He was pushing down with all of his might. I easily held him at bay. I looked over at the rocker and saw that the springs were stretched to the limit. I then looked up and saw Ethyl's fat feet wiggling around. She was trying to get out of the chair. She finally got her body over the side of the chair enough to make it tip on its side. She just lay there trying to talk. She couldn't, though; her jaw was broken.

I turned my attention back to Bert. I envisioned that my hands had the same crushing force that a mature male lion would have when crushing the bones of an antelope. I squeezed Bert's wrists. He soon began to scream in pain. He dropped the electric carving knife, and it landed right next to my head. I continued crushing his wrists until each one was no more than the diameter of a quarter. He passed out from the pain. Ethyl, seeing what was going on, headed, crawling on all fours, toward the bathroom. I let her make it. I heard her slam the door and lock it. From the noise, I knew she pushed a chair up under the doorknob, believing she might be safe. I shoved Bert off of me. As he lay there, I got up and went into the kitchen and got a rag and soaked it in the dishwater in the sink, and then came back into the living room. I wrung the dishwater out on Bert's face and sat next to him as he came around. He could not move his arms. He begged me for mercy.

I said, "Mercy? Did you offer mercy to those in your basement?" I picked up the electric carving knife and held it up to his

throat. I cut him, but not enough to kill him. I said, "I don't want to defile my hands by getting your blood on me." I thought for a few seconds about how I would kill him. I glanced to my right and saw the pillow that Ethyl had been sitting on. It smelled like urine and shit. I took it and put it over Bert's face. He did his best to fight back with his two broken wrists, but to no avail. I suffocated him.

I left him there and went to pay Ethyl a visit. She was leaning up against the bathroom door with her back to it. I guess she thought with the locked door and the chair plus her body weight that she was safe. I watched her for a few seconds through the shower door and then I pushed it open. She screamed out in terror as she looked at me. She tried to open the bathroom door to escape, but she suffered a fatal heart attack before she could get the door open. I left her there and walked back through the bathroom wall the same way I had entered. As I came back through the wall into the living room I saw a shadow on the porch.

The doorbell rang, and I opened the door to see a Girl Scout and her mother standing there. I had opened the door only slightly so that they could not see Bert lying on the floor. With a radiant look on her face, the little girl said, "I have Mr. Walla's cookie order."

I said, "I can take it for Bert."

She replied, "That will be eight dollars please. Mr. Walla told me he would pay when we delivered the cookies." The mother stood there smiling at me.

I said, "Just a minute. I'll get your money for you." I closed the door and went over to Bert's dead body and turned him over and took out his wallet. He only had a twenty dollar bill in it. I went back to the front door and gave the kid the twenty. She said she did not have change, so I told her that Bert wanted her to keep the rest for the Girl Scouts as an extra donation. She said

that I could have an extra box of cookies. I accepted and had her put in a box of the mint cookies with Bert's order. I thanked her and closed the door and went and sat down on the couch and took out the box of mint cookies. They were very good. I went into the kitchen and looked through the refrigerator for something to drink. I found a Coke and went back into the living room. I walked around the house eating and drinking.

I decided to drag Bert's body down to the basement. I took hold of his legs and pulled him toward the basement door. The door was actually locked. Bert had told the truth. I slammed my fist down on the doorknob and broke it off. The door swung open, and I pulled his body down the stairs, with his head bouncing off each step. I though about putting his body in with his victims, but decided against it. I left him there by the stairs—more food for the rats. I was going to go back up the stairs, but something drew me to the hole in the floor. Bert had covered up the hole with a blue plastic tarpaulin. He had done that to keep the smell of rotting flesh from going through all of the house.

I yanked off the tarpaulin and saw, amid the corpses in various stages of decay—Brenda. I looked at her and, to my amazement, she opened her eyes and looked back. The Eternal had given her life back. She had been allowed to touch the face of God and live to tell about it. Maybe her father's prayers persuaded the Eternal, and then again, it could be that God wasn't going to allow Bert to destroy one of his beloved children. I climbed down into that pit in Bert's basement and carefully picked Brenda up and carried her out of the house, stopping only long enough to get all of the Girl Scout cookies.

I took Brenda down the street to an all-night convenience store. The clerk looked at me as I took her into the store and said, "What is the matter with her, man?"

I said, "Nothing you need to know about. Call the police and tell them that the young woman, Brenda Ayler, whom they

are looking for, is in your store."

I said, "You will be famous, my friend."

Brenda couldn't talk because Bert had tried to strangle her. I asked the clerk to get her a cup of coffee and to stay with her until the police got there. As I left the store, I thought: "Kill the fatted calf, prepare a joyous feast. The prodigal daughter has returned home." I now must return home, too, for Geraldine's life is almost over.

Chapter XVIII

Dear Diary, I went back to Geraldine's house. As I came up the walk, Doris came out to meet me. She had a sad look on her face. She said, "Geraldine is not here."

I said, "Where is she?" I knew Geraldine would die tomorrow, but that was another 19 hours away.

Doris said, "Geraldine had a stroke after you left the other day, and she is in St. Anthony's Hospital."

I told Doris that I would go see Geraldine immediately. As I turned to go, Doris said, "Your numbers didn't work. Not one number was right."

I glanced back at her and said, "Have a little faith. Keep playing them. Maybe your faith could turn into luck."

I went to the hospital, and as I walked up to the entrance, I thought I had not been in a hospital for many years, although I had seen the priests of ancient Egypt prepare bodies for mummification. The priests also doubled as doctors, especially taking care of the wounded in battle. I went into the hospital, and an old nun asked me if she could help me. I asked her where I could

find Geraldine. She directed me to the elevator and told me to go to the second floor. She said I should check at the nurses' station. As I waited for the elevator, two young men in their late teens were talking about their girlfriends. The bigger of the two bragged that his girlfriend's dad had a password on his computer so that his daughter could not use it. He went on to say he showed his girlfriend how to go in through the "back door" and bypass the password. Both of them then had a good laugh at how stupid the dad was. We all three got on the elevator, and the shorter of the two asked me which floor I wanted. I said I would be getting off on floor two. The big kid said, "Hey, that's the dying floor."

I said, "Well, son they are all dying floors eventually."

He pushed the "two" button for me. As the elevator started up, I said, "You pushed the three button for yourself. What is that—the living floor?"

He said, "Yeh, the babies are on that floor. My sister just had a kid."

As I got off the elevator and the elevator door began to close, I said, "I want to thank you boys for that back door information."

They both looked startled and the one who was seeing his sister said, "No problem, man."

I went over to the nurses' station and leaned over on the counter. The lady working there did not even look up. After being polite by saying nothing for a couple of minutes, I said, "Excuse me, ma'am, could you tell me which room Geraldine Donato is in?"

She said, "Room 206. The poor woman has only had one visitor—her housekeeper."

I thanked her and went down the hall looking for 206. There were people in their eighties and nineties in the rooms leading up to 206. I thought: Death is the kindest god of all. He

takes away their suffering. I found 206 and went in. Geraldine was lying in bed on her back with her eyes open and had only a sheet over her and a plastic mask which supplied her with oxygen. She moved her eyes and looked at me. I looked at a plastic bag that kept inflating and then deflating as she breathed. I was all of a sudden struck with grief. I hated the place. Geraldine could not speak, but she could think. I sat down on her bed and took her hand. I spoke to her in her mind, and she knew I could read her thoughts.

She said, "I'm so glad you have come, Horus. Horus, I'm so afraid."

I said, "I'm going to get you into heaven. Don't be afraid."

She said, "How? I can't make myself believe that strongly in the Eternal. Horus, I keep having these images flash in my mind—scenes of myself lying in my casket. It is so cold and dark. I scream to get out, but I can't. I know my parents are somewhere, but my casket is the only one there."

I said, "Geraldine, that is not going to happen to you. You will be in heaven with your family. I have a way to get you to the celestial paradise. I'm going to tell you what is going to happen to you—and what you must do. The Eternal changes with his creation, but all that has come before still remains. The heaven that you seek, Geraldine, is the same that the Egyptians sought. The Eternal Amun gave them a way to get there. His ancient method of getting there is as valid today as it was then, but I'm going to modify it. We are going to get you in through the seven gates to heaven. Trust me, Geraldine. Remember when you asked me all those years ago, 'Did I ever love anyone.' I said, 'No.' Well I lied. I love you, Geraldine. I won't desert you.

"When you leave this place, you will be in a pleasant place for three days. You will have some of the earthly pleasures that you now enjoy. You will not be afraid or be alone there. After three days you will find yourself at the edge of a river that is

going so slowly that you will think it is made out of glass. As you look into the water, you will find yourself looking at a beautiful young Geraldine in the water's reflection. Out of the warm mist you will see coming toward you a henu boat. This boat was created by the Eternal to navigate the waters of the River Styx. The oarsman of the henu boat will be reluctant to give you a ride. He will say the boat is in disrepair. He will be pleasant though. Demand that he take you on the boat, and he will. As you are taken slowly down the river, you will see images of your past life on the banks of the river. The experiences will be pleasing for you. You will even see me from when we visited in 1934. The boat will come to the seven gates.

"You are to whisper in the ear of the gatekeeper a name that I will tell you. When you have passed by the seven gates, the oarsman will put you ashore in a beautiful field and there you will find your family. As you get out of the boat, the oarsman will put out his hand for payment for the ride. You will see that all of a sudden you are wearing a gold necklace. The bottom part will be a cartouche with precious stones. The inscription inside of the cartouche is the magic of the Eternal. Take it from your neck and give it to the oarsman as payment. You will then look back at the river and think this life that you now endure was only a dream and I was only a part of that dream."

Geraldine blinked her eyes and thought, "I never knew you loved me, but I will always love you and, if I can, I will remember you in heaven." A tear ran down from the corner of her eye to her cheek. I wiped it away and kissed her cheek.

I then said, "When you pass away, I will evoke an ancient Egyptian prayer that will allow you to pass into the Egyptian land of the dead. The Eternal will not abandon you to the fleeting reality of the universe. The worst thing that will happen is that he will pour out his wrath on me. I'm not human, so there will be no heaven for me—only oblivion some day. In a few

hours, Geraldine, you will go to sleep, and your earthly life will be over."

She asked, "How can you be so sure this will work?"

I told her, "Geraldine, when I was very young, I watched my mother walk bent over and with both hands on her belly. She went down to the Omo River. She sat down in the reeds and pulled some of them up to make a cradle in the mud. After she had fashioned the reeds into a mattress, she squatted over them and screamed in agony, being great with child. The child was my brother. She stayed that way for hours. As the sun set, she brought forth Seth. She took the umbilical cord between her teeth and bit it in half. She then lay down next to him and rested for a few minutes. She crawled over to the Omo and washed herself off. She went to lie back down but saw something in the darkening sky. She sat back up and put her hand in the blood of the afterbirth. Using her finger, she wrote a name on Seth's forehead. Mother then picked Seth up and held him up to the sky and said, 'You will not take this son from me—just like you did not take Horus from me.' I remember thinking she might drop him since she was so weak. Seth's body took on a glow from the sun's rays that broke through the clouds. My mother's face now had a look of contentment. She then lay down next to Seth and was soon fast asleep.

"I quietly crawled over to where they were and looked at the name she had written in blood on my brother's forehead. The name was seven letters long. My mother woke and saw me there beside her. I was much upset by all of the blood since I was only a child. I said, 'Are you going to die, Mother?'

"She smiled and said, 'No my son.' I then asked her what the name on Seth's forehead was for.

"I said, 'Is that what you have named my brother?' Her smile vanished. She now had a look of hate on her face. She took me by my shoulders and shook me and said, 'Never repeat that

name again! It is the name of the Eternal. It is an ancient and secret name—a name spoken only in heaven.'

"I said, 'Mother, if the holy and secret name of the Eternal is only spoken in heaven, how do you know it? Were you able to go to heaven?'

"My mother said, 'No, my son. I needed to find a way out of the garden. I hated it there. Adam and I had both been created out of the dust of the ground. When the Eternal became pleased with his work, he called our souls out of oblivion and put them in our bodies with his breath. At first, my son, the garden was paradise—paradise that is until I realized that I was to be subservient to Adam. I asked the King of the Universe, who was walking in the garden one day, why this should be. Surrounded by a ring of angels, he looked at them and said, 'Depart.' They all fled at his command. He then told me I was to be Adam's helpmate because that is what he decreed. I said, 'Lord, did you not create Adam and me from the same dust? Let him be under my yoke!' He then said, 'You were created to bring forth children. He was not.'

"The Eternal knew what was in my heart, so he left two angels to watch me. Wach-el, the superior of the two angels, watched my every move. If I got too close to the boundary of the garden, he was always there to turn me back. He would even watch while Adam satisfied his sexual urges with me. Adam was the king of piousness. He would put his hands on my bare breasts and say to me, 'It is time for us to do the Lord's work and begin to create humans to praise his holy name.' When Adam said that, it made me think. I had heard the angels speak of the Eternal's secret and holy name spoken only in heaven—a name so powerful that if spoken in anger, the entire universe would crumble—a name so holy, if written on the forehead of a human, it would become a shield that could withstand even the wrath of the Eternal—a name that was the Eternal's when only

his face existed and he traveled to and fro across the waters of time, looking for the perfect place to begin his creations of worlds without end.

"So, my son, I devised a plan. I would make Wach-el fall in love with me and then I would get him to tell me the name. Every morning I would go to a beautiful lagoon and take a bath and wash off Adam's seed. I would chuckle to myself as I thought Adam would never see me bring forth his offspring. One day I asked Wach-el to come and join me in the lagoon. At first he was shy and resolute in his duties. After much coaxing, he came into the water. I waded over to him and put my hands on his arms. I said, 'You are so strong and powerful—no wonder the Eternal has made you the king of the angels.' He told me that he was not the king of the angels—that they were all of the same rank. I smiled at him and said, 'That's really a shame. He put you in charge of keeping order in his garden. Isn't that a big responsibility?' Wach-el turned away from me and got out of the water. I knew he was thinking about what I had said. As I lay with Adam that night, I looked up at the tree we were lying under and saw Wach-el staring down at me. As Adam kept up his pious thrusting, I kept looking at Wach-el. I blew him a kiss. I knew he was jealous.

"The next day as I sat on a rocky cliff looking down on the Euphrates River, Wach-el came up behind me and covered my eyes with his hands. I said, 'Adam?'

"He quickly took his hands away and said, 'You know it is me.' I told him that I did not like him watching me and Adam when we made love.

"Wach-el picked up a small rock and crushed it in his hand. He said, 'That is what I could do to Adam.'

"I said, 'Then you and I could be together—if you did kill Adam.'

"Wach-el said, 'The Eternal would destroy me and, Lillith;

he might kill you, too.'

"I looked at Wach-el and said, 'You don't know that for certain. The Eternal has never destroyed anything that he has created. Maybe he will realize that creating Adam was a mistake and will thank you for correcting his error. Maybe the Eternal might even give me to you as a reward. Then we could be together forever.' Wach-el then tried to kiss me, but I turned my head and said, 'I will never be yours while I am here in this garden. I belong to Adam. There is another way, Wach-el, where the Eternal will forever withhold his anger. Tell me his secret and holy name that is only known in heaven.'

"Wach-el got up and ran yelling back at me, 'Begone, woman!' I knew he would be back. He could not stand seeing Adam and me together in our nightly sexual ritual.

"I told Wach-el one day that maybe I would lie with him if he would make us some fig wine. He saw no fear in brewing up a batch of wine. He said, 'The only problem that I could have is that the fig tree is very vain, but I'll play on its ego and say to it that its fruit is the sweetest and tastiest in all the universe; and, therefore, the fig tree should be worshipped before it gives up its fruit.' I did not see him for a few days. Then, as I sat in a field surrounded by the rays of the morning sun, Wach-el came through the grass carrying a large pot. He had a radiant look on his face. He set the pot down next to me. It was full of fig wine. I put my finger in the pot and then put my finger in my mouth.

"I said, 'It is very sweet, and so are you, my love.' I dipped my finger in the pot once more and then put my finger in his mouth. He sucked on my finger. He became amorous, but I refused his advances. I said, 'We must not make love, but we can enjoy the wine.' We drank the entire pot of wine. Wach-el , then drunk with the wine, lay down on his back—his long blond hair covering part of his face. I brushed aside his hair and looked into his cobalt blue and glazed eyes and said, 'What is the Eternal's

secret name? You told me once, but I have forgotten.'

"He said, 'I told you?'

"I said, 'Yes,' as I rubbed his massive chest. The wine was taking effect.

"He said, 'Come here.'

"I put my ear next to his mouth. He blurted out a name that I knew was a lie. I said, 'That is not the name that you said to me before.' Wach-el lay there looking puzzled. I let him put his hands on my breasts. I beguiled him to whisper to me the secret name. I said, 'The Eternal does not care if his secret name is spoken in this garden. After all, he did not destroy you when you told me before, now did he, my love?'

"Wach-el looked as if he were in deep thought and said, 'Yes, you are right. The Eternal must not care. After all, I am his first and greatest angel in the universe.' And with that he said the name of seven letters that would be my freedom.

"The next day, while Wach-el was still sleeping off the fig wine, I left the garden. Adam looked everywhere for me, and when he could not find me, he cried to the Eternal, 'My helpmate that you have made for me is gone.'

"The Eternal asked Wach-el if he knew where I had gone.

"Wach-el said, 'I will find her. She must be hiding.'

"Wach-el took two other angels and scoured the earth looking for me. They finally found me sitting on the shore of the Red Sea. Wach-el came up to me and said, 'You must return to the garden. It is the command of the King of the Universe.'

"I said, 'I will never go back. You can tell him that for me.'

"Wach-el grabbed my arm and said, 'Then we will take you back.'

"I said, 'Leave me be or I will shout his holy and secret name so loud it will echo off of the walls of the four corners of the earth. Then every demon in the universe will have a powerful weapon to wage war against the lord of the hosts.' Wach-el

and the other two angels became sorely afraid. They departed, leaving me to a life of my own making. As Wach-el turned away from me, I ripped the amulet of the heart necklace from his neck. I told him it was payment for having to put up with him. They told the Eternal that they could not find me. The Eternal had been watching and knew they were lying. Wach-el was cast out of heaven. His arms were cut off and his voice was taken away and his tongue was split in two because he lied to the Eternal. He would never again speak the holy and secret name of the Eternal. He would never again touch another human in an act of love. He would strike out at them only in hate. The light of day would become abhorrent to him, and in the darkness he would sulk with the demons of the night, waiting for the rising of the moon. His beautiful cobalt blue eyes had been replaced with deep red pupils and he would suffer in that state forever. The Eternal would forgive the other two in one thousand years, for their crime was not as great. The Eternal gave Adam another woman to be his wife, only this time he made her flesh from Adam's flesh. He named her Eve, and he made known to her that since she was flesh of Adam's flesh, she would always be subservient to him.

"Geraldine, the Eternal never did forgive my mother. He made an example out of her for all of his creation to see. He allowed her to keep her beauty, but he turned her into a demon goddess who craved sexual contact with humans, and he made her suffer. Every time she gave birth, her children would die. The sons would die the day they were born; the daughters would always die within twenty days. Then she had an idea. She would write the secret name of the Eternal on the forehead of her children the day they were born. It protected Seth and me. If the Eternal destroyed us, he would be breaking faith with himself. It also made us immortal in a sense. I have spoken the Eternal's secret name only twice in my lifetime, Geraldine. The first time

was when I was with my mother when she gave birth to Seth. The second time was when I consecrated the stone knives that I made for my brother and myself. I discovered later that the knives had the power to kill immortals. I am going to tell you the secret name of the Eternal. Remember it and whisper it only to the gatekeeper. Say nothing to the oarsman—nothing! The secret name is for the gatekeeper only."

Dear Diary, I told Geraldine the secret seven-letter name of the King of the Universe and sat with her all night, holding her hand as I had promised. The next morning at 22 seconds past 9:31 a.m. on 5-28 Geraldine Donato's soul took flight for the river and field of eternity. I kissed her on her forehead and then I invoked the sacred prayer for Geraldine as I said I would. As I got up to leave the hospital room, Doris came into the room and I told her Geraldine had just passed away.

Doris cried and said, "I took care of her for the last eleven years, and she never had a cross thing to say to me. She was a good person." Doris, looking very forlorn, then said, "Well, I guess I'll start looking for work now."

I said, "You won't have to. Geraldine did not have any next of kin, and she told me before she died that in her will she left everything she had to you. Geraldine's estate was worth about $12 million. I had made one mistake in my conversation with Geraldine in her office in 1934. I told her that in the future there would be electronic computers that could help her in her search for a Tay-Sachs cure. She must have remembered and invested in computer stock. As I said goodbye to Doris, I thought, "Guess Doris won the lotto after all." When I got back to my home, I took the picture of Geraldine and Frank and taped it up on my mirror. I will miss her.

Tomb of Geraldine Donato, 1903-1999

The bamboo plant

Chapter XIX

I spent the next three days going over Geraldine's notebook. She did a great job of explaining what Tay Sachs disease was. She had some ideas that could work—work that is if someone could manipulate individual genes. The problem is no one can do that now. Geraldine did have a habit of repeating several times in her notebook the following, "The sins of the father fall on the son." Was this something she just kept thinking about or was she in a subtle way telling me how to cure Joshua? I took a break from reading her notebook and turned on my television set. I like to catch Reverend Dennis's show whenever I can. It is interesting watching the lying hypocrites at work on his show. Today, though, he had a fill-in preacher—Reverend Joyce. It seems that Dennis had gone to the Mayo Clinic. Reverend Joyce said we should all pray for Reverend Dennis. He had a stomach problem. She went on to say that Dennis would be back soon. I don't think so. There is nothing wrong with his intestines. It is those lesions that have appeared on his leg that have him concerned. The good news is that he is now going to get a lot worse. The sand in the hourglass of his life is now mainly in the bottom of the glass.

I changed channels and watched the news. The news told of the ever-increasing terrorism in the Middle East. It got me to thinking maybe Seth was at work already. It was now time to go to Geraldine's tomb one last time. I walked the few blocks up the street and thought about what all had transpired in the last 100 days.

I had not attended Geraldine's funeral. I went into her tomb. There were now fresh roses on her coffin. I took them and put them on Sophia and Emilio's coffins and lifted the lid on

Geraldine's casket. I looked at her and said, "You are safe now." I then put my hands to my neck and took off my amulet of the heart. It had been around my neck for thousands of years since my mother gave it to me when I was a kid. I looked at the cartouche. The stones had become worn with age—no more beautiful and sparkling as when it was created and given to Wach-el by the Eternal. I gently lifted up Geraldine's head and put the necklace around her neck. I performed the Egyptian ceremony of the opening of the mouth so that she would be able to speak the sacred words in the afterlife. I said, "Remember this is payment for the oarsman." I won't need its protection any more.

Then I got to thinking, why did I say that—she is no longer here. I never existed for Geraldine now. I guess maybe that is hard for me to accept. I looked at Geraldine one last time and watched my amulet of the heart slowly disappear. It was with her now. I thought the dead may soon be the luckiest of them all. I closed the lid on her coffin and put one of the roses on the lid. As I walked out of the cemetery, I passed by that would-be cop. He stared at me. I said to him, "You have a good day, sir. And, in answer to what you are wondering, no we have never met."

Chapter XX

Dear Diary, I decided to get up and write a few pages. It is 4:36 a.m. I can hear the birds beginning to chirp outside in anticipation of the new day. On the other side of my bedroom wall there is a vaporizer working away in Joshua's room. He had a slight cold that at least did not have anything to do with his deadly problem. I turned on my radio, which amazingly still

worked, considering that it had been bounced off the wall awhile back. On the overnight show that specialized in the paranormal, they were discussing what was going on at Khufu's pyramid. One of the callers said he was there with his wife and daughter, and he was pretty sure that half of the people on the tour were not tourists—they were agents of the American and Egyptian governments. He said he knew a couple of the Americans, and he asked what they were doing and they were very evasive. They actually got it pretty much right. The host of the show did come up with the usual government cover-up. It is not exactly a cover-up. The U.S. government just knows something ungodly and alien is there.

Some archeologist came upon something by pure chance. It seems that several of them had gone into Khufu's pyramid with a small self-propelled robot that had a camera attached to it. It was designed to fit into the small, four inches by four inches, shafts that are in Khufu's pyramid. They wanted to see where the shafts might lead. They put the robot camera into one of the shafts and set it on its merry way. It did not show anything extraordinary on the video monitor as it went up the shaft—just bare granite walls.

But then the operator stopped the robot and asked a question of his three companions who were drinking coffee and paying no mind to the video monitor. He said, "What the hell is that?"

They all looked at the monitor. One of them said, "It looks like a face." They increased the brightness of the light on the camera and, as they did, the face opened its eyes and stared back. They were the first 20th Century humans ever to look at a person of the dark face to face. People all over the world think they have seen them, and probably have. They appear as a blur in the corner of one's eyes, but by the time they turn their heads to look, they are gone. So most people think that maybe they

imagined it, or if they are outside at dusk, perhaps it was a bird flying by.

Khufu had seen them—dead—thanks to Seth and me. This one that they were looking at did not stay around very long. It took off like a shot—heading in reverse since it had no desire to go past the robot. The archeologists all stood there speechless—not believing what they had seen. They then all thought the same thought, which I picked up on a half a world away. They thought, "Was that a ghost?" They called it quits for the day. They could not get out of that tomb fast enough. Too bad they could not get the papyrus of Menkaure. His scribes wrote in great detail of the people of the dark. Most of the writings about the people of the dark were lost in the great fire that destroyed the library of Alexandria during the reign of Cleopatra VII, the last of the Ptolemies. Some writing still exists, locked away by the Egyptian government. Maybe the Americans should ask the Egyptian government for the sacred writings. But the Egyptians believe that their country will rise to great prominence soon so they probably would say they know nothing of it.

The Americans returned the next day with two armed Egyptian security guards and made the discovery that even the Egyptians did not know was there. They ran their robot up to the end of the shaft—only to discover that it opened up into a much larger vertical shaft going down to bedrock. They lowered the camera to where it could look down into the shaft. At the bottom of the shaft they saw a black right angle triangle in the bed rock. It was and still is the same door to the universe of the people of the dark that Seth and I entered all of those centuries ago. The Americans don't know what it is exactly, and they can't take apart the pyramid to get to it to find out. They have had all-night brain-storming sessions and have come up with what to them is the unthinkable: What if that face they keep watching over and over on the video tape came out of the right angle

hole—if it is a hole. They are not sure of that either. They considered the possibility that it might be a black hole. They reasoned that it must not be, however, because by now the entire earth would have been destroyed. They have run tests checking for radiation and have come up with nothing except traces of a form of negative energy that is there, and then when they check again it isn't there. This really has them upset because it is defying physics. They now have a camera stationed around the clock videotaping the hole.

Well, the people of the dark will eventually start to come through again, and they will be captured on videotape. Then the Americans will not know what to do to stop them and how to plug the hole. Right now, though, they are exploring the idea that maybe Khufu put it there somehow. Fortunately, they have discarded the idea of trying to blow it up with a small atomic bomb. I doubt the Egyptians would like that idea, but the Americans may resurrect it. If they do, they might want to keep the idea a secret. Well, the world is full of brilliant physicists, so maybe they can figure it out before the pyramid is sealed on the day of judgment.

I went to water my bamboo plant. I picked it up and put water in the pot. The pot had been sitting on a piece of paper. The paper remained stuck to the bottom of the pot. I pulled off the paper and put down the pot and examined the paper. I rubbed my fingers over the paper. The paper was sticky. I had not done anything with the pot since I had picked it up from young Joshua's bed where Seth had left it. I had not touched the bottom of the pot until now. There was no reason for me to. I'm glad I did now. I smelled the sticky substance on the pot. It was a smell that I remembered from a distant past. I think I will take another trip to the Middle East. But first I have something else I have to take care of.

I went to a dilapidated building in a run-down section of

Denver. I stood leaning over a railing on a bridge looking down on the building. On the side of the three-story red brick building that was built in the early nineteen hundreds was a sign that read "Denver School Book Supply Company." The white paint was faded with time and only the second floor was occupied with businesses, none of which was the Denver School Book Supply— it had died out long ago, along with its owners. I was more interested in what I would find in the basement. I climbed up on the freight dock, which held the odor of urine courtesy of the transients who lived around there. I went through the dock door and found myself in a large room with nothing in it except a card table with a light fixture dangling down from the ceiling with a 100-watt bulb, which was turned on. I went over and turned it off. As I did, I thought to myself that this one would not have held up Father Michael either. I looked at the dust on the floor and saw small toeless footprints leading to a space in the floor about one inch between the flooring planks. I quietly walked over to the freight elevator. I reached my arm through the slats on the door and pushed the lever so that the elevator would go down to the basement. There was a handwritten sign on the elevator that was amusing to me. It read: "When you get off the elevator, put the gate down. Otherwise no one on the other floors will be able to bring the elevator to their floor. So remember that, stupid!"

As the elevator started on its way, making a loud humming noise in protest for having to work, I went down the dark stairs. The basement was dimly lit with only the light of day shining down through the elevator shaft. I made my way through the dark toward the elevator. I had to be careful. There was junk everywhere—one match, and the whole place would have burned down in an hour. I went from one white support post to the next until I was only 15 feet from the elevator. I just stood there and waited.

Out of the darkness came two people of the dark. They cautiously went over to the elevator and looked up the shaft. I started to creep up on them. As I did, I made a blunder and stepped on a beer can left there by some drunk. The noise made them turn around and look straight at me. They took off in panic. I knew they would not head for the daylight. I picked out the one I wanted and chased him down. I must have run around that basement five times trying to catch him. I was jumping over boxes of rags, going through the support posts, and finally in panic the creature doubled back and ran smack into me. I grabbed his arm before he could get away again. He squealed like a frightened mouse. I dragged him over to a couple of boxes and I sat down on one of them. The box collapsed, but I did not let go of my quarry. I got up and pulled him over to a 55-gallon drum. I sat him on it this time. He was absolutely terrified. I told him I was not going to harm him again. I looked at him and said, "Remember when we met in that tomb, my friend. I tore your head off, but lucky for you that was in another time and place. Why, you have been born again. Do you want to live this time or do you want me to kill you twice? I'm going to let go of you— if you try to run I will catch you and take your head off—again." I let go of him. He sat there on that drum and held out his hands, palms up in submission to me. I looked at his hands. Only the tips of his fingers could move. The people of the dark have webbing between their fingers that comes up about two thirds of the way on their fingers. It does make catching light rays more convenient.

I said, "I am going away for awhile. If you or any of your friends bother the people who live in the home I share with them, I will kill you all. I will then wait outside of your door to this universe and kill each one of your brothers and sisters as they come through the threshold." He covered his eyes with his hands and bowed. I said, "One other thing, my friend, tell your

buddies what I just told you. No matter where I am in the world, I will pick up on any danger to Joshua, Sara or their grandmother. Now get out of my sight." He was more than happy to oblige.

I walked over to the elevator and started to leave the elevator gate up so that the guy who put up the warning sign would have to walk down to the basement to get the elevator to work. But then I thought better of it and decided that I could have some fun if I just sent it up to the third floor, so I did—and the elevator was sent up to the third floor. As it went up I heard a female voice coming from the second floor say, "You bums get out of here or I'll call the police." I should not have frightened the lady. I guess I must have a mischievous personality sometimes. I went back home to take a bath. I was covered with dust, and my hair had some sort of industrial fluid in it. After I had showered, I lay down in the bathtub and thought about what Seth was planning. I must say it was pretty ingenious. It was also an idea that was a product of his imagination based on his ancient past.

I went over and knocked on Mrs. Bloom's door. Sara answered the door and invited me in. I gave Thelma my rent money for the next month, and I gave her my bamboo plant to take care of for me because I would be gone for a while. I looked over at baby Joshua asleep in his rock-a-bye baby chair. I told Thelma that I was sure something good would happen to baby Joshua. She asked me if I believed in angels. I said I surely did—good ones and bad ones. She told me she had a dream that Joshua's disease would be taken away by an angel of the Lord.

I said, "See there. This must be proof that the Eternal will give him a long and healthy life. Otherwise, why would we both be thinking the same thing?" I asked Thelma if I could give Joshua a toy model that I had picked up in the Middle East. She agreed. It was a little statue of the goddess Best, the protector of

children. I put the statue on the windowsill in his bedroom. I told Thelma that it was a symbol of faith by the people in ancient Egypt and it would remind her when she looked at it to keep her faith, and that all would be well.

Now I don't know if Best could really help save Joshua; I only know that in the reign of King Nepherites a children's plague spread throughout the land. The children would literally cough themselves to death. It was heart-rending for their parents watching their children gasping for breath when nothing could be done to save them. It was especially deadly for the very young. Great were the cries of the mothers of Egypt. In desperation the women began to make statues in the shape of Best to pray to. Someone had remembered the legend of the godly woman whose children had been spared when the same form of plague had struck during the reign of King Horemheb. In their prayers they begged Best to intercede on their behalf to Amun to save their children. The plague soon ended. Maybe it would have anyway because perhaps it had run its course. At any rate, Best can't hurt Joshua. I said my goodbyes and then left for the ancient land of Kush. Seth always did love that place. They used to worship him as a god there.

Chapter XXI

Well, Dear Diary, I'm back in Kush—an ancient name for northern Sudan. This is a poor country and lawless in some areas. It has always been poor. Hell, even the Romans did not think this place was worth fighting for. My brother did fight here twice, though. The first time was for the Egyptian King

Amenophis I, and the second time was for King Thutmose I. Seth was rewarded by the king by being named the governor and with a title, "Son of the King of Kush." He stayed there for 20 years. He did not build any shrines for Thutmose—but he managed to build one for himself at Musawwarat—not much left here at Musawwarat now. I remember when he built this shrine. Now there are only two pillars that used to hold up the roof plus an obelisk in between them that foretold of what a great god Seth would become and how he would rule here forever as the warrior god. If he is in this country, it might take me awhile to find him. He would probably be in the south. It is there that he will find the material that he needs. It may be here in this forsaken country that the first battle of the end of the world will take place. The colossal powers of the earth will hardly take notice at first. They regard this part of the world and what goes on here as only an annoyance—nothing more.

I decided to go to the Nuba Mountains, located in the middle of the country. I walked down a road that was nothing more than two ruts. As I came around a bend, I saw a bus about 50 yards ahead of me. It was painted a bright yellow and piled on top of it were the personal belongings of the passengers. I walked up to the door of the bus, which was broken and jammed open, and looked in. There was no one in it, but the engine was still running. I climbed up the two steps inside the bus and stood there looking down the empty rows of seats. It was an eerie feeling even though it was midday. I glanced out the door and noticed several hyenas milling around outside the bus. I reached over and turned off the ignition. There was no sign of a struggle and there were no bullet holes in the bus—that rules out the Sudanese People's Socialist Front and their adversary, the Mandari Militia, the local guerrillas that infest this part of the country. I walked down the aisle, and as I got to the last row of seats, I saw a small black face looking out from under the seat

at me. Whoever had taken the people off the bus had missed one.

This kid looked about the same age as Sara. I had brought along a knapsack with me that had a couple of bottles of water plus some of Bert's Girl Scout cookies. I sat down next to this kid and held them out to him. The bus was terribly hot. One of the hyenas, probably the leader, was brave enough to climb up the steps and look down the aisle at me. There was a basket sitting on the seat in front of me. I picked it up and threw it at him. He beat a hasty retreat. Dear Diary, I thought to myself: Shit, I can't leave this kid here. The damn door won't close for one thing, plus he would die of the heat. The hyenas will be back when the sun sets and they will be more aggressive. They would have him for dinner. The kid downed a whole bottle of water. I tried to converse with him. I went through several sub branches of eastern Sudanese languages. I finally struck a chord with the Kurdufanian language.

It seems according to my little friend that the bus had been full of children who had been taken to see a wrestling tournament between two competing villages. Wrestling here is more than just a form of entertainment. It is a rite of passage to manhood for boys. They start learning how to wrestle when they are about thirteen. This little boy, whose name was Sebo, was too young to participate, so he could only watch. I asked him what had happened to the other boys on the bus. He told me some men that spoke Arabic had stopped the bus and had taken them and the bus driver away. He said they had not noticed him hiding under the last seat and that his brother had distracted them from checking the last row by attempting to climb out the window. I asked him if he knew the direction of his village, and he pointed out of the window in the bus—south. I decided to turn the bus around, but as I did, one of the rear drive wheels got stuck in a rut. I turned off the engine and told Sebo we would

have to walk.

The hyenas were still outside the bus, so I picked up Sebo and sat him on my shoulders. We got out of the bus and I started walking. One of the hyenas got a little too brave and tried to snap at the back of my leg. I turned and kicked him in the side hard enough that it lifted him off the ground. He let out a yelp and they all ran off. I walked with Sebo sitting on my shoulders for about four miles. He then started beating on my head and pointing at a small village ahead. The village consisted of six cone-shaped houses with thatched roofs. The mud houses were built in a circle with a wall leading from one house to the next, as a form of protection. There was one common entrance that led into an open courtyard. We walked in. I had gotten tired of providing transportation for Sebo, so I put him down on the ground and he ran into the open courtyard. In the middle of the courtyard sat a lone woman. She was sitting on her haunches and was in mourning. She had covered her hair in white ash and had painted her eyelids with white paint Sebo ran over to her, and she hugged him. She was his aunt. This was not his home, but she knew where he lived. I asked her where everyone had gone. She told me that the devil had taken all of the children, and the men had gone to look for them. I left Sebo with her and, as I left, he came over and asked me if he could have the rest of the cookies. I gave them to him. I like to eat, but I don't have to eat to maintain my life.

I headed for the "Sudd"—the world's biggest swamp. You can hide almost anything in that swamp. I spent the night in a large tree. I lay down on a large branch with my head up against the trunk and beheld the beauty of the universe. As I listened to the music of the creatures of the night, I was grateful the Eternal had no assignments for me—then again, maybe this is an assignment from the Eternal. The next morning I continued on my way south. I came across several more villages that were

minus their children. There are dense jungles in the south, and the further south I went I saw more and more wicker baskets high in the trees. This was an ancient way of harvesting honey from wild bees. Put up a basket in a tree and eventually bees will use it as a hive. Of course, it is a little risky robbing the hives—unless, of course, you have an army of children to do the work for you—slave children that the Sudanese government pretends don't exist. If you lose a few kids to bee stings, just let their bodies float away in the Sudd. The crocodiles will get rid of the victims. In a poor country two and one half times the size of Egypt, the world does not take note of the misery.

I saw several young men in their early teens climb out of the back of a four-wheel drive pickup. Each one had chains on his ankles. There were two adult males who got out of the cab of the truck. One of the teenage slaves said something to one of the men and received a beating with a whip for his trouble. The others went to work harvesting the honey-soaked beeswax. Each of the slave children carried a pot to put it in. They appeared oblivious to the bee stings. One of them, however, fell trying to ward off the bees. He lay on the ground writhing in agony for about twenty minutes. All the while one of the men kept kicking him in his side and telling him in Arabic to get up. The men were with the Arab Murahaleen Militia and were armed with Soviet Kalashnikov AK 47 assault rifles—compliments of my brother. I guess Seth has come a long way from the Asian bow of the Hyksos invaders. (The Hyksos had conquered Egypt during the XV Dynasty in 1660 B.C.) The young man died a few minutes later. I was watching this from a small hill looking down on the road.

I decided that they now would have an opening for a new slave. I left my knapsack there and became a black teenage African, stark naked. As they walked back toward the truck, they turned and looked back. I then made sure the two men saw

me taking the dead boy's clothing and putting them on. I let them chase me down and clamp a set of chains on my legs. I half-heartedly protested and begged for mercy. They slapped me around and told me to take the dead boy's basket and climb back up the tree that he had fallen from and collect the beeswax and honey. I did. When I came down from the tree, they did not notice that I did not have any bee stings on me. I went up several trees before we were through for the day. The only food we received was three pieces of bread that we were allowed to smear a little honey on. We washed it down with rainwater that had collected in the pockets of large leaves. We all got into the back of the truck and headed south to the Sudd. One of the slaves criticized me for being stupid and getting caught. He told the slave next to him that I would not last a week.

When we got to the edge of the Sudd swamp we boarded a flat boat, composed mainly of one and three-quarter inch plywood, with a small aircraft engine rigged up to the back to provide the power to propel the boat across the swamp. The slave who had been critical of me thought he had a chance to escape, so he jumped overboard—but the slave master stopped the boat and shot and killed him. He then walked among us, slapping us and warning that we would receive the same treatment if we tried to escape. The Sudd was a natural prison.

We reached our destination in about an hour. There in the middle of the Sudd was a floating platform about the length of a football field and square. The place was hell on earth for the children. The flies and mosquitoes were everywhere by the thousands and the heat was almost unbearable. The place consisted of a common living area in the center and a work area where we squeezed the honey from the beeswax combs, and sheltered living quarters with air conditioning for the slave master. I know Seth did not care about the honey. He only wanted the beeswax. The honey, once harvested, was a bonus for his henchmen. We

would work until all of the honey was separated from the beeswax. Then we were allowed to eat six pieces of bread with honey and all of the swamp water we wanted to drink. The Sudanese were working with Seth, but they regarded him as just another terrorist leader—one that they could control. They might find they have made a bad bargain. The bee's wax was put into cartons and then loaded back on the flat boats. I kept thinking maybe my brother would show up to check on his operation. But he did not.

I remembered what an asshole he had been when he was governor here 3500 years ago. He did not care for the people then. They were only pawns in his grand scheme. After about two weeks, one of the guards came over and asked us if any of us had artistic talent. I raised my hand, and he and his friends laughed. One of them grabbed me by the hair and said, "Get on the boat." I did, with several other slaves. As the boat made its way back to shore, we passed several rotting bodies of children floating in the water. The bodies in the warm water of the Nile gave off an odor that permeated our clothing and attracted the crocodiles. The boat kept bumping into the corpses. One body, minus its arms, was thrown up on the boat. I put it back in the water and said, "Peace be with you." Eventually, we were put in the back of a large truck with a canvas top. It looked like an old American military two and a half ton truck. We drove for about five days and nights until we reached a large building on the outskirts of Khartoum, the capitol of Sudan. We were herded into the building. We walked past sacks of flour marked, "Food for Peace from the people of the United States."

We were taken to a large room with long tables in it. There were probably about 300 slave children there—both boys and girls. Each one was chained to a leg of the table with a chain just long enough so that they could reach one of the holes that had been cut into the floor so that they could relieve themselves. The

guy who was in charge was known as Mohammed, the most common name in the world. Since we were new here, we were shown by other slaves what we were to do. Two of the new slaves went to work at a table where the beeswax was heated and melted and poured into cylinders about two inches in diameter and six inches high. After the wax cooled, it was taken out of the cylinders and was distributed to the slaves. A little Dinka boy showed me.

He said, "You are to be a carver like me. You take a piece of beeswax and a knife and try to cut it into the shape of that wax figure of a man."

I said, "I'm not too good at carving."

Staring at me with fear in his dark brown eyes, he said, "You must learn quickly or they will first beat you."

I said, "What happens second?"

He said, "Sadik will take you to that room over there and you will never come out."

Pointing to the opposite wall, I said, "What is in that room over there?"

He said, "That is where they take some of the girls to pleasure at night—sometimes."

I practiced my carving and then about two in the morning they turned out the lights. All of the children lay over the tables and went to sleep. No one was allowed to use the toilet holes in the floor until morning. My young friend told me to not let my chain rattle or they would turn on the lights and beat everyone for making noise. I sat there straight up in my chair, thinking about my brother. In the darkness I heard sobbing from the children and laughing from behind the door where the slave masters were raping the young slave girls.

Dear Diary, I stayed here living among the stench, filth and despair waiting for my brother. My little Dinka friend told me how he had been captured. He said in the middle of the night

men came into his village and woke everyone up by firing their guns. He told me they put all of the young children in one circle and all of the adults in another circle and then shot all of the adults and put the children into a truck (like I had been in). He said as the truck pulled away from the village, the hyenas, attracted by the smell of blood, were sneaking into the village. This was the last vivid memory he had of his parents—and that he had been here ever since.

I guess Seth had built up a pretty good network. He always was good at organization. The local Sudanese officials know he is good at improving their living with hard cash. I am leaving here tomorrow. Seth will find I left him a present. However, I'm sure he will have other factories turning out assassins. A form of magic that was handed down in Egypt from king to king was the ability to create living assassins from wax figures fashioned into the shapes of men. Once blessed by a priest of Egypt, they became living, breathing men—only men with the souls of demons. Western civilization would say, "That is impossible— only fantasy" while all the time believing in a savior who sup-posedly could turn water into wine.

If the Americans tire of losing their young men in battles around the world, maybe they should study the writing of Nectanebo, the last native king of Egypt, and the last of the ancient dynasties: XXX. He was the last king to use the wax assassins. Then the Americans, with the help of the Egyptians, could fight demon assassin against demon assassin, without families crying back home for their dead loved ones. Of course, there are only two priests of Egypt who are qualified to utter the ancient words in the right order to bring life to the wax assas-sins.

Tomorrow came. We received our morning ration of food, and then we began to work. One of the slave children, a young man of perhaps 14, had developed dysentery during the night

and began to defecate all over the floor. Since his chain got tangled up, he could not make it to the hole in the floor. On his way to beat the young man, Sadik, one of the slave masters, came by me. I picked up one of the wax figures and bounced it off of his head. He turned around, rubbing the back of his head, and yelled, "Who did that?"

I smiled and said, "I did."

He came toward me, and he started flailing away with his whip. I stood up and broke the chain loose from the table leg. All the time he was swinging that whip at me as hard as he could. I put my leg out and tripped him. He fell to the floor. As he tried to get back up, I took my chair and started hitting him at the base of his spinal cord, knocking him back down to the floor. I kept yelling at him in Arabic, "How do you like this, huh?" I think I broke his back, because he could not move his legs. I took the chain and wrapped it around his neck and pulled it tighter and tighter and watched his eyes begin to bulge. It did not take too long for him to die. I dragged him to one of the holes in the floor and shoved him head first into the hole. One of the other slave masters came running over and held a pistol up to my stomach and pulled the trigger five times. Pandemonium had broken out in the place.

He should have pulled the trigger one more time, and then he would have run out of bullets—but he did not. I broke loose his fingers that were holding the pistol. I took the gun and put it up to his head and pulled the trigger and watched part of his brain splatter all over the table. With that last bullet, he fell like a rock and lay dead on the floor with his eyes staring at me. The slave children were all yanking on their chains trying to get the chains loose. They were still afraid of their slave masters, even though they were watching what they perceived as one of their own killing the masters that they feared so much. The children's legs were bloody where the chains were hooked to the leg

clamps. I busted up the tables, and the slave children freed themselves and ran out of the building, holding what was left of the chains still attached to their leg clamps.

I caught Mohammed in his office. He had just come into the building and had no idea what was going on. He liked to torture slaves by soaking them in a bathtub of ice water for an hour until they were suffering hypothermia and then beating them. I saw that he had a tub right in his office and it was still full of water—no ice in it now, but that was okay. I threw him toward the tub. There was water on the floor. He slipped on it and fell backward into the tub by himself. I was on him in seconds. I held his head under the water in the tub. He held his breath for a good two minutes before the bubbles of death made their way to the surface of the water. I let go of him and his body slowly turned over on its right side, gently bobbing up and down.

I decided to check out what was behind the door that the little Dinka boy had told me about. I opened the door to find that it led to a closed-in courtyard where the last of the slave masters was hiding. I found him behind a small open pit where they had burned the bodies of slaves that had displeased them. I had resumed my normal form. I came over to him and told him to undress. He did. I put on the rags he was wearing. He got down on his knees and put his hands together as if praying and begged for mercy. I pulled him up and held him up so that his feet were off the ground. I said, "I am not going to kill you. I want you to wait here in Khartoum. Soon your master will come and ask you what happened here. You tell him Horus did this." I said, "Your master will reward you for this information." I thought: Seth will reward him all right. Seth will become enraged. Seth does not hold with the theory that you don't kill the messenger for the message.

I went back into the now vacant building and took three five-gallon cans of gasoline and poured them all over the boxes

of wax assassins and dropped a match on them. Within minutes the place was an inferno. I watched as the place burned down. As I walked north to the confluence of the White and Blue Niles, I saw nine of the slave children trying to get off their leg clamps. I stopped and helped them. I used my stone knife (which I had concealed from the slave masters all this time) to break loose the clamps. I told them to try and make their way to Kenya because there was nothing left for them here in the Sudan. I went to a local store and bought some western clothes with money I had taken off of the late Mohammed. The shopkeeper held the money up to the light since the bills were still wet. I guess he wanted to make sure they were not counterfeit. I like to think of it as overtime pay. I decided to make my way east now. I will follow the Blue Nile to its headwaters in my ancient homeland of Ethiopia.

I soon grew tired of walking by the Blue Nile, so I transformed myself once more into a falcon. I flew into the sky and slowly flew east toward Ethiopia. I flew to Lalibela. I knew a priest there who was the guardian of the "tomb of Adam." The tomb of Adam was built over the "tomb of Eve." They had both been disinterred and brought here from the land of Nod to be reburied by Enoch, a servant of God. Even in death that occurred thousands of years ago, Eve was still subservient to Adam. His tomb was on top of hers. Maybe she was buried in the missionary position. Christians, Muslims and Jews alike would love that idea. At least my mother did not have to endure that indignity.

I met my friend at the entrance to the church that housed the tomb. Unlike Westerners who announce their faith to the world on bumper stickers and crosses around their necks, the Christians of Ethiopia wear their faith on their forehead. Usually it is in the form of a blue cross. My friend had gone one better. He had a cross branded on his forehead. Though his faith was

in that of an ancient usurper, nevertheless his heart was pure—and he possessed the power of prophecy. He carried a book of the Psalms of David, which I know he reads daily. He came down the five steps of the church to meet me. Each step that he took was painful to him. He had a boil on the side of his right foot that he had treated with an ancient remedy: Lapis Lazuli ground up and mixed with honey and milk. He stood six feet, two inches tall with a gaunt appearance. He wore a white turban and a white embroidered robe that reached to his ankles, almost covering the sandals on his feet. He offered me a cup of tea. I accepted. He then looked at me and said, "What brings the ancient avenger to the door of the Lord?"

I said, "I have questions that only you can answer." I asked, "Do you know where my brother is?"

He stared as if in a trance and said, "At this very moment he is lying with that demon harlot whom you freed, when you transgressed on holy ground."

I said, "Where?"

The priest said, "Why, at the throne of Solomon." He kept pushing his hand into my chest to emphasize the points he was making. He spoke to me in Geez, an ancient and obnoxious language. and was beginning to piss me off. "Ironic isn't it? You came here to kill if necessary to steal the secret of Solomon and your brother at this very minute sleeps on the ancient bed of King Solomon, surrounded by an army of assassins. Go home my friend—tend to the little one whose life you want to save. The time is not right for you to do battle to the death with your brother. Not right! Not right! He must do his evil here first, and his henchmen, on his behalf, will do that evil in the infancy of the next century. With the arrival of the new millennium will come the anti-Christ, disguised as the new prince of the West. He will wage war with the zealots of Islam, and the fruits of their combined labor will be the blood of the innocent. The pillars

that reach to the sky will be brought low. The anti-Christ will seize this moment. He will cause a veil to cover the intelligence and wisdom of the people, who will be stricken with fear. The people will become confused and will not know what is righteous and what is unrighteous. The people will look to the anti-Christ for guidance and assurance that all will be well. The angels in heaven will weep and shout in unison, 'Now it begins.'

"Vengeance and hate will pervade in the West, and even the kindest heart will become its victim. The prince of the West, having no stomach for battle himself, will send forth his troops eager for battle and the taste of blood. He will turn a deaf ear to the cries of the families of his dead soldiers. He will be hell bent on victory at any cost. He will conveniently keep safe at home his own offspring. In a thousand ships on the sea and in the air his troops will come to our ancient lands. They will come with a determination to extract justice that would make even Achilles and Menelaus proud, but he who wears the red and white crown will withstand their fury and slowly diminish their numbers while increasing his own. Hailed as a champion, he will be, for defeating the West. He will consolidate the countries of the East into a hammer to crush the head of his adversary. And then on the brink of victory, in the year 2032, on the day of the winter solstice, he will wage a battle with his own bloodline at the first crossroads of commerce in our ancient land. There, like two scorpions circling each other, they will fight to the death. I don't know who will prevail, but one will die. This is all that I see. Lastly, my friend, leave our national treasure alone."

I thanked him for his advice and the tea and then took my leave of him. I thought how his prophecy mirrored that of my nightmare.

I headed for Lake Tana, the headwaters of the Blue Nile. I decided to rent one of the reed boats that still navigate between the churches around the shores of Lake Tana. I had thanked my

priest friend. I had not said I would leave. After all, this is the land of my birth. In fact, maybe I have more of a right to be here than he does. After all, longevity should count for something. I thought to myself there was no point in asking him where was the hiding place of the treasure of Solomon. It was taken away in the middle of the night centuries ago and carried off to Ethiopia because Israel had offended the Eternal—when Solomon gave in to his new wife and allowed her to worship gold and silver idols. The ark was hidden by Solomon's son, Menelik I, a son from the union of King Solomon and the Queen of Sheba, an unbroken line that supposedly stretched all the way to the 20th Century and ended with the death of Haile Selassie, the Lion of Judah. My friend would not have told me even if it meant his death. I admired him for that.

I enjoyed my time on Lake Tana. I thought about what the priest had said. He was wrong though. I did not want to steal their only treasure. I just wanted to see it. I thought it might be on Tana Cherqos Island in Lake Tana, but it was not. I decided, Dear Diary, to go to Aksum to see if it might be in the holy of holies, the church of Mary of Zion. The church was guarded by priests carrying automatic rifles. The priests don't really know if the ark is there either. They were told just to guard the church. Obviously the Jews don't believe it is here, or they would come and kill everyone to get it back. There is only one priest who is allowed to pass through the seven rooms and enter the sanctuary and bow down before it. He is pure of heart like my friend. He never leaves the church compound. I will go see him in a little while. I will walk up to the green wrought iron metal gates of the church and ask the guard for entrance. I will be respectful, but I will see for myself if it is here. So perhaps it would be unwise for the guard to turn me away. I will wait until the sun begins to set.

Now, though, I find myself at the shrine of the dog star. The

dog star and the southern cross could be seen by the naked eye when I was young. Seth built this shrine for me in honor of my birthday. I remember he kept it as a surprise for me. He had been acting very mysteriously for several months, and he would go away for weeks at a time and not tell me where he was going. He and I could have been kings of the earth back then if we wanted to. He built my shrine during the reign of King Tcheser of the Third Dynasty. The king had commissioned him to take a small party of men to seek out the source of the Nile. A famine had fallen upon the land. The Nile had not risen in its annual flood stage for seven years. The crops withered and died. The people began to fight among themselves because they were on the edge of starvation. Their prayers to Khnemu, the god of the Nile, came to no avail. The people brought their complaint to King Tcheser. They reasoned that since he was a god-king he would make everything well.

King Tcheser was very upset because he knew he could not make the waters of the Nile rise, and, therefore, he would lose face in the eyes of the people. This was the only thing bothering him. He really did not care if the people starved. He knew he would not starve. It is just like the rulers of the 20th Century. They just want to placate the masses. King Tcheser called for his priests to be brought before him. Seth and I went along just to watch and listen to what the priests had to say. They came up with an outlandish tale of how the annual flood was due to water flowing from caverns located on Elephantine Island. They told the king that Khnemu, the Nile god, had beseeched the gods Osiris, Isis and Nephthys to help him withhold the flood waters because the people had let his shrine fall into disrepair.

Seth and I looked at each other and laughed. He and I had traveled all over the world and we knew the source of the Nile. We told the king that the Nile is really the offspring of the Blue Nile (mother) and the White Nile (father). Since the priests said

we were lying, the king asked Seth to prove this by taking a party of the King's choosing to the two sources. We told the king that the drought was caused by the lack of rainfall in those two countries. The king said that if the caverns at Elephantine were not the source of the annual Nile flood, then that means his priests and the governor of Elephantine lied. He said the penalty for lying to the king would be death. We went along with the king's command. He was willing to pay us with enough beer, bread, onions and barley to last us for seven years.

In our party were two priests, bearers bringing supplies, and the scribe to the king—the rest were soldiers for protection. The priests were agents for the king in all political matters and were in over-all charge, unless we got into a fight with the locals— then Seth was in charge until the battle was over. We told them that we should follow the Blue Nile. We also said we knew where the source of the White Nile was, so there was no point in going there. The priest demanded we take them to the source. We did. The source was Lake Victoria and the Mountains of the Moon. We had to back track to where the White Nile met the Blue Nile. We followed the Blue Nile to the land of Punt (Ethiopia) all the way to its headwaters, with the scribe taking notes every foot along the way. We encountered some of the worst rainstorms of our lives. Seth and I knew the drought was over. Seth told me that we should go to Aksum, since there was a shorter way home. I remember as we came into the town, he said, "Look, brother, what is that?"

I said, "It looks like a new shrine. Maybe it has been built for Hapi, the local name for the god of the Nile." As we walked up to it, I saw it was a tribute to the dog star.

He looked so happy as he grabbed me by my shoulders and said, "It is for you, my loving and good brother. This is where I have been, my brother. I was not out doing the bidding for the king like you thought. I love you, Horace, for truly no one could

have a better brother."

Dear Diary, I guess I should forget those memories now. Most of it is gone now, torn down centuries ago by invaders from the north.

I leaned up against the broken obelisk and watched some young boys playing soccer. One of them kicked the ball and it rolled up next to me. I picked it up and handed it to a young man who had come over for it. I looked at him, and he smiled back at me. I thought, he will be in Seth's army some day—just like his counter parts in America will be in their army. Perhaps they will meet in battle. There will be much gnashing of teeth on both sides before the 21st Century sees its third decade. Seth wants to rule the world from his kingdom in Egypt. He believes it is his right. The West wants to rule the world for their dead savior. However, they will claim as they go to battle that their real cause is freedom. The West won't succeed—unless I help them. I am not sure, Dear Diary, whether I will or not. I only know that I want to see my brother face to face again. He did not try to kill me before; maybe Amun stopped him. Maybe Seth cares something for me after all. Obviously, not all of our memories are bad. I must finish with my quest to save Joshua's life. Then I will deal again with Seth.

I got up from the obelisk and went to the church. I decided there was no point in going to the front gate. I went through the brick fence and in through a side wall of the church. The place was empty. There was only the smell of incense to guide my way. I quietly made my way past the back of the altar and through a locked door. There was a space of about seven feet to the next door. The place was really designed as a maze. I finally made it to the final door. I went through the door into the last room. The room was empty except there was a dumbwaiter on one of the walls. I climbed in and lowered myself down by the rope that held it up.

I got out into a small damp room maybe ten feet square with a dirt floor, and there before me, in the center of the room, was a wooden box. The box was about two feet wide and three feet long and two feet deep. Carved on the side of it were angels with their wings spread wide. One angel was on each corner of the box. The angels' wings touched each other as if offering protection from all sides. The box had a lid on it. There were candles positioned around the box, providing enough light to see the box clearly. I stood there and studied the ark. I thought: I wonder if it really contains the tablets given to Moses. I started to pick up the lid on the box to see what was inside. As I reached for it, I heard a voice behind me say, "Touch it and you will surely die." I drew my knife and spun around. My first thought was: How did I miss this guy? I must have walked right by him.

I saw there was a cut out in one wall that had been made to accommodate a mattress. That is where the keeper of the ark was lying. He lit a candle and held it up to me from where he lay. He was a small frail man of about 70. As he sat up, I heard the keys around his neck make a tinkling noise as they rubbed against each other. He looked at me through the dim light and said, "You cannot steal God's ark. He won't let you. It is ours to keep until God himself comes to claim it."

I said, "Listen priest, I don't want to steal it. I want to know, does it have the power to heal?"

He said to me, "I don't know. No one has ever tried it."

I said, "Is it true that if someone is truly innocent and pure of heart that they can touch it and not die? Tell me priest, if you were to lay a young child down in the box, he would surely not die—for he is truly innocent. Whereas even an old priest like you must have impure thoughts. You are not pure and yet you have not died when you've touched it. So surely, a true innocent and offspring from the house of David would not perish now would he?"

He looked up at me and said, "What makes you think I have touched the box?"

I said, "I guess I assumed you had."

He replied, "You have assumed wrong. You came in peace, now go in peace."

I said, "Wait a minute. I did not come here to be told to get out by a so-called servant of God. Maybe I'll bounce you off of the ark and see if you die. What do you think of that?"

He said, "I think if that is the will of God then you will do so, and I think if it is the will of God for you to leave then you will leave."

I said, "I am going to leave, priest, but if I think that box will cure my young friend, I will bring him here and you will put him in the box for me or you will surely die." The old priest lay back down on the mattress on his side with his back to me, ignoring my continued presence. I left, but this time I jumped up and grabbed one of the support beams and pushed my legs up through the ceiling and put my arms through the ceiling. I was back in the room with the dumbwaiter. I hope the priest saw what I did. It will give him something to think about.

I walked past the startled guards and out the front gate. I can't remember the last time I had allowed someone to order me out of a building. I have some other ideas that could help Joshua. If those ideas don't work, I will come back, but I would not kill the old priest and watch his blood soak into the dirt floor. I don't kill the righteous even if the cause is just—but the old priest does not know that. I doubt, though, that my threat would frighten him into action on my behalf. So I guess I will have to find another way to lay Joshua down in the ark.

Chapter XXII

I spent the night next to a candelabra tree on the outskirts of Aksum. My thoughts turned once more to my brother. So he (as the priest said) was at the ancient throne of Solomon high in the mountains of Hindu-Kush in Pakistan. So he is there with Ishtar. Well, he is probably having a great time. She is probably teaching him some tricks that he never imagined. Maybe he is planning on cornering the market on lapis lazuli. It is in great abundance there. Solomon, in his old age, used to take his women there on occasion. He believed that the cold air would act as an aphrodisiac and make them want to lie with him. Now there is a Muslim shrine there. I suppose it would not be a bad place to operate out of. The area has been the home to assassins and terrorists for four thousand years. Even a modern army would play hell rooting out Seth's army from there. Alexander the Great tried, and all he was able to come out of there with was a bride: the fair Roxanne. I must give this a lot of thought before I go there. I have mixed emotions. Why should I help out the West so they can shove their religion down everyone's throat. Of course, that is what Seth's army would like to do to the West.

The descendants of Ishmael, the son of Hagar, the slave girl, have a right to their way of life and their religion. I wonder why the Eternal commanded that Ishmael's descendants should be despised so, and yet the descendants of his half-brother, Isaac, should be blessed, and his descendants multiplied in numbers greater than the stars? It was not Hagar's fault if Abraham's wife Sarah could not bear children. It was Sarah's idea that Abraham should lie with Hagar in the hopes that Hagar would become with child—and he was only too happy to submit to Sarah's wishes. Sarah had planned to raise the child as her own. Maybe

she took her rage out on Hagar because even when Hagar's belly began to grow Abraham still wanted to lie with her. Sarah confronted Abraham one day in his tent screaming at him to "Leave that whore alone. She is already pregnant."

Poor Sarah would look at her own reflection and see only an old woman with drooping breasts and a fat and barren belly. In despair, she would cry out to the Eternal and he decided to not only answer her prayers, but he would tell her in person. In her old age, she brought forth Isaac, the blessed one. The Eternal then looked the other way as Hagar was cast out of Abraham's house along with her son. Sarah would not tolerate Hagar staying there, and she worried that Abraham might lie with Hagar again. No wonder Hagar turned away from Abraham's idea of the Eternal. She did not owe him anything—the Eternal had made his decision. I guess she felt betrayed. The hatred that she possessed was transferred to her son and to each succeeding generation of his. Maybe the Eternal made all of this happen because he craved a good fight for some unknown reason. Well, he is going to get one.

I made my way east across Eritrea and the Red Sea to the port city of Jizan in Saudi Arabia—and then farther east to the "empty quarter"—the one place on the planet where practically no life exists—two hundred thousand square miles of sand and no rain. I did not come here for nothing. I lay down on the warm dry sand and waited for the night. I kept picking up a hand full of sand and then letting it slip through my hand as if my hand were a funnel. It was just a habit of mine. I was biding my time. Around midnight the light of the full moon appeared as bright as day on the dunes.

I lay on one side of a dune and looked directly across to another dune. The sand soon appeared to look pock marked—and the pock marks were coming toward me. Soon the sand next to my right shoulder began to form into a face—then another

face on my left. I was soon surrounded by faces coming up out of the sand. The one face on my right asked, "Why do you come here to bother us? We leave the world alone, do we not? We picked this place because of its desolation to avoid humans!"

I turned to my right and lay on my side with my right arm propping up my head. Using my left hand and my index finger, I put some brows in the forehead of the face. I said to the face, "You, the Archons, are the children of Ishtar. I only want to know if Mom has been to see you. Besides you demon children should thank me. I set her free, remember? I'm sorry that whereas she has a beautiful body, to which I can attest, that none of you have a body at all. Tell me, when she gave birth to your formless bodies, how were you born?"

The demon said, to me, "How would we know? Tell us, Horus, did you give yourself your body? Whatever you are, is it all of your own making? When only the face of the lonely Eternal moved across the endless waters of time, were you there to console him and give him advice? Was it your idea to create the universe from the nothingness of space? We think not! You are what you are because that is what the Eternal had decreed. We are what we are for the same reason. Do you think we like being here hiding in the sand since the dawn of creation? We are the misfortunate of all that God has created. We are neither angels or humans or lesser ancient gods created by the Eternal to do his bidding—and yet we are despised by all! So is that what brings you here to ask that question? Or is it to ask how long you have to live until Seth kills you!"

I said, "Well, right now Seth is screwing your mother isn't he? Maybe he will knock her up and you will all have another demon brother!" I took my hand and pushed his sand face back into the sand and said, "Get the hell away from me! You all would just lie to me anyway!"

I sat up and the sand all around me was smooth and silent

once more. I yelled at them to come back. They did. I said to Ialdabaoth, the eldest of the demons, "I have a proposition for you. You mentioned my brother. What do you think will happen to all of you if he succeeds in becoming the god of the earth? He will come here with evil demons and kill all of you. You know I speak the truth. Maybe I will stop him, but I need the services of one of you who is brave enough to walk among your counterparts in Seth's army."

The youngest, Eleleth, said, "I will go!"

Ialdabaoth said, "He is too young, even in our years. He does not know all of the ways of man. We have sheltered him from that."

I said, "He is the only one courageous enough to help me." Therefore, I agreed. I took out a small vial of water—water from the Nile—and then I took from my pocket one of the wax figures that I had taken with me from the slave room in the Sudan. I laid the wax figure in the sand and drew a cartouche around it. At the left side of the wax figure I wrote in the sand the first name of the holy trinity of the ancient Egyptian gods: Ptah. He brings forth the glow of the morning sun and the beginning of a new day. On the right side of the wax figure I wrote the hieroglyph of Seker, the god who releases those who have been shut in the darkness. Lastly, at the head of my wax figure I drew in the sand the hieroglyph of Ausar, the giver of life. Then as I poured the water from the Nile onto my wax figure, I evoked the sacred prayer of the goddesses of the Nile and consort of Ausar. I stepped back and watched my creation grow. My wax carving slowly sunk into the desert sand and soon I could see the outline of a man. The desert wind began to blow and the sand began to be stripped away from my creation. First his torso and head took shape, then his arms, legs, hands and feet. He was now complete—skin, flesh and bones. He pushed himself up from out of the sand. He stood there next to me looking at everything: the

desert, the sky, and me.

He said, to his brothers, "This is fantastic! I can hear my heart beating, and all that I behold has depth and color in it. I can smell the sand. I can feel the heat of the desert. May all of you, my brothers, get to experience this feeling of being human someday." He shook his head back and forth, casting out the last of the sand.

My creation looked at me and said, "What is thy bidding?"

I said, "Well, first put on these clothes. You can't go around naked." I had bought a set of clothes in Jizan in the market there. Now I will need some more for myself. I sat down in the sand with Eleleth and said to him, "I want you to travel to Pakistan, to the city of Islamabad. There you will find ample opportunity to join with other recruits who will be heading to the mountains of Hindu-Kush to become part of Seth's assassins. I want you to become my eyes and ears. Do whatever they require of you, short of dying. Get as close to my brother as you can, but never look directly into his eyes. He will find you out if you do, and he would kill you. My thoughts will come to you at night. We will converse in the dark and in secrecy. Do all that I ask and maybe the Eternal will take pity on you and your brothers. Lastly, if you see your mother, say nothing. She will betray you for her own sake. Now go, my friend." I watched him go off into the night.

The next day I sat at the top of the sand dune for most of the day. I pondered what the old priest had said. So Seth now wears the red and white crown of lower and upper Egypt. I must say that is impressive! Even I did not know where it was. I thought it was lost in time forever. Unfortunately, I will not be the only one who is impressed—so will the entire Middle East. With the exception of a few scholars in the West, presidents and prime ministers will think that it is laughable. The West regards the people of the Middle East as inferior to them, and they

believe the religion and customs of the East are nonsense—a joke. They won't laugh long. Egypt, which is slowly turning into a hot bed of terrorism, will consider Seth the reincarnation of Osiris, who is to come and reinstate Egypt to its prior glory. Hydrogen bombs cannot destroy a belief.

I watched a tiny speck in the distance get larger and closer with each passing minute. At first I thought: Eleleth does not know which way to go. As it drew near, I saw that it was a herder and his son with a few goats and several sheep. The herder saw me and waved to me to come down. I made my way down the side of the sand dune to the rocky flat land. We greeted each other with a Muslim welcome. My new friend asked me what I was doing in this desolate place, while all the time chewing on a miswak. A miswak is a centuries-old method of cleaning ones teeth. He invited me to his encampment for dinner. I accepted. My new friend's son set a meal of roasted lamb with a few dates and rice all washed down with a very strong coffee. Omar kept questioning me about how I came here. I told him I was on an "umrah" (lesser pilgrimage) to Mecca to pray at the Kabah, the city that was the birthplace of the prophet Mohammed in the city that was founded by Adam. The Arabs were right about Mohammed, but the story about Adam was not correct—only legend. My mother had told me that. I was actually lying to Omar about going to Mecca, but then he said something very interesting to me. He said that some very unusual "comings and goings" are going on there. My friend Omar asked me to stay the night with them in their tent. I accepted. I went through the motion of praying to Allah with them, but I really was thinking about Mecca.

I rose early the next morning while the two of them still slept. I had thanked Omar before we turned in for his hospitality. I opened the flap of their tent and walked outside and beheld the light of the moon on the barren and silent landscape. The

only sounds were that of the goats foraging for food and the far off noise from a jet passenger plane. Dear Diary, this land is beautiful to me. I saw a falcon in the sky and instantly pulled out my knife—and then I realized it really was only a falcon, not my brother in the form of one. I'm looking for him, and yet I'm sure getting jumpy. I traveled for several days northwest to Mecca and then I saw the minarettes of the mosques in the distance. I had bought a set of clothes from Omar. I did not want to stand out as a foreigner. I even wore the gutra. It is a headdress made of cotton and covers ones head like a hood. This one I had on must not have been washed for months. It smelled awful. Too bad I can't make a trade with Eleleth. On the outskirts of Mecca I came upon a grisly sight: a woman, perhaps in her early thirties, had been stoned to death for adultery. She had a sign around her neck announcing her sin to all who passed by. She lay up against an embankment with bloody stones strewn around her, with her hands tied behind her back. The soft embankment had rocks embedded in it. I guess some of her executioners were not too good at casting not only the first stone, but most of the ones thereafter. Obviously, some stones had hit their mark. I stopped for a moment and looked at her dead body.

I then made my way on down the road toward Mecca. Slowly walking in front of me were four men who had carried out the execution. I read the minds of each. Three of the men believed that they were truly carrying out the will of Allah. The fourth man, however, was thinking how he had gotten away with rape. The woman had reported the rape to the Matawwan, the Saudi Arabian religious police. Women here are treated like shit. So instead of going after her rapist, she was put on trial and found guilty of adultery, which is punishable by death. Her accuser (her husband) threw the first stone. This guy in front of me kicking up dust on the road and blabbering to his three friends was the real murderer and rapist. I followed them to

their homes. Along the way, he kept picking up rocks and throwing them and making gestures to his friends about how she deserved to die. I decided that I was not in that big of a hurry to get to Mecca, so I waited in an area where I had a clear view of his house. I waited all night.

About seven in the morning the man came out. Fortunately, he decided to go back toward where the woman lay dead. He stopped and went over to her fly-infested corpse and pushed her over with his foot. I guess he wanted to make sure she was dead. He then continued on down the road. I followed him. I once again watched him kicking up the dust on the road. As a car passed, he looked back and caught sight of me. He started to walk faster and faster, and he would turn and look back at me to see if I was really following him. He attempted to make it look as if he was looking for someone rather than seeing if I was following him. He then started to run. He thought he had waved down a car, but it sped past him. He then headed up an embankment and ran as fast as he could. He turned and no longer saw me behind him. He felt safe for a moment. As he turned his head back, a falcon came right at his face. He dove to the ground and put his hands over his head to ward off the falcon. He waited on the ground a few minutes until he thought the falcon was gone. As he got up on all fours, he looked right at my feet. Then he looked up at me and put a weak smile on that hypocritical face of his.

He stood up, and with fear in his voice, he blurted out an Arabic salutation to me, "Salaam Aleikum." I just stood there and pulled back my smelly gutra headwear and stared at him and did not say a word. I then hit him in his face with my fist, and he fell and, through his bloody lips, he begged for mercy. He held out the money he had on him and said, "Take, take all of the money!" I looked down at him and thought what a coward he was.

I said in Arabic, "Get up—up!" He got up and I made him go and lie down on his stomach in a small gully. He wondered what I was going to do. Well, he did not have to wait long. I told him to turn over. I said, "I am going to cast the first stone." He screamed for mercy because he looked up to see me holding a hundred pound rock over him. I brought it down on his chest with every ounce of strength I could muster. His scrawny arms, which he had held out in defense, were unable to ward off the rock coming down on him. I heard all of his ribs cave in—in unison. He did not die right away. I took my right foot and kept pushing his head back and forth with it. He looked up at me through glazed eyes. He tried to speak, but could not. He was strangling on his own blood. Then he died. I took his money and his gutra, which did not smell as bad as the one I was wearing. Of course, it was a little bloody. He had offered me his money, and when I get to the Kabah, I will give it as an offering. I wrote on the stone that I had killed him with: Here lies a murderer, a rapist and a liar—all in Arabic and in his blood.

Dear Diary, the Eternal allows me the honor of exacting retribution whenever I feel it in my heart without waiting for his command. I am grateful for that.

I left him lying there with the rock on his chest. I traveled back down the road toward Mecca and past the dead woman again. A woman sat next to the corpse grieving over her. It was her mother. I looked at her as I passed by and I tried to comfort her. I said, "Remember that God is merciful."

The mother held up her hands to me, which were covered in her daughter's blood and said, "Is this mercy? My heart has been torn out. There is no God for me now."

I told her, "I am sorry. All I have to give is pity. I will pray Allah will grant you peace."

Through her tears, she said, "If you want to pray, then let your prayer be that the evil people who did this to my daughter

be killed and roast in hell this very day—and let me meet their executioner some day so I can thank him. Now please leave me to my grief." I did what she asked.

I completed my journey to the Kabah. It is a black cube that is open on the inside allowing room for hundreds to pray. There is always a crowd of people there. I saw many imams; they are prayer leaders. I now know what my desert friend meant when he said something unusual is going on here. I remembered what my little slave friend had told me. When we were carving our wax figures, he showed me in confidence how he would put his mark on the face of each wax figure he made. He would always put the mark in different places on each figure so that it would be hard to be noticed by the slave masters. Now as I made my way through the crowd, I kept seeing my little slave friend's handiwork on the faces of some of the imams. It looked like a birthmark. It was really the mark of the beast. One might have it on his chin—another on his cheek. One even had two birth-marks under his left eye and his right. My friend had done me a great service by putting his mark of the beast on each of Seth's demons.

After the nightly prayers, I followed five of Seth's assassins, along with some new converts to his army, to a cave on Mount Hira. We all sat around in a circle outside of the cave entrance. The spokesman was the local Hamus leader, Abdel Aziz Rantisi. He began to speak about the cave and Mohammed. Making gestures with his hands, he said, "Brothers, it was here that the prophet hid from the Jews and Christians who were bent on killing him. In this very cave he sought refuge! As he hid in the dark, he asked Allah why did the Jews and Christians despise him so. He said to Allah, my brothers, 'Did I not go to them with open hands? I offered them my friendship, but they secretly sought only my death.' They hated him, my brothers, because he brought the light of truth to the world.

"Today, my brothers, the Jews and the Christians still hate his descendants—they hate you, my brothers. They want to defile our women with their wicked ways. Their children are brought up to cherish all that is worldly with no respect for Allah, the giver of life. They are all in league with Satan. We must wage jihad until they have all been erased from the earth. My brothers, Allah, the merciful, heard the prayers of the prophet and sent the angel Gabriel to protect him. Gabriel told several spiders to join together and spin a web over the cave opening. They did. The assassins came looking for him, but upon seeing the cave opening was sealed over with the silken web of a spider, decided the prophet could not possibly be in the cave. They reasoned he could not have torn down the web because the spiders could not possibly have spun a new one that quickly. Allah be praised. So they sought the prophet elsewhere. They made their way to Medina, their evil hearts thirsting for blood. But whereas Allah had mercy on the prophet, he caused the assassins to fall asleep on the road to Medina. As they slept, Gabriel raised up an army of thousands of camel spiders, and they fell upon the assassins and devoured them. The assassins tried to fight them off, killing some spiders, but there were too many of them. As the morning sun rose, it glistened off of their white bones. That was all that was left of them. Allah be praised. My brothers, we must be like the camel spiders and fall upon our enemies in great numbers and we will conquer them for Allah." I looked around, and everyone in the circle was nodding his head in agreement.

Abdel then gave each of us an assignment. I was to go and live with a family on the west bank in Jordan. Abdel then gave us food and drink and blankets, and we spent the night out on the ground. As I lay there, I decided to commune with Eleleth. He told me that he had hitched a ride in a plane to Islamabad by bullshitting the airline ticket seller. He was more resourceful

than I had thought.

He said, "Master, I was walking down a street and I passed a wedding party only to be dragged by the groom to have my picture taken with the wedding party. I did not know what to say, Master, so I just kept congratulating them on their marriage. They would not let me leave, Master. They had me stay for their wedding feast. The food was really good, Master. At least I think so. I have never eaten food before, so maybe all of it is good. They gave me some tasty meat. I took a bite out of the meat, and it was crunchy and spicy. I asked them if it was the body of a scorpion that had been deep fried, and they all laughed at me and said it was fried shrimp." Eleleth was so excited about his new found freedom, I decided to let him continue. He said, "We ate for hours and then the bride and groom went into a room by themselves. I went over, Master, to join them, but a man who kept looking into the room through a crack in the partially open door, stopped me and told me to go back to my table. After a little while the man who had been guarding the door was handed a bed sheet from the groom. He took it and ran around the room pointing to blood on the sheet and shouting: 'Victory, Victory!' Did the groom kill his wife, Master?"

"No," I said. "Now tell me, have you seen anything suspicious?"

Eleleth said, "Only a couple of truck loads of men carrying weapons riding in brightly colored trucks."

I said, "If you see a truck full of men heading northwest toward the mountains, join them. And be careful, my friend, you are in one of the most dangerous cities in the world. I will contact you again soon." The next day I bid farewell to the terrorists and made my way to Jerusalem.

Chapter XXIII

Dear Diary, I arrived in Jerusalem as the setting sun cast an orange glow over the city. I sought out the home of Louis and Karen Cohen. I had time to spare, so there was no rush in getting to the West Bank. The Eternal had never gone this long in giving me a new death command. Maybe when I go back to the United States he will call on me again. The Cohens lived in west Jerusalem in a very nice apartment complex. I rang the doorbell and their son Joseph answered the door. I told him I was here to see his father, Dr. Cohen. He let me in.

I heard him say, "Hey, Dad, there is some guy here to see you. He looks like an American."

Louis Cohen met me in his living room. "What can I do for you, Sir?" he said.

I said, "My name is Max Karsh, and I came to see you on a most important matter." He took me into his office and closed the door. I lied about Joshua being my nephew and said my sister's son had Tay-Sachs disease. "I understand that you are one of the leading experts in the world on the disease. That is why I am here." Louis leaned forward in his chair and said, "Thank you for the compliment, but I don't know if I can help you with any more information than you could have obtained in the U.S."

Dr. Cohen said, "I assume your family must have ancestors of eastern European descent."

I was not prepared for his question, so I thought fast. I said, "Yes—Lithuania."

He said, "Lithuania—that's interesting."

I thought he might be on to me so I said, "We also have relatives in Olsztyn, Poland." I remembered that Thelma Bloom had mentioned something about relatives in Poland once.

Dr. Cohen said, "I wish I could offer you some real hope, but about all we can do is prolong the life of the patient for a few years. Of course, as I'm sure you know, the disease can be completely irradicated by having people who are carriers of the defective gene not marrying another carrier and having children. There is a simple test to see if one is a carrier or not. I realize this is not going to help your nephew with the disease."

I told him, "It is my understanding that the disease is nothing more than a gene having a different type of sugar or lack of one on a gene. Is that right?"

He said, "Well, you are close. That is pretty much correct. But that one defective gene can cause awful problems. It is as if you built a house on sand without a foundation and then said, hey the house is slowly falling apart and will soon collapse. Then someone said, well the only problem is that there is no foundation under the house. We still can't solve the problem of Tay-Sachs, and, unfortunately, about all you can do for your nephew is just watch and pray for divine intervention."

I said, "A friend of mine in the U.S. who has done a lot of research on the disease kept saying about the disease that the sins of the father fall on the son. Before I could question her about her statement, she passed away. Do you know what she meant?"

"Well, I have already said the disease is genetic, like other diseases for that matter."

I said, "Well, someone had to be the original carrier, correct?"

He said, "Maybe. Sometimes, though, several people can develop a genetic defect at the same time."

I looked at him and said, "Let's, for the sake of my theory, say that the disease started with one person. If it were possible to change the lifestyle of that one person, you could stop a disease it its tracks, could you not?"

"Perhaps that could work, assuming you could go back in time and knew what to change. I don't understand how this conversation can help your nephew."

"Obviously, it cannot. I was just curious. You told me, doctor, that there is a simple test to see if one has the disease. What is required for that test?"

"A drop of blood. We can break it down and check the chromosomes."

"I see."

We did not speak for a few seconds. Then Dr. Cohen said, "Why don't you have dinner with us?"

I accepted. During dinner he told me that he was going to his son's basketball game that night. He said, "The way things are in Israel these days, I try to attend all of his games." He invited me to go along. I know he was thinking I would decline, but I did not.

I said, "Sure. I would enjoy watching his team play."

At the table, along with Dr. Cohen and Joseph, were his wife Karen and their 24-year-old daughter Elizabeth. Joseph said boastfully, "I think I will score twenty points or better tonight, Dad."

I said, "You must be pretty good then."

Joseph said, "I am!"

Turning to Dr. Cohen's daughter, I said, "So Elizabeth, what do you do?"

"I am a computer programmer for El Al Airlines." It was obvious that Karen was very proud of her family. Elizabeth was going to move out to her own apartment, but with the terrorism, she had decided to stay here for a while longer.

Dr. Cohen said to me, "It looks like the Clinton administration does not look upon Israel with the same friendly attitude that the former administration did. What do you think the people of the U.S. think about the Israeli-Palestinian problem?"

I said, "Well, I think most Americans hope for an equitable solution—soon."

Dr. Cohen said, "We all hope for that, but the big stumbling block is Hamus. They want us all dead so they can have the land back. My friend Yehoshua came out of a market heading for his car. He took too long in finding the key to his car. Two Palestinians shot him in the back of his head. The bullets went through him and shattered the glass on the window of his car. He left a wife and eight young children. He did nothing to deserve this. Of all of us, he was the most kind to the Palestinians. Death is a daily occurrence here. We live in fear of the phone ringing at night or the doorbell. Whenever there is a terrorist attack that we hear about, we immediately contact all family members to make sure they are safe. When we can't reach one of them, life becomes a living hell—until we do."

I said, "I'm sorry for all of your troubles."

Karen said, "My god, they let their own children become suicide bombers. It is just awful—what mother would let her son do such a thing?"

Elizabeth interrupted, "Well, we have to do something about the settlements on the West Bank. We cannot keep taking their land. It makes us no better than the Nazis."

Dr. Cohen, his face blood red, became enraged and slammed his closed fist down on the table, making all the dishes rattle. He said, "What do you know about the Nazis! Comparing us with them is ridiculous! The Nazis wanted to kill your grandparents."

Elizabeth said, "I'm just saying we cannot keep taking their land and allowing none of the rights we enjoy and at the same time expect them to do nothing."

"And so suicide bombers are the answer?"

"No," she said, "and neither is having our military retaliate after every bombing with helicopter rocket attacks, killing some

of their women and children, and then saying we are sorry."

Dr. Cohen said, "The women and children were accidentally killed."

Elizabeth said, "The bottom line, Dad, is that they are all dead Israelis and Palestinians, and with endless deaths on both sides the hatred grows. What would you do, Dad, if Joseph or I were killed?"

He said, "I would kill some Palestinians, as God is my witness—and I wouldn't care if they were innocent Palestinians or not."

She said, "You just made my case, Dad. Killing begets killing." Dr. Cohen appeared relieved to see that it was time to go to Joseph's game. He apologized to me for getting mad at dinner. I accepted his apology.

We drove to the game. Dr. Cohen told me he avoided public transportation nowadays, due to the fact that you never know who is on the bus with you. Joseph's team lost 42-37. He did not get twenty points. He had to settle for eight. As we got back to their home, I asked him if we could meet tomorrow for one last time to discuss the Tay-Sachs disease again. He agreed.

I retrieved my small bag that I had brought with me. I had purchased some more clothes in Mecca. I started to leave. He walked me to his front door and, as an after thought, asked me where I was staying. I told him I would find a hotel. He assumed that I would answer in the affirmative, so he was taken aback when I said, no, but that I would find a place.

He said, "This is not the U.S. It is not that easy. Be our guest for tonight."

I thanked him and said yes. He showed me to my room.

Joseph was busy playing a video game. He was intently blasting the bad guys on the t.v. screen. It reminded me of what my mother said about Seth, "See how he plays at killing." Well, I hope Joseph only has to play at killing and never participates

in the real thing. I lay down on my bed, wearing just my shorts. I heard Dr. Cohen telling his wife how foolish I was not to have had a place to stay. She asked him how I could have gotten away with it since the Israeli security forces keep track of everyone entering the country. He said that he had no idea.

I soon discovered that I had a visitor. Through the open window that was letting hot, though fresh, air in, the Cohen's Abyssinian cat came in. I guess this was his room, and at first I don't think he was too keen on sharing it. He jumped up on the nightstand and sat there looking at me. I looked back. He left again and then came back about an hour later with a dead rat in his mouth. He got up on my chest and lay the dead rat on my chest. I guess he was bringing me a snack. He waited for me to enjoy the dinner. When I didn't, he started licking the rat and began to eat it. The cat was about eight years old. He had little black spots all over his nose. He also possessed something else. He was related to the ancient cats of Egypt, which means that he possessed a memory of all of his ancestors going back five thousand years. He might not have known it, but I did. That is why he warmed up to me. I renamed him "Miu." I didn't bother to find out what the Cohen's had named him. He thought that we had met before and that I had been kind to him. Egyptians worshipped the cat.

When Ramses II and I imprisoned Seth, the people of Egypt asked where Seth was. After all, he was a general in Ramses' army. He had saved Ramses at the battle of Kadash against the Hittites. Of course, Ramses took credit for the victory, which really was more of a standoff instead of an Egyptian win. And Ramses' father, Seti (which in Egyptian literally means "of the god Seth"), had taken that name in honor of him. Naturally, the Egyptians wondered what happened to Seth. Ramses came up with a great line of crap. He said that Seth had become the incarnation of evil and had turned himself into a giant snake. As a

snake, he began to devour the people's souls in upper Egypt and was now coming north to the Nile Delta and us. The people panicked because they, like the fools of today, believed their government.

Ramses let his people stew over the coming disaster and then he allowed a rumor to spread over the land that Osiris was sending a warrior to destroy Seth. I was the warrior. The people gathered outside of King Ramses' palace, demanding that he send me to do battle with Seth. In front of all of the people, his priests and army, he asked me if I would go do battle with the evil one. I held up both of my arms and said, "Great King, I accept." The people went wild with cheering. Alone, I left in a chariot pulled by Ramses' two black horses. I stayed out in the desert for a couple of weeks, and then returned.

Standing next to Ramses, I told of how I had turned myself into a cat (much like the Cohen's cat) and that I waited in the rushes by the Nile north of Elephantine, knowing Seth would come my way. He did. I pounced on him. We did battle. At first Seth got the better of me. He wrapped his body around me and tried to crush me. I bit into his flesh, and as I did, I heard the souls of men who were imprisoned in his body cry out for help. I sunk my sharp teeth deep in his flesh. He writhed in great pain, so he released me and tried to slither away. I followed him as he plunged down into a hole. We looked for each other in the darkness. He came up behind me without my knowing. It was his chance to kill me, but as he opened his mouth to strike, the souls of the men in his belly spoke and said, "Please save us." I turned and bit off his head. In the darkness, I saw coming back up through his throat the illuminated souls of all those he had devoured. The people were saved. Dakulah's mother came over to me.

The crowd became silent, for she was of the royal family. She said, "Did you see and hear the soul of my daughter?"

I replied, "Mother of sorrow, let not your heart be full of sadness. The gods of Egypt have not and will not ever abandon the true daughters of Isis. This very day Dakulah is in that heavenly paradise, for she did speak to me in a voice filled with everlasting joy."

Once more I held my arms up over my head, and the crowd went wild with excitement. I can still hear those long-dead ghostly cheers of adoration. They wanted to believe that what I said was true. From that day on I was worshiped as the god of justice as well as the god of the kings.

Dear Diary, the last thing out of Pandora's box was hope—and, for the Egyptians, their gods were the epitome of that hope. I had never been such a phony in my life. I felt bad, though, about lying to Dakulah's mother. Ramses announced that from this day forward all cats in Egypt were protected by the gods. He went on to say that anyone including priests and members of his court would suffer death if they ever hurt or killed a cat—even if it were done accidentally.

I went to sleep with the cat sleeping on my chest. I woke up the next morning and the cat was gone. He had left me a present—the tail of the rat. I threw it out the window, and as I did, I saw Dr. Cohen going outside with his daughter, telling her to always be careful. He asked her to look me up on her computer at work, although he was sure I was okay. I knew the fear he had in his heart and how he prayed to God to protect his family every day. I wished him well, but I cannot change the fate of the Middle East—or the world for that matter.

After breakfast we met again in his study, but all he could offer as hope was that maybe some cure for Tay-Sachs would come along before Joshua died. Dr. Cohen did say he had given some thought to our previous conversation. He told me that if a woman were to drastically change her lifestyle three months before she became pregnant, that might have an adverse effect

on her fertilized egg. He said, "I know this won't help Joshua, but you were curious, so I thought you might like to know."

I thanked him and then asked him what was under the cloth on the table. I had not noticed it before. He looked at me and said, "Here I will show you." Dr. Cohen removed the sheet, and under it was a pretty accurate scale model of Solomon's temple. I asked him how he was able to build it to such exact proportions. He said, "I'm going to confide in you as to how we did it. Besides, the world will know soon enough. One of my friends discovered in an earthen jar buried beneath the city in an ancient waterway the original architectural drawings from the age of Solomon. The government has put together a secret committee to build this model and to come up with a feasibility study for constructing the real thing. It will displace a lot of people, so we are taking our time."

"You would have to displace more than people. The Islam Dome of the Rock sits there. I don't think the Muslims would like that idea."

Dr. Cohen sheepishly said, "You are correct."

I said, "It could start World War III?"

He took off his glasses and looked into my eyes and said in a solemn tone, "My friend, World War III is already here. Haven't you noticed? If we are to die as a nation, then let us die in the temple of our god. The Eternal will either send a Messiah to save us or we will have found that our faith was nothing more than the house we talked about being built on sand."

I said, "Let's hope it does not come to this." I shook his hand and left for the West Bank. I guess I will have to try some of my other ideas to save Joshua after I return home.

Chapter XXIV

I made my way to Hebron, the city an ancient legend says was named by Abraham and which means "friend" in both Hebrew and Arabic, and is in the occupied territory—friends and enemies living side by side. I thought about Dr. Cohen and truly felt sorry for him. I went to the home of Abu Adaibe. He shares the home with his wife and his son, Nasr, and daughters Jasmine, who is 24, and Riza, who is 11. Nasr is 15. Abu invited me into his home. The place was nowhere near as nice as Dr. Cohen's home. Abu asked me if I had any trouble getting by the IDF (Israeli Defense Forces). I told him I did not have any problems. I said I was sent here by Hamus to help with the suicide bombing plan that involved his son Nasr. Since I had arrived in time for the noon meal, I ate with them and then Nasr and I took a walk. He showed me around Hebron.

As I listened to Nasr, I thought about Eleleth and wondered how he was doing. I had conferred with him briefly at night when I was in Dr. Cohen's home. He informed me that he had managed to join up with some of the local Taliban soldiers that were heading to the mountains of Hindu-Kush. I asked him to tell me of his experiences.

He said to me, "Master, being in human form has some drawbacks. One is that you get hungry, and you get hot or cold, and you feel pain. The only food we have to eat is a large bag of walnuts and we only get a small ration of them. We also eat the green moss that is on the rocks we find in the icy cold streams. I woke up the other day, Master, with someone trying to steal my boots. I caught him and he begged for forgiveness. He showed me his feet, which were all bloodied and had large cracks in the skin. I told him I was sorry for him, but he could not have my shoes. Master, we ran into a large group of refugees composed

of women, children, and old men. They were all trying to get back to Afghanistan. Some of them were sick. One of the women gave birth on a rocky road high in the mountains. She was bleeding very badly and knew she would not live, so she begged for someone to care for her new son. No one offered to do so, so we left her and her baby by the road. It was a sad sight Master." Eleleth then told me that they should reach the base camp in about two more days. He said he would contact me then.

Nasr interrupted my train of thought. He said, "This is where my grandfather used to live."

I looked at the rubble of what had been his grandfather's home and said, "How did he die?"

Nasr folded his arms together and said, "The Israelis thought he was a sympathizer of Hamus so they bulldozed down his house—with him in it. We pleaded with them to stop, but the soldiers kept us from helping him. They knew my grandfather was in the house that they were demolishing, but they pretended that they didn't know he was there. They ran the bulldozer right over his body." Young Nasr, with clenched fists, then said, "That is why I'm going to kill some of them."

I said, "Yes, but you are young and you will die too."

He replied, "But I will be with Allah, and I will be a living martyr to our people and they will never forget me."

I said, "Your sisters and mother and father will miss you very much. They will feel sad every day. Besides, what if you kill innocent people?"

Nasr said in a cold and matter of fact tone, "No Jew is innocent. My mother and father understand and so do my sisters. We are in a war of survival."

I said, "How about your sister Riza—does she want you to do this?"

"No, but she is only 11; she will understand eventually. The

video tape I left will comfort her."

We went back to his home. It was to be Nasr's last night on Earth. We sat, his father and I, discussing the problems of the occupied territory. Abu had the same hatred for the Israelis as Dr. Cohen had for the Palestinians. He said the Israeli government regarded the Palestinians as vermin to be destroyed and that in the Israeli schools the maps showed one Israel as if the Palestinians didn't exist. He said to me, "Ironic isn't it—the Jews love to cry about the atrocities perpetrated on them by the Nazis, and yet they practice the same methods."

He told me he also hated the West. He said, "Without Israel's big brother, things would be different here. Then Israel would have to make peace with us." All the time he and I talked Riza and Nasr were laughing and chasing each other around the yard as if nothing was going to happen the next day. I heard Abu's wife Manoa softly crying in the next room. Abu heard it, too. He said, "Of course, we don't want to lose our son—we only want the same things that the Israelis want—to live in peace, own property, raise our children, and worship Allah, and make a decent living for our family." He said, "We will fight for this until we are all dead or we win." He then said something that caught me by surprise.

Abu told me that there was a rumor going around here in Palestine that in the mountains of Hindu-Kush there was a prophet: Abu Al Qasim Muhammed. It would be he who would brings together the middle eastern countries and bring justice to the Palestinian people and drive out the infidels. So, my brother had taken the name of Abu Al Qasim Muhammed, passing himself off as the reincarnation of the "Hidden Imam" who lived in the 12th Century. The Muslims have been waiting a long time for him to come back. They have dreamed of his return. It is said he is supposed to usher in a golden age of peace that will last for 1000 years. What it really means is my brother is taking advan-

tage of the despair, the plight, and the hatred of the people here. Abu showed me to my room. As is their custom, he gave me the best room they had. I did not sleep all night. I kept thinking about Dr. Cohen's family and Abu's family.

I got up about 6 am. Nasr's mother had fixed him his favorite food. They all sat around making small talk and remembering especially pleasant moments from the past. Riza had made a picture of herself and Nasr for him to take with him. Since they believed that I was the Hamus representative, they expected me to put the explosive charges on Nasr. He put on a shirt that was made to hold TNT and plastic packets of benzene, nails and rat poison. I pulled the shirt up tight on him and buttoned it, and as I did I looked into his sad, young eyes. I carefully attached the TNT in the packets of benzene. He had a detonator with a battery to supply the electricity to the detonator. It was rigged up under his left arm with a concealed wire going down to his hand. All he had to do was close his hand at the appropriate time. He was to get on the bus at Hebron at 11:15 am. It was now 10:45. His mother hugged him and went crying into her bedroom, saying she did not want to watch as he went to his death. His older sister told him he would always be loved and remembered. Abu hugged and kissed his son. Riza, though, began crying and begged him not to go. She clung to him as he and I left the house. He pushed her away and yelled, "I love you." She sat down on the ground crying. Many of their neighbors were watching; they knew exactly what he was going to do.

Nasr and I waited for the bus about 20 minutes. I told him to do nothing until I gave the word. I said, "When we get on the bus we will try to sit in the middle of the bus." Amazingly when we got on the bus, which had about 12 Israelis on it, no one even noticed him. We took our seats. Nasr was extremely nervous. He kept running his right hand over the railing on the back of the seat in front of us. The bus made more stops. People got on and

off, but soon most of the seats were taken. I whispered to him, "Remember, two more stops and then I get off. I will tell your family how brave you were." The bus slowly made its way about another 250 feet and came to another bus stop. A family of five got on the bus. Nasr stared at them as they sat down in front of us. The family was headed to the United States and then for a cruise to Alaska. They were all very happy. Nasr sat listening to them. I read his thoughts. He was beginning to get his courage up. He whispered to me that he would enjoy killing them. Though his low voice was filled with hatred, he did not sound very convincing. An old man and woman sitting directly across from me were on their way to see a dentist. The husband was complaining that his dentures still did not fit right. He just bitched to his wife as if she were the dentist.

I decided to end this charade. I reached over and hugged Nasr. I grabbed his wrist and pulled the detonator and the wire from his sleeve. I yelled, "My god, this kid has a bomb." The bus driver slammed on the brakes. I had actually already disarmed him. Several passengers held him down and took off the rest of his explosives while I said that I would summon the authorities. As I got off the bus he yelled at me, "Why, why?" I didn't answer, but I thought, well the Israelis will lock him up for a while and they will plaster his picture everywhere. He is never going to blow himself up. They may bulldoze down his father's house, but at least Nasr and the Israelis on this bus will be alive—and maybe at least for this day there will be no killing in Israel—no phone calls of death to Dr. Cohen and his friends—no rejoicing of death in Palestine. I'm going to make one more stop in Israel before going home. I'm going to go to ancient Jericho, and then I will go to Kenya. I will write later of Jericho.

Chapter XXV

Dear Diary, I have come to Kenya. I suppose it could be considered on the way to the United States in a roundabout sort of way. I had been thinking for a while that I should come and pay homage to the Neanderthal family that I had buried here all those years ago. Now, at what was the burial place, is a museum. I went inside, and there was the skull of the male Neanderthal. There was a sign stating how the skull had been found by Louis Leakey, the world-reknowned paleontologist. Well, I guess I found the skull when it was still attached to the body. I thought it was interesting how I had buried the Neanderthal and his family in haste, whereas archeologists and university students took months digging them up and trying to find something in the burial that never existed. Archeologists thought it was some sort of prehistoric burial rite. They believed that each item buried with them was of great significance. That was not the case. What one sees is not always the reality they think it is. I looked at the skull and said in a whisper, "You have outlived the ages of man. You and I and Seth are all that remain of the time of the dog star."

Dear Diary, after several more days I was now back in the States—only not at home yet. I had been gone longer than I had planned. Today is November 28, 1999. Time is running out for Joshua. I'll let Eleleth keep me apprised of what Seth is doing, and I'll do my best to let Joshua live. I stopped in Utah and went back to the restaurant where they served "the best Mexican food in southern Utah." I had told Jack, the owner, months before that I would come back if he mistreated Penny, his wife. I guess he did not believe me. He should have. His restaurant was closed up. Plywood was over all of the windows. There was a sign that

read "For Sale." It was probably a good idea for Jack to have gotten out of the restaurant business. It is a tough way to make a living.

I went across I-15 to a gas station that looked like it had been there for a long, long time. I walked into one of the two garage bays. The owner, a guy about fifty, was putting on the last of a set of four new tires on a 1984 Ford pick up truck. A man, his wife and young son were standing outside looking into the garage as the tires were being put on their truck. The garage owner stopped working and asked me what I wanted. I hesitated before I answered. I thought: This guy has a tattoo on his arm—it kind of looks like the ones Jack has. I said, "I just want to ask you about the Mexican restaurant across the highway."

He replied, "I've got to finish this job for these people. Go wait in my office, and I'll talk to you."

I said, "Where is that?" He pointed to a small room practically hidden behind a vertical air compressor. I went in and waited. I think his "office" had seen better days as a bathroom. He had removed the bathroom fixtures and capped the pipes and stuck a tomato can down in the sewer drain to seal it. He had the usual nudie pictures up on the walls that you find in most garages.

I sat down on his desk and waited about 15 minutes. I listened as he tried to sell the family of three an oil change to go with the tires. The dad said no, and they left.

The garage guy came into his office and promptly asked me to get off of his desk. I did. He said, "Now what do you want to know about the restaurant? Are you interested in the property?"

I said, "No, I am actually more interested in getting in touch with Jack, the restaurant owner."

He said, "I was hoping you were interested in buying the place—I own the property."

I said, "Do you know where Jack and Penny went?"

He didn't answer that question. Instead he asked me one, "Do you know what that S.O.B. did to Penny? You know she was pregnant. He got mad at her and slugged her so hard in the temple that she miscarried the baby and suffered water on the brain. It was touch and go for her for a while. When she got out of the hospital, she had a shunt in her skull to drain the water out. The doctor said she might have to have it in her head for the rest of her life. I really feel sorry for her."

I said, "So what happened to Jack?" The garage owner said, "He took off for parts unknown—the cops never got him."

"So where is Penny?"

"Well, she lives with her dad in the town of Summit just west of Brian's Head ski resort." I thanked him and left. It was only about 30 miles to Summit.

I went to a small convenience store and asked the clerk (a young man in his early twenties) if he knew anyone named Penny. I had forgotten to ask the garage owner what her last name was.

He said, "We have two Pennys in town—which one do you want?"

I said, "The lady who has a shunt in her head due to an accident."

He said, "Oh, you mean Penny Smith. She lives across the street. See that sign that says 'Indian pottery for sale.' Well, that is her place."

I went over and knocked on the door. Her dad answered the door. I said, "I am here to see Penny."

He said, "Just a moment, Sir." He left me standing in the doorway. He then came back with a shotgun, which he put up to my face. He said, "You tell all of your polygamist sons of bitches to leave us alone, you understand—or I'll blow your damn brains out. Penny has suffered enough. You tell that ass-hole husband of hers she isn't going to testify against him. She

still loves the jerk."

I said, "You have got me wrong. I'm with the Justice Department. We are going to put him away for the rest of his life, but we have to find him first." I convinced him.

He said, "She got a letter from Colorado City in Arizona. It was unsigned, but I recognized Jack's handwriting—and the post mark was from Colorado City."

I said, "Sir, I want to thank you and rest assured, justice will be done for Penny." I went back to I-15 and hitched a ride with an independent trucker who was heading south on I-15. We listened to the radio show that comes on nightly with topics on the supernatural and the paranormal. Most of the discussion was once again about Khufu's pyramid. The truck driver dropped me off in the town of Washington, only a few miles west of Colorado City. I walked the rest of the way.

The Utah desert is not as nice as the Egyptian desert, but I like the solitude. I got into town about seven at night. I discovered most of the townspeople were at a dance. The adults were not dancing—they were all standing around watching their children dance in a circle. Mainly the adults were women, and none of them were smiling. The children were doing a dance that had been done in Israel during the reign of Solomon. I guessed they were really hard up for entertainment. I tried to enter the building, but one of their elders stopped me at the door. I asked where I might find Jack Smith, but he would not tell me. I did not need for him to tell me, though. I read his mind. I said, "I apologize for bothering, you, Sir."

I went straight to Jack's place. He had moved up the marital ladder since he had tried to kill Penny. He had two new wives now. They were both at the dance. I jumped over the white picket fence surrounding his gray two-story house and went up and opened the unlocked front door. I went inside. There was no one on the first floor, but I saw that there was a light on in a bed-

room on the second floor. I quietly made my way up the stairs to the bedroom. There on the bed lay Jack—without a stitch of clothes on. He did not see me. He was engrossed in a Playboy magazine. As he turned the magazine sideways to see the center fold, he caught sight of me standing in the open doorway with my arms folded. I said, with a smirk on my face, "Hello, Jack— remember me?"

He jumped out of bed and grabbed a straight razor that was lying on the dresser next to the bed. He said, "You are that son of a bitch who sucker punched me!" He said, "I'm going to slice you up with this razor you old bastard."

The dumb ass ran at me just like he had done in the restaurant. I jumped up on his bed and then off on the other side as he swung the razor at me. Seeing how pissed off he was really cracked me up. I ran around the room laughing while he chased me. As he got close to me in the corner of the bedroom, I laughingly said, "Please don't hurt me Jack."

Then, I nailed him in the gut just like I had done in the restaurant. This guy was one real dumb ass. He dropped the razor and staggered around the bedroom holding his gut and moaning. I threw him to the floor and pulled a 300-pound chest of drawers down over him. I sat down on it. Most of the top of his body was covered up. Only his thighs and legs were sticking out. He was trying to push the chest of drawers off of him, and as he did, the drawers kept pulling out and hitting him in the face. He was cussing and kicking until I grabbed his nuts and squeezed. He then screamed for mercy.

I said, "Remember what I said I would do to you, Jack, if you hurt Penny ever again. Well, Jack, I'm going to alter my original plan. I'm not going to deep fry your head after all. No deep fryer—no restaurant. Jack, you wouldn't happen to have a deep fryer in your kitchen would you? Hey, don't answer—that was a silly question. I guess, Jack, you moved here to do a lot of

procreation, huh—and to evade the law. Well, Jacko, you can tell your wives they won't have to secretly take birth control pills anymore—they can thank me for that. Hell I'm sorry Jack, you didn't know they were on the pill now did ya?"

Jack was pretty strong. He finally got that chest of drawers off of his chest and then actually managed to kick me in the face. I let go of him, and he ran toward the open window. He was trying to climb through it and out on the porch roof when I caught up with him. He was half way through the window when I reached up and slammed the window down on his back. He let out one loud yell. His dog, a white pit bull, was down in the front yard. He looked up and started barking in a vain attempt to help his master. Jack liked to keep the dog as a pet because he thought it added to his machismo. He didn't have any machismo. He was really a gutless asshole. I pulled the window down a little more to where I could lock it. He kept reaching back with both of his legs trying to get leverage to push himself all the way through the window.

I said, "What do you think I'm going to do with your razor, Jack?"

He said, while still struggling, "I don't know."

I told him, "I'm going to cut your balls off. What do you think of that?"

He pleaded with me and said, "Penny would never want that."

After considering his answer I replied, "You are right! Penny would not want that even after all you have done to her."

Turning his head, trying to look back at me, he said, "I lost my temper with Penny because she disrespected me."

I yelled at him and said, "Disrespect? No one can disrespect shit, Jack."

Hoping that he was beginning to convince me, he went on, "Penny is one good woman, and I'm praying she will take me

back some day. Every night I read the Book of Mormon, trying to straighten my life out."

Well, with that I had enough of Jack. I said, "You are nothing but a liar—you have never picked up the Book of Mormon in your life, and, Jack, I'm not Penny, so you are shit out of luck."

I took the razor and with one slice cut off his nuts. He screamed bloody murder. I then grabbed both of his legs and yanked him back into the bedroom. The window came with him and came crashing down on his back and head. To put it bluntly, Jack had been turned into one bloody mess. He said, "Why didn't you just kill me?"

"Because, Jacko, you will now suffer as Penny suffers. Penny was good to you. She tried really hard to please you. She would tolerate whatever crap mood you were in. You would put her down in front of others in an effort to build yourself up. It hurt her a lot. Truly God in heaven would like to have the faith of the human race in him that she had in you, but you brushed her aside. You were one real ass, Jack. She thought she was marrying a real man, but all she got was a self-centered prick. Well, Jack, you are still a prick—only a prick who doesn't have a set of balls under it any more. No woman will want you now. They will look the other way when you walk by. They will whisper to each other and snicker about your 'condition.'" I took the Playboy magazine and dropped it down on him and said, "Let's see you get yourself off now. You can still piss to your heart's content, though, Jack!" I threw his bloody razor at him and said, "Here is your razor back, stud. Be careful you don't cut yourself."

He said, "You have to get me to a doctor."

I said, "You didn't get one for Penny; she barely made it to get help for herself–without dying. I think if a small pregnant woman can survive on her own then you can too. On the off

chance you don't bleed to death, don't go after Penny. Perhaps I should say if you get brave enough to bother her, take a gun with you—you will want to use it to put a bullet in your head. Remember, I have visited you twice. If I have to make it thrice, I will take that crosscut saw by that tree stump in your yard and very slowly cut off your head with it."

Jack lay there praying to God. I don't think it will do much good. I did a little dance going down the stairs. I was in a really great mood. Fred Astaire would have been proud of me. I hummed the melody from The *Wizard of Oz*: "If I Only Had a Heart." I thought up new and appropriate words for the occasion: "There is a man who thought he's clever; Now his balls are gone forever. Ain't that an awful shame. But he'd not be sad and gloomy if he'd only listened to me—only got himself to blame."

Dear Diary, I always feel like this when I dispense justice, and Jack seems to bring out the song writer in me. I stopped on his porch and admired the Arizona night sky. I felt something licking my hand and I saw that it was Jack's dog. It was licking Jack's blood off my closed fist. I said, "Sorry, boy, you can't have what's in my hand."

I went back over to the dance that was now breaking up. I walked over to the same guy who I had talked to earlier. He was talking to two other elders behind the dance hall. I said, "Here, I have a present for you." I grabbed his left hand and pulled it toward me. I then deposited in the palm of his hand Jack's testicles.

He said, "My god, what's this?"

I said, "It is Jack Smith's nuts. Now spread the word to all of your asshole buddies, that they had better leave Penny alone or their wives are all going to be widows. Remember what I did to Jacko." As I walked away, one of them shot me in the back with a 38 caliber pistol. I felt the thud of the bullet as it hit me, quickly followed by the crackling sound of the gun firing. I

turned around and held my arms out wide and said, "Don't do that again." He didn't. They just stood there staring at me in silence.

The head elder said, "Maybe he has on a bullet-proof vest."

I said, "Don't have a vest, boys. Maybe I'm one of those demons you like to preach about when you want to scare the hell out of your kids. Fire one more time, and maybe you will find out whether I'm a demon or not. By the way, boys, don't bother running over to Jack's place and rushing him to a doctor to have his nuts sewn back on. I washed them off with paint thinner that he had on his porch. That is why they smell the way they do. I don't think they will work too well now, plus he probably has already bled to death." I then pointed at them with my right index finger and said, "Ya'll keep in touch now—you hear?"

There was now a small crowd of mostly women, all dressed in the same style and color of clothing, who had come to see what the ruckus was all about. I said, "Excuse me ladies," and I made my way out into the Arizona desert. I couldn't get the words of my new song out of my head, so I whistled it all the way to the Grand Canyon. I will commune with Eleleth once more when the sun is high. He should be sleeping in Pakistan by then.

Chapter XXVI

On the north rim of the Grand Canyon I sat among the weeds and the stifling heat and gazed down into the canyon. My mind and that of Eleleth's became one. I relived that which he had seen. I did not have to say anything to him as he was asleep in Hindu-Kush. I looked out at the Grand Canyon, and it became blurred into a mirage of what Eleleth and the rest of Seth's army of assassins were told by Seth. I saw the leaders of all the countries of the Middle East come forward through the chanting crowd at their base camp. Each one bowed down and swore allegiance to my brother. One by one they kissed his hand and called him the blessed Iman. Next to Seth's throne, which was made of alabaster, sat my old friend Ishtar. She wore a pure white linen robe with gold trim, and on her feet were gold sandals. On her head she wore a crown of gold with embedded diamonds in the shape of seven stars. She had around her neck a gold collar, and hooked to the gold collar was a gold chain about six feet long. The other end of the chain was hooked to a golden bracelet that Seth wore on his left wrist. She was like a dog on a leash. I never imagined that she would bow down to him, but now I guess she really was his harlot. I'm sorry for that.

In my vision Seth spoke and said, "The middle eastern countries of the Sudan, Egypt, Saudi Arabia, Iraq, Iran, Pakistan, Afghanistan, Syria and Lebanon will be brought under the control of one man, me, by the year 2015. I will bring them together as one nation, which I will call Kittim Islam, as it is foretold in the stars. At first I will appear peaceful to the West— at last, a man with the best of intentions—a true holy man. I will even find favor in the eyes of Israel. I will decry the actions of the terrorists, although they will really be our assassins doing

our bidding."

One of his assassins in the crowd interrupted his vision with a question. He said, "There are but seven stars on the crown that the great whore of Babylon now wears, and yet you have named nine countries that will band together to drive out and destroy the infidels. Why aren't there nine stars?"

Seth answered, "That is because in the early part of the new century two heads of our hydra will have to be sacrificed to appease the West for a while, but they will not die in vain, my brothers. They will buy us time and overconfidence to the fools in the West. The seven remaining heads of our hydra will be enough to prevail in battle. For 3200 years, my brothers, I sat in the dark waiting for this moment. In the dark I sat alone; therefore, our army will be known as the army of darkness. The pious fools of the west will think of themselves as the sons of the light. One of their politicians will even call them that as they prepare for war. They will say they want to bring the light of freedom to the Islamic nation. We will allow the fools of the West to feed our seven-headed beast. They will feed it in appeasement, for they don't really want war. Their people don't want to sacrifice their sons in battle, and their governments don't want to sacrifice their goods and money. My brothers, we must be prepared to fight a war for 40 years."

My vision of Seth's meeting was temporarily interrupted when a small sight-seeing plane, which bore a slogan on the fuselage which read "Grand Canyon Tours," flew through my line of vision. When my vision of Seth returned I saw Ishtar looking over the crowd. She gazed at them, not looking at anyone in particular. She then stared intently at a man 12 rows back from the front. He was dressed much like Eleleth. In fact, I was afraid it was Eleleth at first, but then it dawned on me that I wouldn't be reading his mind now because he would already be dead. She stood up and pointed at him and announced that he

was a spy.

He was seized upon and brought before Seth. He was stripped naked, and though he protested his innocence, Seth slowly cut off his head and threw it into the crowd. The people in the crowd kicked it around like a soccer ball. This was a practice that had started a long time ago and was resurrected by Seth. Seth then announced that this first meeting was over because the sun was beginning to set. He took off the bracelet on his left arm and attached it to the throne. He announced that all the representatives of the nine countries were welcome to take their turn raping the whore of Babylon. They all eagerly accepted his offer. They drew lots to see who would be first. I knew Eleleth was crying to himself. I must warn him again or he will wind up like the spy they caught. Ishtar is not the mother that he wished she would be. I saw no more. I guess Eleleth could not stand looking any more at what was going on—or at least cast it out of his mind.

Chapter XXVII

My half of the duplex was a welcome sight. I went into my living room and saw that the books that I had checked out from the library had dust on them. I should have taken them back. Since they had been checked out on the assistant librarian's card, she has probably caught hell over the books. I'll take them back tomorrow. I'm sure she will be able to get the over-due fines waived. Tonight I will take a quick look through the books to see if I can find anything of interest. I had not closed my front door. I saw Sara standing in the doorway. She had a whimsical

look on her face. I said, "What's the matter, Sara?"

She handed me my bamboo plant and said, "My brother did not water the plant, and it died."

I said, "Sara, your brother is a baby and I asked you to take care of the plant."

She asked me if I was mad at her.

I told her, "No."

She told me that her grandmother thought that maybe Joshua would die. She said, "Horus, do you think he will die?"

I said, "No, Sara, he will live." I told her that I would even bring the bamboo plant back to life. She appeared relieved because she wanted to believe me. She ran home to tell her grandmother. I did not tell her that it would only take six bucks and a trip to a WalMart store and then a transplant into the base the old plant was in. She will never know the difference. I wish Joshua's problems would be so easy.

Dear Diary, I went to Colorado University Medical Center in Denver. I walked past a half-awake guard and over to the offices listed in the glass case on the wall by the elevator. I found what I needed listed there: Rose Fernandez, Clinical Cytologist, and Charles Foster, Cellular Pathologist. I went up to the second floor and walked down what seemed like endless halls. I asked directions from a small, skinny Mexican woman about 40. She said, "Follow me." She walked right to Suite 209. She unlocked the door and said, "Come on in." I had run into Rose. She was carrying a large notebook. She put it down and said, "Okay, what can I do for you?"

"I know that you are a friend of Dr. Cohen of Jerusalem."

She replied, "So?"

I pulled out two 12 x 18 white linen cloths. I said, "Dr. Cohen would like you to test the blood stains on these cloth samples."

Rose said, "Test them for what? By the looks of the cloths

you have here, they should really be handed over to an archeologist."

I said, "Dr. Cohen would like them tested to see if the DNA carries the Tay-Sachs gene."

Rose said, "He said, that, huh?"

I said, "Yes, he did."

Rose countered with, "Why didn't Dr. Cohen test them in Jerusalem?"

I said, "Rose, I can't answer that."

She said, "I'll call him and ask him."

I told her, "That's not possible right now—he's on vacation. I will be going back to Jerusalem soon so I was hoping to take the results with me."

Rose picked up one of the pieces of cloth, looked at it and said, "Are you a colleague of Dr. Cohen?" I said, "No—just a friend."

She said, "I didn't think so. You don't sound like you know much about genetics."

"I don't, Rose. I'm just retired and a world traveler. So, Rose, what do I tell Dr. Cohen? Will you do it?"

She begrudgingly said, "All right—if I can get Charles Foster, a colleague of mine, to help."

I said, "What kind of a time frame are we looking at?"

Rose said, "Next week—how about Thursday?"

I said, "That would be great. I want to thank you in advance for helping Dr. Cohen."

She said, "Just tell him he owes me a favor."

I smiled at her and said, "You can count on it."

I went by the WalMart store on the way home and picked up the new bamboo plant. I found one that actually was very close in appearance to the old dead one. I took it home and transplanted it in the old vase. I took it over to Thelma Bloom's home and showed it to a truly amazed Sara. I squatted down

and handed it to her. I made her promise that she would water it and not let it die—again. She took the plant, and, taking great care, walked very slowly to her bedroom and put it on the table. Thelma was in Joshua's room. I told her that in the morning I would be leaving again for a trip in a few days. I went home and lay down on my bed and thought about the Eternal. Maybe Amun has turned away from me and now I am no more than a convict on death row waiting to die. If that should be the case, I hope my earthly remains someday will be lying in the soil in Egypt.

My thoughts reached through time and space and embraced the thoughts of Eleleth. I saw only images of darkness and over-whelming sadness. He was taking the plight of his mother very hard. I got up and went into my living room and looked through the library books. I glossed over the books and then noticed a picture of the oil cartel. In the picture there were six men seated next to the king, but only the names of five men were listed in the caption below the picture. I took a magnifying glass and studied the picture, but the image was not clear enough, and the one person unidentified had his head turned. I was about to give up. I thought the person in the picture could be anyone, but then I dropped one of the books on the carpet. It lay open on a page with the same picture that I had found in the first book. This picture was different. The unidentified man was sitting with his arms folded, but everything else, including the time on the clock on the wall, was exactly the same. I guess Seth has been doing some time traveling of his own. He hasn't been traveling back before 1996, though. His tomb became a barrier that he could not cross. I guess he is having the oil cartel of the Middle East provide the funds for his needs—funds that come from the West. The West will be unwittingly paying for its own destruction. I took the long overdue books back to the library.

Once again I waited for the rising sun, rising in the east and

escaping the darkness of the underworld and bringing a new day. I would soon be back in the land and time of my ancient past and the age of Osiris. I closed my eyes and felt the centuries rush by in reverse. I opened them when I felt the cold wind once more of Holy Illium and saw 50 feet ahead of me a man sitting down by a campfire. I was looking at myself. There is always something forlorn about seeing yourself because I now know what I did not know then, and my former self would never know once I had returned to the future. For my old self all of the endless centuries lay ahead.

I was back outside of the city of Bab Edu-Dhru, the city that would forever be known in modern times as Sodom. My former self and I caught each other's glance and merged into one being. I looked at the city and walked towards the gates. I was greeted by one of the guards. He looked down at me from the wall and asked what I wanted. I almost made a mistake and replied in English—but I caught myself. I said, "I want entrance to the city." He asked me what I could pay. I threw three silver coins on the ground. I looked up and he had disappeared, only to open the gate and run and gather up the coins. I had forgotten what primitive people lived here.

I asked him where I would find the home of Lot and his wife and two daughters. I gave him another silver coin. He took the money and directed me to a small home built into the city's wall. Lot was not there. He and his family had left to visit his uncle—Abraham. He had left a caretaker to guard his possessions, for the city was full of thieves. The caretaker told me they would be back that night, for they only had to travel a short distance and they had been gone for two days already.

The caretaker was an old man, bent over and using a cane of sorts. I knew he was not an evil person. Perhaps Abraham should have bargained a little more with the Eternal. Then this old man would have had more than one day of life left. Well, at

least in the morning he would not die alone. All of the other Sodomites would be with him. I considered: When the Eternal passed his death sentence on this forsaken place, did he factor in my returning from a future time? And if he did, then he knows why I'm here. I convinced the caretaker to get me some wine, unleavened cakes, and cooked meat from a freshly slaughtered calf—enough to last for five days. I gave him two pieces of silver to pay for the food. Once he had left, I searched the home for the cloth that contained the virgin blood that was proof of Lot's wife's virginity, the cloth taken from their bridal bed. I found it. The old man soon returned with the wine and the food. I left it there and told him I would come back for it later. He put the food on the floor along with the wineskin. His left hand was missing a thumb and index finger. He had cut them off because of an arthritic condition. The fingers on his right hand did not look any better. Soon his hands will be open and motionless and they will hurt him no more.

I took a stroll through the stench-filled narrow streets of Sodom. I wandered over to the town square. Most of the people of the city were there. I stood next to a woman of about 30. She was holding a small baby that was nursing on her right breast. She had three other children who were doing their best to push through the crowd to see what was going on. King Bera was passing a death sentence on 12 women. They were all accused of adultery. They were also all of his wives. They ranged in age from about 13 to 40. The oldest one was about eight months pregnant. She was his mother. She begged her son for mercy. Her cries did not sway him. Maybe he originated the Oedipus complex. Hell, the Greeks would not be around for another 2000 years, so they did not start it. King Bera pointed to each one of his wives and pronounced her guilty. They were all put into a cart that had wooden bars around the sides and on the top, and with a door at the back. The bars at the top had purposely been

spread apart far enough for the condemned to stick their heads through. They were all screaming and crying as the cart was pulled through the city streets. The crowd had worked themselves into a frenzy. The woman who had been nursing the baby ran over to the cart and put the baby in through the bars, where he lay wiggling at the feet of the women.

Well, well, maybe his mother considered it a very late term abortion. I guess it wasn't that bad. He would have died tomorrow anyway. The cart was pulled down to the Dead Sea. This whole fiasco was really only special entertainment. The women in the cart fought each other for the chance to stick their heads out through the bars on the top of the cart, trying to prolong their lives if only for a few seconds from drowning. One of the women stepped on the youngest wife and stood on her body in an effort to get higher through the bars. Another, taking a cue from the first wife, did the same with the baby, but it did not lift her up that much. The cart was taken deeper and deeper out into the Dead Sea until only the head of the woman who was standing on the body of the youngest wife could be seen. Then she, too, went under the waves—they were all dead. I felt no sorrow for them.

Now they got down to their usual entertainment. The Sodomites made the old and infirm draw lots to see who would live or die. The old were of no use to the Sodomites so the unlucky ones who drew the lots poorly would be drowned in the Dead Sea. The survivors would be allowed to live until the next darkening of the moon. It would then be the day of Sheol again (the day of hell). I climbed up the stairs to the outer wall and looked out at the carnival of death taking place. Some of the old would be buried in the sand with only their heads sticking out of the sand. The waves of the Dead Sea brought death closer with each wave. The condemned begged for mercy, but their cries were only met with laughter.

I have found that it is usually the young who can be the most cruel—but not here. Everyone got into the act. I saw two of the survivors who had been spared holding an old woman face down in the sand suffocating her. I looked straight down at the base of the wall and watched three dogs tearing apart the remains of two small children who had been thrown to their deaths from the very spot where I stood. King Bera then announced that there would be a wedding feast that night because he would be taking 12 new wives. Well, he better make love to all 12 tonight because there won't be any opportunity to do so tomorrow. I did not want to encounter the crowd as they returned. The guard at the gate was more than happy to open the gate for me. I think he thought I was going to give him a tip.

I walked over to my abandoned campfire, and I passed Lot and his wife and daughters on their way back home. Lot and I acknowledged each other. The rest of his family was looking at the slaughter that had just occurred. Lot's wife Zoe was complaining to him that if they had only gotten an earlier start they would have made it back for "the entertainment." Lot, being a good man, suffered much over Zoe's selfish and uncaring heart. She was only content when she was ordering someone to wait on her. His two daughters had to listen while she would berate Lot and tell him how lucky he was to have married her. Though she was no raving beauty, she claimed that suitors had been waiting in line when she magnanimously gave herself to Lot. Her vanity was such that she would have her daughters in tears by telling them that they would have to settle for the first men who would want them because their beauty was no match for hers.

No matter how sad someone's plight might be, she would show no sympathy—no words of comfort. Instead she would pour forth lamentations about her supposed various illnesses and how hard she had worked when she was younger helping her ungrateful husband. Although her life had been pretty good

for the times, she claimed she never had one good day ever. She never thanked God for anything. If death had come to her door, she would have gladly offered up Lot and both of their daughters if it would have saved her life—or even prolonged it for one miserable hour. I thought it was a crying shame she had missed out on the "entertainment." I knew Seth on the morrow would be outside of Gomorrah.

The next morning, just like the first time I was here, I allowed Lot, his wife and two daughters to escape. As it was before, the youngest daughter lost her sandal, but did not look back. They hurried north to the cave of Zoar. Most of the Sodomites were sleeping off the party from the night before. The ground began to shake and the yellow sulfur mountain that was part of the walls of Sodom began to heat up. I could hear the screams of the people trapped in the city. Fissures opened up in the barren desert around Sodom, cutting off any means of escape. The heat was very intense. I saw the city caving in on itself. The sky became black as a night with no moon. People trying to flee the carnage tried to jump over the fissure, which was about eight feet wide. One almost made it. It was the guard of the gate whom I had met before. He grabbed hold of an ancient root that became exposed by the earth opening up. He begged me for help. While hanging on to the root with one hand, he threw the silver coins at me with his other hand. I watched for a while and, as he tried to pull his way up to safety, I took my stone knife and cut the root and watched him fall into the abyss. He was quickly incinerated in the lava that was beginning to reach the surface of the fissure. The mountain of sulfur, aided by a ferocious wind, had become a wall of fire. I picked up my silver U.S. quarters that now lay on the ground where the guard had thrown them. I saw Lot's wife, who was about 100 yards from me, turn and look back—and, as she did, she disappeared. She had fallen in a sinkhole created by the fissure and water

rushing in from the Dead Sea. Lot and his daughters panicked trying to get her out. It was to no avail. They watched her die, and ran for their lives.

Then in an instant it was all over. The fires were gone. There was only an eerie silence and the smell of burned flesh. The fissure closed up and the heat dissipated. Along with the silence, the cold Asian breeze returned.

I walked over to the sinkhole and looked down on the body of Lot's wife. The water from the Dead Sea had been sucked back out leaving her body encrusted in salt. I sat there by the sinkhole for two days waiting for Lot to come back and claim her body. They did not bring any food with them, so they were beginning to starve. Lot had his daughters pull her body up the side of the sinkhole. He then took out his knife to cut off pieces of her flesh. The first time I was here I had witnessed them having parts of mom for lunch—but not this time.

From the opposite side of the sinkhole I yelled at them, "Don't be afraid. I mean you no harm." They recoiled with fear anyway. They tried to run, but I cut them off. I came over to them and gave them the wine, the cakes and the meat from the slaughtered calf.

Lot said, "We have no money or anything of value with which to pay you."

I assured him that he owed me nothing. He had an incredulous look on his face. He was used to the ways of Sodom where no one would ever offer charity and kindness for any price. They took the food and drink and ran, leaving the corpse of salt behind to be preserved forever.

In the night, I watched and listened while the two daughters conspired to get their heartbroken father drunk with wine. They believed that all human life on earth had come to an end. The eldest said she believed that I was some sort of a demon and responsible for the disaster that struck their city. The two of

them sat by a fire at the opening of the cave and made a pact. The eldest daughter would lie with their father in hopes of becoming pregnant to repopulate the earth with humans. The next night the youngest daughter would lie with their father in hopes of conceiving. The oldest lay her virgin cloth on the ground and lay down on it naked and her drunken father lay with her and satisfied himself. She waited until he was asleep and then took her virgin cloth and laid it outside of the cave. The following night her younger sister lay with their father. She put her virgin cloth outside of the cave just like her sister had done. They both prayed to the Eternal to let them conceive.

I came up to the cave entrance and the two women, seeing me, went farther back into the cave, leaving their sleeping father lying at my feet. They threw rocks at me and shouted for me to go away. I told them the world had not been destroyed after all, only these two wicked cities. I pointed north and told them to go to the Jordan River where it flows into the Dead Sea. "There you will find human beings just like you." I picked up the virgin cloths. They begged me to give them back. I said, "Do you really want your father to see this? What will you say to him? He is a man of honor. He would kill himself out of shame."

They did not answer my question. The youngest daughter said, "We think you're lying. You want us to go to the Jordan River to die."

I said, "Your food will run out in a few days. Hunger and thirst will drive you there and you will see that I speak the truth."

The eldest daughter spoke again, "Our father will see in the coming months that our bellies are growing larger. What shall we say to him?"

I came into the cave and looked at their partially hidden faces in the dark. I would not have been able to see them at all if it had not been for the campfire. I pulled their drunken father

away from the campfire. In his present state, I thought he might catch his clothes on fire. I said, "When your father awakens, tell him some Sodomites who survived the destruction of the city came to the cave and raped both of you while he slept. I will put a thought in his head that he had offered both of you to them the other night in Sodom."

The youngest daughter said, "Why would he do that?" I replied, "I'll let him think that the honor of his household was at stake and this was the only solution. He will think that they had come to the cave to take him up on his earlier offer. In his heart he will forgive both of you for your condition. He will blame himself and want to kill the men who he believed raped you. Both of you will still find husbands, and your bloodlines will live through the ages. The Eternal himself has written it in the stars. May he who created himself be with you always."

The eldest ran over to me and took hold of my arm and said, "Wait, wait. Why can't you take us as wives?"

"Me!" I replied. "Earlier you were calling me a demon." I pulled away from her grasp. I said, "Remember—go north to the twin sister of the river of life—the Jordan." I started to leave, but then I remembered I still had the youngest daughter's lost sandal. I gave it to her.

I left them and took my cloths. As I turned to go, Seth was standing right behind me. I almost ran into him. He was hunting for me as well. He paid his respects to Lot's daughters and glanced down at drunken Lot sleeping. We went to the southern end of the Dead Sea and made our way back to Egypt; we slept out on the desert. Before going to sleep Seth told me of how he chased down Birsha, king of Gomorrah, and cut not only the king's throat but that of his two wives and eleven children. Seth was very happy. I watched Seth while he slept. I thought how he trusted me. I remembered all of the centuries that we had already lived and thought about the 1685 years Seth had in front

of him before he would be betrayed by me. I slowly took out my stone knife and thought that maybe I should do us both in here and now.

Dear Diary, as I held my stone knife close to Seth's chest I remembered what he had written on the wall of his prison tomb: "I returned the compliment—you spared me and so I spared you." This made me pause in reflection of his statement. I turned my head and saw an apparition walk by. They're not like the people of the dark. Their universe just touches ours from time to time, and so we glimpse each other once in a while. The same apparition had appeared in the exact time and place as the first time Seth and I were here. Obviously, changes in our universe don't affect theirs.

I put away my stone knife. Seth could not wait to get back. King Narmer had made Seth vizier of Upper Egypt. He had been given the job because of all of the corruption going on, and King Narmer knew Seth would make an example out of anyone caught pilfering from the royal treasury, because Seth would have absolutely no mercy for the guilty. When we reached the Egyptian border, I left in a blinking of an eye. He was once again with my former self. They were happy. Neither of them knew what was ahead.

Dear Diary, I've never felt so depressed in all of my life. I'll try to put these thoughts out of my mind. One more stop in time and then I go home.

Chapter XXVIII

I went back to the University of Colorado Medical Center. Rose had everything ready when I got there. She handed me a large brown envelope. I thanked her and asked what she had found. Rose said, "Both samples carried the Tay Sachs gene."

I said, "I'll get this information to Dr. Cohen."

Rose said, "Why bother? I called him yesterday. He does not know you, so he could not have sent you here—so what do you really want?"

I said, "Well, you found me out. I don't have bad intentions. I'm trying to save a little boy's life. He has Tay Sachs"

Rose said, "You have a fat chance of doing that now don't' you?"

I said, "What did running this test cost you? Did it ruin your week—put you behind schedule?" Now Rose was on the defensive. I said, "I have some more samples I hope you will test." I had my five cloths wrapped up in a box. I pulled out my stone knife. I cut the tape on the box and, as I did, I accidentally cut my hand. My blood dripped on one of the five samples. I quickly circled it with a magic marker. I didn't want my blood to be the one tested. "Rose, I believe if you test these samples and test also the DNA that is on this baby's bottle and maybe compare them with the first two, you may find something amazing. What do you have to lose—a few more hours taken from your week can't hurt now can it?"

Rose said, "Okay, but this is the last time. It won't do any good, you know. I can test these samples until hell freezes over and it won't make whoever this kid is any better. He will still have Tay Sachs."

I said, "When can I meet with you to go over the results?"

Rose said in resignation, "How about next Wednesday?"

I told her I would be there. I went home and rested.

Two days later I went outside on my front porch to enjoy the autumn morning. There was a box sitting next to my front door. It was wrapped up like a present in blue paper with a pink bow. A present for a kid must be for Sara, was my first thought. I picked it up and shook it. Sara, who loved to come and visit me, was once more at my open front door looking in through the screen. I saw her and said, "Come on in."

Like all children, she was full of curiosity. She said, "You got a present. Is it your birthday?"

"No," I said. "There is no name on the box."

She said, "Then maybe it's for me." She asked me if she could take off the ribbon and open up the box. I said that would be okay. Kids love that sort of thing. Sara opened the box. It was full of sand. She said, "I'll bet there is something in the bottom."

As she reached her hand into the box, I grabbed her hand and yelled, "No, don't do that!"

She looked shaken and began to cry. The box fell on the floor on its side. The sand went all over the rug, and out of the box came a two-foot-long asp. It was very deadly. It took off slithering under the couch. Sara screamed and ran into the dining room and got up on the dining room table. She panicked and yelled for me to make it go away. I went over and picked her up. She clung to my neck. I took her home and explained to Thelma that it must have been a prank and that the snake was harmless. Sara told me she would never come to my home again because the bad snake might get her. I told her I would catch it and take it to the zoo. She liked that idea.

I went back to my living room. I absolutely had to find the asp. The last time I saw it, the snake was going under the couch. I reached my hand in under the couch and began to feel around. Nothing! Snakes don't need much of a space to hide. I started

moving furniture all around. All the time I was thinking about who would send me that snake. Seth did not do it—that was not his style. He also would not try to kill Sara. I checked all of the heating and air conditioning vents. An asp would not want to go out into the cool autumn air. It would hole up in a place that was warm and damp. Next I tore up the bedroom in my search. I thought I should have known better and not let Sara open that box. I hunted for that little poisonous son of a bitch for hours.

Dear Diary, I was about to give up. I went into my kitchen. I had left a two-quart pot that I had cooked spaghetti in lying in the sink. I looked down to see the asp curled up in the pot. I don't make it a practice to kill anything for no reason. This time, though, the asp had to die. I decided to make it quick, but then it bit me several times in my hand. I got a little annoyed over that. I took the pot out of the sink and stuffed the asp down into the drain. The snake kept working its way back out of the garbage disposal. It managed to get one last strike at my arm. I pushed it back down and put my hand over the opening of the drain. I waited a couple of minutes and then took my hand away from the drain. I turned on the garbage disposal. The asp's head and part of its body sticking out of the drain started flying around in a circle. The rest of the snake was pulled down into the disposal. The disposal made one loud racket as it chewed up the asp. Blood came splattering up from the drain. As the disposal ran, I took the washer/sprayer and washed off all of the blood. I will ask Wadjet, the snake goddess, to forgive my transgression.

Now that the asp had been dispatched, I straightened up my home. I scooped up the sand and put as much of it as I could on my coffee table. I kept thinking about who would send me that box. No one knew where I lived and only a very few even knew I existed. I looked at the box the asp had been in. I looked at the wrapping paper and the bow, and thought only a woman would

wrap up a box like that. The snake had been an Egyptian asp—the same kind that had done in Queen Cleopatra VII. Women don't like bloodshed—another reason to believe this box was sent by a woman. I started spreading out the sand on the coffee table until I had a thin layer. I asked Thoth for divine help. I slowly blew gently on the sand. Soon a word began to appear as the sand scattered from my breath: Petra. I will go to the long deserted city only when the moon is full. I will have to be careful that I am not walking into a trap.

Dear Diary, I had just finished straightening up my home when the doorbell rang. I opened the door to see two smiling faces. One was a woman about 45. The other was, as it turned out, her husband. He looked about 50. The wife Eleanor was holding a Bible. They asked if they could come in because they had some "good news" to share with me.

Because of my upbringing, I said, "Sure." You don't dishonor your home by being unpleasant to guests—even uninvited ones. They came in and sat down on my couch. I had not had time to clean off my coffee table. The word "Petra" was still spelled out in the sand on the table. Mel, the husband, commented on it. I said my next door neighbor's granddaughter had written it. Mel asked me my name. I told him. The wife was a scrawny-looking woman with black hair with gray streaks in it. She was wearing bifocals, and she got right down to business, looking up something in her Bible.

Mel said, "We are canvassing the neighborhood."

I said, "Canvassing for what, Mel?"

He said, "Horus, we would like to invite you to our church."

"Which church is that, Mel?"

"Well, Horus, it is the Church of the Risen Jesus. We are a Bible-believing church. Do you believe in Jesus, Horus?"

I said, "Well, I met him. I believe he was executed for sedi-

tion on Monday, August 27. It was 2005 years ago."

Mel said, "Well, Horus, you are off a little with your date, but you are pretty close. I take it to mean you are a born-again Christian."

I looked at Mel's chubby face and said, "Actually, Mel, I'm not a Christian at all." I kept looking at their faces. There was something interesting about them. Trying to be polite, I said, "I guess I'm too old to change now, but I appreciate you two stopping in." I thought they would get the hint and leave. I was wrong.

Eleanor said, "It is never too late to accept our Lord as your personal savior."

Before I could open my mouth, she said, "Have you ever heard of Reinhard Heydrich?"

I said, "I think maybe I have. Why don't you elaborate?"

Eleanor said, "Well, Heydrich was a Nazi who was head of security police."

I said, "Wasn't he called the 'Butcher of Prague'?"

Eleanor said, "I'm impressed, Horus, because that is exactly right."

I found this amusing, so I said, "Please continue, Eleanor."

She said, "Well, he was riding in his car during World War II in 1942. The English sent two soldiers to kill him."

I said, "Well, Eleanor, did they succeed?"

She said, "Yes, they did. They threw a hand grenade into the front seat of his car and the grenade exploded."

I said, "Is that so?"

Mel said, "You know the remarkable thing was what went through his mind as his car blew up?" Then slowly repeating himself, as if his question was really brilliant, said again, "Do you know, Horus, what went through his mind?"

I said, "Let me guess—the transmission?"

My answer made Mel hesitate. Then he said, "No—he

accepted Jesus."

I said, "Mel, how would anyone know that?"

"Well, Horus, he did not die right away. He lived for a few days and then died of his wounds."

I said, "That's too bad. If he could have stuck around a little longer, why he could have been dangling at the end of a rope in Spandeau prison."

Eleanor piped in and said, "As he lay dying, he told his doctors that he had accepted Jesus as his personal savior." Eleanor then started spouting off different verses from her Bible. I thought I should tell them the real story of Reinhard Heydrich. I didn't, though.

I thought back to those days. Reinhard was a first class murdering asshole. For the Eternal to issue a death warrant during the time of war, you have to be a real bad boy. He was. I had planned to kill him myself, but the British agents Gabcik and Kubis tried to beat me to it. Their explosive device blew pieces of steel and fragments of the car's upholstery into Heydrich's body. It put a wound in his spleen. Even with these wounds he would have recovered. His doctors did a good job. His only problem was with me. I went to the hospital when he was recovering. I stopped outside long enough to pick up the feces that a German Shepard police dog had just deposited on the hospital grounds. I took them with me. I thought it would be a nice get-well present. I went to his private room. It wasn't hard to get by the two S.S. soldiers guarding his door. When they saw me I made them believe they were looking at an S.S. General. I said to both of them, "You two clean up that dog shit over there, and do it now!" I had conveniently left on the floor a few feces for them. They did what I said.

I went into Heydrich's hospital room. He was lying on his right side. The doctors had put him in this position due to the wound in his spleen. I went over to him. He could not speak very

loudly. He looked at me and said, "You!"

I said, "Yes, it's me."

What he was referring to, Dear Diary, was that he and I had met before. I had allowed myself to be taken prisoner and put in the labor camp at Theresienstadt. I wanted to see just how rotten this asshole was. The S.S. took one look at me and decided that I was of no value to them. I was loaded onto a truck and taken to a wooded area with about 25 women and children and old men. We were told to get down into a trench. We did. Just an hour earlier Heydrich had been playing with his two sons. His best friend, Heinrich Himmler, the head of the S.S., and Heydrich's pregnant wife looked on at the children. They were such a happy and loving family. Of course, dad was a murdering son-of-a bitch. Heydrich drove up in his Mercedes, got out and came over and looked down into the trench. He was the perfect Aryan—six feet tall, well built, blue eyes, blond hair, and a devoted Nazi who loved the Fuhrer. He stared at the people waiting to die. They were all huddled together. Some of them were children about the age of his son. He was very annoyed that he had to leave his family to come to this execution. With a smirk on his face, he then told his soldiers to "Get on with it." They opened up on us with machine pistols. I can still remember the screaming. I yelled at him to remember my face. After the firing stopped, I lay there as if I were dead. I heard Heydrich say to his troops, "Vergrabe den stinkischen, Juden Scheissdreck! (Now cover up that stinking Jewish shit!)" After they left, I dug my way out of the now filled-in trench. The dirt had been turned into a combination of mud and innocent blood.

Thinking back about all of this, I said to Heydrich, as he lay there temporarily paralyzed, "It looks like some of that stinking shit has come back to see you." There was no way he could summon help. His voice was too weak to attract attention because he had also suffered a wound to his throat. With the

remaining dog feces on my hand I began to work it into his wounds. I worked it in really well. I wiped off the rest on his face. The smell of it must have got to him, since he vomited all over the bed sheet. He lay there gasping for breath. "I guess I've turned you into stinking dog shit this time. On the bright side, though, it is at least German Shepard police dog-shit." When I left I gave instructions that he was not to be disturbed for the next 48 hours. He lasted for another three days before succumbing to blood poisoning.

Eleanor said, "Were you listening to me Horus?"

I said, "I'm sorry, I guess my mind wandered." I offered Mel and Eleanor some refreshments. They accepted. I kept looking at Mel. After another hour of their bullcrap, they finally departed.

Dear Diary, Thelma asked me if I would watch Sara for her. She told me that she was taking Joshua to the doctor because she believed that he was doing better. I told her that I would be delighted to watch Sara and that, with her permission, I would take Sara to the Museum of Natural History. Thelma told me that would be fine. So off an excited Sara and I went. We took the bus. The bus was not much of an improvement over the trolley car of 1934. It took almost an hour to get to the museum. Sara babbled on for the whole trip. In fact, she told everyone near us on the bus where we were going. It is nice to be young and full of enthusiasm. We got off the bus and Sara made a bee-line for the door. I ran to catch up with her. Sara liked the dinosaur exhibits. I found it interesting that the museum had a special exhibit from Egypt.

Sara and I went up to the third floor of the museum and began to look around. There was a black obelisk with engraved hieroglyphs. Sara ran over and touched it. It was okay for kids to touch it, so she ran her little fingers into the crevices. The hieroglyphs were part of the text from the Book of the Dead. This obelisk had been carved for a junior official from Thebes

during the reign of Kamose, who freed Egypt from the yoke of the Hyksos invaders. She asked me what the symbols meant, so I read some of it to her. Sara looked up at me and asked once again what it meant. She said that she didn't understand. I said what the Egyptians were saying was that once you get to heaven you don't want to run out of food because you might get so hungry that you would eat almost anything—like a bug or a frog.

Sara said, "Yuck, I would never get that hungry."

I smiled and said, "Would you ever get so thirsty that you would drink water that a cow was standing in?"

She said, "No, I would go thirsty."

"Well the Egyptians were saying that they would drink water that dirty." I said, "I'll tell you what, see that café over there? Why don't we go get some real American food?" Sara got the kid's special and a big drink. Then we went back to see the rest of the Egyptian exhibit.

There was a red granite head of my old friend Ramses II. Next to it was the mummy of a small child. Sara kept staring at that mummy in silence. Sara said, "When my brother dies will he be wrapped up like that?"

"No," I said, "He will live to be an old man like me."

She said, "Grandmother thinks he might die."

I reassured her again that Joshua would not die. We then went into the next hall. There was an ankh of Amenhotep II; next to it was a statue of a falcon carved out of granite. Below the falcon was the inscription: Horus, sun god of ancient Egypt, son of Osiris and Isis. Sara was thrilled to be able to tell me that the falcon had the same name as I did. I looked around a little annoyed. I guess even I have somewhat of an ego. There was not any mention of Seth or me. The Egyptians had blotted out most of the writings of our exploits. Once Seth was imprisoned he was forgotten after a while, and I became something of a non-

person to the king of Egypt. All the kings liked the idea of keeping the glory to themselves, so Seth and I were stricken from the historical records, along with anything else that could be embarrassing to the king.

Moses, the Jewish prophet, who led a minor uprising against Ramses II, was also erased from their history, along with any military defeats suffered by Egypt. Any scribe writing anything detrimental to the king would face death, not just for himself, but for his entire family. I bought Sara a few souvenirs. As we were ready to leave, I looked down into a glass case. There before me was the third stone knife that I had made—when I had made the ones for Seth and me. I had lost it in Sakara centuries ago. I just assumed that it was gone forever. This knife also possessed the power to kill immortals. I thought maybe I should come back when the museum was closed and take back my property. I'll think about that some more.

As we left the museum Sara did her best to get me to take her to the zoo. I told her that we would have to do it another day. Sara asked me questions about everything. I was aware of a young man in his late teens following us. I thought about him as Sara said, "How did the animals get their names—do you know?"

I said, "Well, have you heard of Adam and Eve?"

Sara said, "Yes, Grandma told me they were the first people who ever lived."

My thought pattern kept getting interrupted with the thoughts of that punk following us. I said, "Yes, Adam named all the animals. God let Adam and that mean devil Satan get into a contest as to which of them knew the real names of the animals, and the devil lost and got really mad."

Sara saw a little girl on the museum lawn sitting with her parents. She went over to talk to her. I said, "Hello," to the little girl's parents. The girl's father told me that they were here vis-

iting from Omaha, Nebraska. I knew that they were good people. I also knew that worthless piece of crap was watching us. He walked by and stared at Sara and her new friend. He went into the men's room. I asked the couple if they would watch Sara for a couple of minutes. They agreed. As I walked over to the small outdoor cinderblock men and women's bathrooms, the girl's dad yelled, "The toilet's broken."

I turned and held up my hands and said, "Just going to wash my hands." I quietly went into the men's room. It stunk like hell. Graffiti was all over the walls, and crap was on the floor. He was in the one and only stall with the door partly shut. The latch was broken, so he couldn't lock it. I bent over and saw under the door that he was on his knees. I don't think he was praying. In fact, I knew exactly what was on his mind. I kicked the door on the stall as hard as I could. I heard the door hit his head, and he let out a loud scream. The stall door started trying to close again, so I kicked it again. I heard another scream. I bent down and looked under the door. His head was shaved on both sides, leaving only hair about an inch tall in the center. In the old days it was known as a Mohawk. He had it dyed blue, and he wore a ring in his nose. The ring had gotten caught on a loose bolt on the stall door, and he was trying to get it loose. I started to yank on the door, but at the last second I decided he had suffered enough for his transgression. I said, "Hey, sorry, man. Didn't know anyone was in there."

He said, "You broke my nose."

I said, "I'll get you help. Be back soon." I picked up an open bottle of aspirin that someone had left by the sink and took the jar and put it on the floor and kicked it under the door. The pills went everywhere. I told him that the aspirin could tide him over until I could come back with help. He muttered an expletive at me as I left. I thought maybe I just saved him from being killed by me later—perhaps he will turn his sorry life around. I doubt

it though. This country, and much of the world for that matter, has become obsessed with sex and all things material, and the young low lifes like this kid have made these things their god.

I saw Sara chasing after her new friend Jessica, who was running around waving a blue ribbon. I told Sara we had to go home now. Sara was getting worn out. By the time we got off the bus she was sound asleep. I picked her up out of the seat and carried her the four blocks to our duplex. Thelma looked distressed. She told me the doctor thought Joshua's disease was advancing quicker than he had originally thought. I told her to keep praying and then I went to my half of the duplex. After all, I had to get ready to go to church the next day.

I went over to Mel's church. The building his church was in had been a carpet store in the past and was now masquerading as a Christian church. Mel had a pretty good crowd there. As he began to preach, I read his mind. He believed what he was saying and so did his followers. He preached of the immorality of the country and of its government officials. And like all good Christian zealots, he got around to the subject of abortion and the great evil that it was. He announced that there would be a rally at a Planned Parenthood office tomorrow at 8 a.m. He sent around a signup sheet for those able to attend. He then recognized me as a newcomer to their church and wanted me to stand up. I did. He also introduced a "god-fearing, born-again Christian" who was running for congress on the premise of getting this country back its moral values. Mel then went on a tirade lasting about thirty minutes on how Christians must take back the schools, the liberal churches, and local and state governments from the secularists. He followed that up with a question: "Do I hear an Amen?" Someone shouted out "Amen" to oblige Mel.

I thought there was not a whole lot of kindness in this crowd. I saw one woman reach over and slap her young son

because he was getting fidgety sitting through the sermon. So the kid sat there crying through the sermon, with his mother whispering to him to shut up or she would slap him again. Mel began to work himself up into a rage. All of a sudden his eyes rolled back in his head and he began to speak, as the lady next to me said, in tongues: "SHLL TH WRD F TY TRNL SHLM!"

I thought: That is not some secret language of God Mel is speaking, it is the language of the demons of the desert. Their speech isn't that hard to understand once you realize that there are no vowels in their language. Mel and his wife did not know it, but they were actually demons in sheep's clothing. They had been created by Seth—created in the same manner in which I created Eleleth. Seth had just done a good job of brainwashing them. Eleanor was even pregnant—the sure sign to Christian zealots of subservience on the part of women. This time, though, Eleanor would be giving birth to a monster. Seth had created a fifth column of zealots here in the United States to do his bidding. I wondered how many more Mel's and pregnant Eleanor's had he created and sent here. I suppose Seth was using them to flame the fires of hatred, by rewriting the Christian belief. Seth had done that sort of thing in the past. After all, it's easier to defeat a house divided. I shook Mel's hand as I left his church. I felt no hatred for him; after all, he was of Seth's making. It's true, though, eventually I may have to kill him and his wife.

Dear Diary, I kept my appointment with Rose. It was an experience that is still sending shock waves through my mind. I went into her office and she said, "Sit down."

I did. I said, "So what did you find out?"

She methodically went over every test with me. She said, "On the sample marked 'Mother' there was no evidence of the Tay Sachs gene. On the two marked 'daughter #1 and daughter #2' there also was no evidence of Tay Sachs. On the samples marked 'granddaughters' there was also no evidence of the Tay

Sachs gene. I don't know why though. The granddaughter's DNA was the same as the samples that you brought in the first time."

I said, "Well, that's good news. I guess the DNA from the baby bottle had the same results."

She said, "No—it bears the Tay Sachs gene."

I was aghast. I said, "That is impossible."

She said, "No, it isn't. The tests are accurate." My heart sank. I was sure I had cured baby Joshua. She said, "There is something else that is very strange—an anomaly—one that I, or no one else, has ever seen before." She stared at me and said, "Just for the hell of it I tested your blood."

I interrupted her, "I don't have Tay Sachs."

She said, "I didn't say you did."

I replied, "Then what are you saying?"

She said, "In every human being is cellular material called mitochondria. If you break it down to its bare components you will find a single cellular thread that goes back to one woman— the mother of the human race. There are sub-groups, but break them down and you keep arriving at the same woman."

"So what?" I said.

Rose said, "I'll tell you so what! Your DNA does not come from the mother of the human race."

I acted as if I were surprised, but I knew my mother, Lillith, was not the mother of the human race. I said, "Well, maybe you didn't run your test correctly."

She said emphatically, "Yes, I did. I ran it several times. There is something else you should know."

I said, "Okay, what's that?"

She pulled out the test results on baby Joshua, dropped them on the desk in front of me and said, "He has the same ancient mother as you! You two are related."

I said, "That is hard to believe!"

Rose said, "You want to bet on it!" Looking pissed, she said, "Even though I have in my hand an amazing discovery that might be worthy of a Nobel Prize, I can't do anything with it. I would have to run more tests on you and your young friend, and I doubt you would let me. I don't even have your name."

"I'm sorry, Rose, but I'm not going to give it to you either. There is a consolation prize for you, though. You may have just helped out the human race far more than anyone who ever lived—that's all I'm going to say except thanks for what you did."

As I walked down Colorado Boulevard, a thought crossed my mind. Actually it was really a question that I will ask my dear brother when I see him. I will say: "Did you screw Lot's daughters?" I guess I already know the answer to that. Seth had taken several trips to Jericho after we had returned to Egypt. Lot and his daughters had moved to Jericho after the calamity at Sodom. I just never put two and two together. Maybe Seth had seen something written in the stars that I missed—or maybe it was just lust. In the dim past I had listened many times while Seth bragged about how he changed himself into the image of some woman's husband so that he could lie with her. The daughters of Lot had to be the only ones he impregnated, though; otherwise the Rose Fernandez's of the world would have run across many more anomalies by now. Some of Seth's exploits had been written down and are now considered fables, just like the fables of Zeus and Apollo, but even fables have their beginnings sown with the seeds of truth. I thought to myself that Baby Joshua had a very interesting blood line—that of King David and Seth, warrior god of upper Egypt, and yet he will die in a little less than two months unless I can come up with something to save him.

Chapter XXIX

A week later I made my way to Petra in southern Jordan. There are a couple of ways to get there, but I took the route through the ever-narrowing gorge. The path led through red limestone, which had been cut out by centuries of water and wind erosion. I looked up at the walls, which in places came so close together that they blotted out the night sky. I could hear the demons that still haunt this place. It had been a bustling city of about 8000 in 3000 B.C. I would hear an occasional rock come tumbling down from the heights. I came out into the Valley of Petra. Across from me cut into the cliffs were the tombs of its long dead citizens. I climbed up and sat down on one of the columns. From there I could see in all directions in case of an ambush. The place was deathly silent. I sat there for a couple of hours. The moon was soon going to be out of sight. I started to leave. I looked down and at the base of the column I was sitting on was Ishtar. I climbed down. She looked beautiful and, unlike the last time I had seen her, she was dressed. She was wearing a purple linen gown lined in scarlet. Around her neck was a strand of pearls. She was wearing gold sandals just like an Egyptian princess would have worn. She offered me a goblet of date wine. She held her goblet over to mine and touched my cup and said, "Cheers."

I said, "You look very nice. I guess being Seth's whore has not been too bad, huh?" She looked at me and held out her cup of wine and poured it on the ground.

I said, "Why did you send me that snake? You knew it would not hurt me."

She said, "Horus, it was not my idea. It was your brother's. He is here and wants to see you."

I grabbed her and spun her around and put my knife to her

throat. I then heard a voice say "That won't be necessary, Horus." Well, I have been saying I wanted to see my brother and now I'm going to get my opportunity.

Seth walked up to me from out of the shadows of two obelisks. I let Ishtar go. He held out his hand to me and I shook it—forearm to forearm. He and I looked at each other in the moonlight. He said, "Horus, I'm not here to kill you."

I said, "That's good. I guess I'm not here to kill you either." We walked around Petra. It was not exactly like the old days. We used to walk sometimes arm in arm. I guess times change. I kept thinking about the slave kids as we strolled around Petra. He said, "Horus, my brother, let's get a new start. Okay?"

I said, "That depends on what you mean." We sat down on a ledge overlooking the valley. I looked at Ishtar standing about 20 feet from us. The wind was blowing her gown, and it was now clinging to her. I kept staring at her. Seth patted me on my back and said, "Why don't you screw her?"

I smiled at Seth and said, "I've got to be honest with you. I was thinking about it."

Seth then said to me, "I want you to think about what I am about to say. We can do anything we want. Who will stop us? Horus, are you really interested in helping out the West? You were, are now, and always will be an Egyptian, just like me." Seth put his hand on my shoulder and said, "Do you still believe in the divine order of the universe?"

I said, "Yes!" Seth asked me to recite it for him just the way our mother had taught us.

I did: "As the face of Amun moved across the pitch black waters of time he saw a small glitter of light from below the surface of the water. He thought for a moment and said, 'Bring forth the light.' The light had been kept prisoner at the bottom of the abyss. His command brought forth a colossal explosion in the water causing the light to come to the surface and the waters

of darkness to recede to the depth, where they are to this very day. He then ordered the stars and the planets to take their places in the sky. Lastly, Amun brought forth dry land on the earth—a large expanse of land pushed its way up through the water."

Seth interrupted me and said, "When the Eternal first put his foot on his dry land, what land was it, Horus?"

I said, "The holy soil of Egypt."

Seth said, "That is correct."

"He said it was his holy ground—though kingdoms would come and go over the earth—Egypt would last forever," I said. "But Seth, that does not make me a follower of Islam now does it? You and I bow down only to Amun, do we not?"

"Horus, I'm not a follower of Islam either. I am just using them for my own needs. Horus, I really want you with me. You and I, Horus, come a lot closer to the people here in the east than in the west. What could you possibly like about the West? The place is overrun with hypocritical assholes who have a superiority complex—maybe it's time to take them down a peg. We have shear numbers on our side."

I said, "I guess that's so—but they have nukes on their side."

"So what! The humans are no more than cattle to be slaughtered. Those fools don't control this planet. We do. The demons of the night control it. The people of the dark control it. The humans only think they control it." Seth spoke the truth.

I said, "Amun ultimately controls it." Seth said, "Right now he doesn't appear too interested in it now does he?"

Dear Diary, I must say, I felt at ease talking to Seth. Seth said, "Are you hungry, my brother?"

I said, "I could eat."

He said, "I have ordered up some cakes with dates like our mother used to fix, and I guarantee they will not taste like dust

in your mouth." Ishtar had set a table complete with a silk table-cloth and gold plates and gold flatware. The food was delicious—even Seth's favorite, the lettuce salad. As we ate, one of Seth's henchmen from Pakistan came over to the table. He was Abu Farat Al Libbi, a real bad ass. Abu held out his hand to me. Seth went into a rage and said, "Bow down to my brother just like you do to me." Abu got down on his knees and bent over to where his head was touching the ground. I put my foot on the back of his neck. I did not like doing that to him—even though he was an assassin. Seth told him to get up and to get out. Abu asked me for forgiveness and kissed my hand and left with his head bowed.

Seth looked at me and said, while pointing a finger at me, "Fear, fear is the glue that holds my army together. Did you notice, Horus, how frightened of me he was? I will eventually allow him to be captured by the West, and he will feed them false information that they will believe. He is part of my chain of command—a chain of fear and deception."

I said, "Well, Seth, I don't fear you."

He replied, "Of course not. You are my brother!"

I said, "True enough, and I am also your equal." As I sat there holding my cup of wine, I thought, "If fear is Seth's ally, then truly ignorance and naivete of the masses is its counterpart for the leader of the West."

Seth took a drink of wine and held out his cup for Ishtar to fill it again and said, "Horus, you always did have an Achilles heel. You have always cared too much for these humans, where-as I don't. I guess you cared more for just about everyone except me."

I did not want to get into a discussion on his imprisonment again so I said, "Seth, I have always just done the bidding of Amun."

He felt of my shirt and said, "You are not wearing the

amulet of the heart because you gave it to Geraldine. Was that doing the bidding of Amun?"

"No," I said.

"Horus, my brother, she tried to find a way to make a bargain with me before she did with you. She would just have soon seen me cut your throat and the throats of the friends next door to you if it would have helped her cause."

"Well, Seth, I guess she was just desperate. She is happy now, though."

"Yes, she is and you are minus a form of protection."

In a somber tone I told him, "It was a form of protection— only against you, so I don't need it now do I?"

"Horus, Mom never gave me an amulet as a loving gift." Staring into my eyes, Seth continued, "The only thing I ever got from her was syphilis!"

I knew Seth was just trying to aggravate me. So I said, "That's too bad."

"Horus, I'm only joking. I never did lie with our mother. Although, Horus, you and I were probably the only ones who didn't screw her."

I said to my brother, "Seth, while we are on the subject of the good old days, I thought about it a lot before I decided to come here. I did not want to wind up in a casket floating down the Nile for all of the world to see!"

Seth stood up and walked around in a circle and said, while making a gesture with both of his hands, "Why would you bring that up?"

I said, "Because you killed Osiris, the first true king of Egypt, because you wanted to screw Ast (Isis), his wife. Remember how you threw a lavish party for him? You invited him into your home with hands open, and then you betrayed him. Put in a box was he, and the lid was sealed shut. He beat on that lid until his air supply ran out. Seth, did you ever see the

inside of the lid once it was reopened by Isis? There were fingernail marks all over it. He deserved better, did he not? Seth, you left it to me to explain to Isis why you killed her husband. I stood up for you because you are my brother. Isis, though, lived out her life and never forgave me either."

Seth said, "That is not the way it happened. I invited him to my banquet and he wanted to possess one of the women who was mine. I refused to give her to him and he took offense and attacked me!"

"You lie, Seth," I said, "but let's forget it. Why relive the past?"

"Horus, you are right, as usual. Let's forget it. They really should have thanked me, though, because I made them gods of Egypt."

"Yes, you did, Seth, and Amun didn't like that and maybe he still doesn't."

All of a sudden coming over the top of the mountain was a Jordanian military helicopter. It came down, kicking up a lot of dust, and landed about 50 feet from us. "Horus, I don't travel the way we used to in times past. I've got to leave for a while, but I will be back. Ishtar will keep you company while I'm gone. Got a little business to take care of. If you were with me in mind and spirit, I would invite you to go along."

I said, "Well, I'll stay for a while and see you then when you return." As he got into the helicopter, the pilot saluted him.

Ishtar came over and said, "Just you and me now. I knew you had nothing to fear. Seth does love you."

I said, "How the hell would you know?" She replied, "Because of the way he speaks about you."

"Well, he spoke well of me in the past, too, and I didn't trust him then."

"But you, Horus, were the one who imprisoned him, not the other way around. So he was the offended party, not you.

You know, Horus, he and I have something in common. We both were imprisoned unjustly."

I said, "Ishtar, how did you wind up in the catacombs of Ur?"

She said, "It was King Nebuchadnezzar who did it. I had lain with him nightly since the day the crown was bestowed on him. He held in his arms that which other men only dreamed of. Still he was not satisfied. Even though I performed every filthy act known to heaven, his lust just grew greater."

Ishtar sat at the table that Seth and I had sat at running her hand over the rim of a golden goblet, talking in a manner just like some 20th Century secretary would about her breakup. It was actually amusing. She continued, "Here I was the aborted fetus of Aphrodite, cast out of heaven and thrown down to earth and forced to make my own way, which I did. My beauty was and still is greater than any woman on earth—and this king with feet of clay abandoned me. Well, I made him suffer. I came to him in dreams at night with thoughts of that which will be and will soon come to fruition. In all of his kingdom there was no one who could interpret the dreams that I gave him, especially not that harlot that he chose over me. So I drove him mad—for a while. He then tricked me with the help of his exorcists, Chaldeans and diviners and Jewish prophets. He cast a statue of pure gold in my image and sat it in the forefront of the gate of Babylon, which he had renamed for me.

"He was able to use my own vanity as a weapon against me. He then took me by my hand and led me into the catacombs of Ur and told me that whichever of three paths I chose would lead me to everlasting joy. I went willingly, since I am an immortal, like you. As I walked forward alone, his priests sealed the door behind me. I never dreamed that I could become imprisoned with no way out. I became afraid and tried to go back, but I could not, and I saw the griffin being ridden by Shedim, the

demon (that you dispatched), coming toward me. I ran for the third path and found upon entering that they could not follow me. The demon could come in by itself. If I wanted to live I had to allow it to rape me once a year. From that union I would bear a demon child every year. Once I gave birth, Shedim would take my beautiful child to the opening in which you and I escaped and would give it to the demons of the desert. These would bury it in the sand. I gave birth 2700 times. I was safe, but I could not leave. I guess that is why I could sympathize with Seth. He had a routine he went through every day of his imprisonment, and so did I. I would go to the bank each day and look down on the garden of stone and I would wonder what was happening in the world above." With a smile on her face, she said, "Then you finally came along."

I said, "Why didn't you just let the griffin and demon chase you into your realm and bring the walls together and crush them?"

"I could not bring the walls closer together. I let you believe that I could." I stared at Ishtar in silence and then I took a drink of wine and chuckled.

I said, "So Ishtar, what happened when I left you?"

"Well, I did what you said. I went to Baghdad. I stole a dress out of a home on the outskirts of the city and the woman's husband chased me down the road and was going to beat me when Uday, the son of Saddam Hussein, drove up in his Lamborghini. He almost hit me with his car. Uday got out and walked over and opened the passenger door. He grabbed his passenger, a young girl about 14, by the arm and pulled her out of the car. He said, 'You're going to have to walk back to Baghdad.' She screamed at Uday and said, 'That is another five miles. Remember, you said you were going to show me your palace.' Uday said, 'Not today—change in plans.' The young girl walked away crying and cursing him. Uday told me to get into

his car. The woman's husband recognized Uday and begged him for forgiveness. Uday just brushed him aside.

"We drove down the road to Baghdad. Until then I had no idea that the world now had machines that could travel that fast. Uday kept looking over at me. He turned off of the road and stopped the car. He reached over and put his hand on my thigh and slowly pulled up my dress. He saw that the dress was the only clothing that I had on. I thought he wanted to make love right there. I was wrong. He said, 'We've got to get you something better to wear.' We drove into Baghdad and he parked the car on the sidewalk outside of a chic western store. We went inside. The store was very busy, but Uday told everyone to get out. They all left except the store's employees. Uday and I walked around the store looking at clothing. He would pick up a dress and hold it up to me. If he liked it he threw it to one of the store clerks and would say 'Wrap it up.' If he didn't like it, he would drop it on the floor. Soon there was clothing littering the whole floor. He was very nice. At that point I didn't know who he really was. I thought he was just a rich Iraqi.

"When we left the store with several dresses and matching shoes we went to a nearby jewelry store. Once again Uday just walked around picking up any piece of jewelry he liked. He never paid for anything. This time though, the shop keeper did not recognize him and called the police. Two policemen showed up and took one look at Uday and told the shopkeeper that he should feel honored that Uday would come into his store. Before they left, they told the shopkeeper that if he wanted to he could file charges against Uday, but they definitely would not recommend it. After taking several diamond and pearl necklaces, with matching earrings and an absolutely stunning diamond bracelet, we left. He took me to a very exclusive women's spa. He gave the attendant one of the dresses and some of the jewelry and told her to clean me up to look like a princess. The spa was a won-

derful experience. After about two hours I came out and walked up to him. I knew from his look that he now belonged to me body and soul. He was such a kind and compassionate gentlemen.

"We then went to a very nice restaurant in a very rich section of Baghdad. The restaurant overlooked the Tigris River. I thought to myself, at last I'm back among the living. After a waiter took our order (Uday ordered for me), Uday accused the waiter of staring at me. The waiter assured Uday that he was not looking at me. Uday did not believe him and became enraged. He picked up a fork and stabbed the waiter in the eye and kicked him. The people sitting at the tables around us all ran for the exits. Uday then calmed back down and smiled at me and took hold of my hand as if nothing had happened. The waiter staggered off with his hand covering up his bloody eye. The meal of mutton and champagne was delicious. He told me that his father, Saddam, was having a party that night for some very important people. He told me he would show me off as the most beautiful jewel in Iraq.

"Baghdad is a beautiful and modern city. Saddam's palace was of opulent splendor that the kings of Persia could never have imagined. There were very influential people from all over the world. A beautiful ice carving in the shape of a map of the Middle East was on the center table. At the party I was having a drink and talking to a couple from the United States (the woman bragged to me that her husband was head of a Fortune 100 company) when everyone quit talking. The room fell silent. I turned and looked and saw Seth enter the ballroom.

"He did not notice me at first. He went around shaking hands and enjoyed a laugh with Saddam. He finally saw me. Our eyes met, and he instantly knew who I was. Seth came over to me and picked up a drink and said, holding the glass high in the air, 'I drink to my new queen.' At that moment I still had not

said a word to him. Uday just looked down at the floor and said nothing. I knew he was in fear of Seth though. Seth invited me to sit at his table. There was much scurrying by the wait staff rearranging the table settings. Seth and I did not talk that much at dinner. He spent most of his time discussing business with Kojo Annan of the United Nations. Finally, he looked at me and said, 'Let's go.' As Seth and I left, I said thank you, to a down-trodden looking Uday, who was now standing next to his wife. He just said, 'Goodbye.' I whispered to Seth that I wanted to get the rest of my clothes out of Uday's car. Seth said, 'Leave your clothes there. I will get you clothing befitting a queen.' Seth and I made love that night in Hussein's palace. Seth asked about you Horus. I told him the truth—that I had tried to seduce you by the garden of stone, but that you refused me. Do you know what Seth said when I told him that Horus? He said, 'Then my broth-er is a fool.' Are you still a fool, Horus? No one will bother us here, and Seth won't be back for several more hours."

I said, "Ishtar, I guess I'm still a fool. So you moved in with Seth. I guess you're planning on being the queen of the Earth. I just hope you don't develop Seth's personality. I know you have seen what he can do when he gets pissed."

Ishtar said, "I will be careful, but tell me Horus, did you really think that I would not recognize my own offspring! As soon as I saw Eleleth I knew he was mine."

"So, Ishtar, did you betray him to Seth?"

"No, I didn't. He is still safe in the mountains of Hindu-Kush."

"Good," I said. "I'm glad Seth did not destroy him. When the opportunity presents itself, tell Eleleth that I don't require his services any more. Now he is free to travel to and fro, wherever he likes—but that he must leave the base camp soon."

Ishtar assured me that she would tell him. I said, "Ishtar, what work does Seth have for you to do now, assuming it is not

confidential?"

Ishtar said, "I will be going to seduce the head of state in the West and discover his secrets."

Dear Diary, Seth returned in time for dinner. We once more had a delicious catered meal. The Jordanian army made sure no one disturbed our privacy. Seth looked at me, glanced at Ishtar, and said, "I really need to know if you will be with me."

I said, "I've got to think it over."

He said, "Don't take too long." He leaned back in his chair and reached over and took out a small vial from his pocket. He pitched it to me and said, "What do you think this is?"

I said, "I have no idea, Seth. Why don't you tell me?" "Okay," he said. "One thing that amazes me, Horus, is that I'm the one who was locked up for 3200 years, and yet I've gone with the philosophy of the 20th Century. Unfortunately, Horus, you are the one who is out of time. You don't fit in this century. Look what you did the other day when we first met again. You instinctively pulled out your stone knife. Horus, stone knives have gone out of date."

I said, "Maybe so, but this stone knife can kill you."

Seth looked at Ishtar and said, "See, I told you I could get under his skin."

I said, "If I don't choose to join up, what are you going to do?"

Seth said, "Well, you would be wise to stay on the sidelines and be only a spectator." He then said, "Oh, we got sidetracked with all this bickering. Take a look at that vial in your hand."

I held it up and looked at it. I said, "So what is it? It looks like water."

"Well, Horus, I would not recommend drinking it. Well, I guess you could drink it, my brother, but the average human would not last too long. Their organs would turn to jelly. It is a keepsake from the XVth Dynasty. Remember when the Asiatic

invaders came to the two lands and conquered all of the sacred soil? Remember what drove them out?"

I said, "Well, I remember your joining them."

Seth said, "That is true, but what destroyed them was the plague of Amun—a plague straight out of the swamps of the Rift Valley of Ethiopia and carried by the wings of death. The plague eventually killed all of the invaders."

I said, "Yes, it did, Seth, but it took 110 years."

"I'm in no hurry, my brother. The true people of the East are immune to the disease. It is another story for the people of the West. They won't know what is happening to them. It does not kill right away. The people suffer, and as they suffer they have to be cared for. The West will bleed money. Their scientists will only know that something is killing the people, but they won't know what."

"Seth, maybe you are the one who is living in the past. Most diseases now can be beaten."

He said, "Well, we will see."

I said, "How did you get hold of it?"

"I sent a messenger to get it for me."

I said, "Let's discuss your messenger. I don't like being watched by beings you and I always considered mortal enemies. So call off your dogs or I will start killing them for you. Oh! And while we are on the subject, I was not all that impressed with your army of Christian zealots that you have sent to the West. By the way, how is your slave factory doing these days in the Sudan?"

"Well, I had to rebuild, thanks to you, Horus."

I said, "While we are being so honest with each other, did you think I bought your lie about being set free by three children? There is only one man in the Egyptian government who could have understood that you were entombed and who could have freed you. What did you offer him, Seth?"

He said, "I promised him that I would make him the first true king of Egypt in 2300 years and of the 31st Dynasty."

"I'm impressed! Well, Seth, what did you propose to give to the kings of Saudi Arabia and Jordan to help you with your worldly plans?"

In a cryptic tone, he replied, "I told them that I would allow them to live."

"Tell me, Seth, what will you do if Amun decides to intervene?"

"He won't. Amun would be going against his own word."

"Seth, if you succeed and become the ruler of the world, what will you do when the end finally comes? Your rule will end then."

"Horus, I will try to make a bargain with Amun—or maybe I will escape from this place through the door of Khufu's pyramid."

I said, "The West is working on that problem at Khufu's pyramid right now."

Seth said, "No they are looking at it and that is all they are ever going to do. But that is in the future, Horus. What will you do now?"

I said, "I have some things to do and I need some time to think. I will let you know on the 26th day of August. Maybe we will be brothers forever."

He interrupted me and said, "Or maybe it will be the war of the gods of upper and lower Egypt, because, after all, that day is appropriate."

Ishtar reached over under the table and put her hand on my leg and said, "We know you will reach the right decision."

Seth said, "Join me now, brother, and maybe I can help you with your problem of the young Jewish boy who is facing death."

I said, "Well, he is my problem."

Seth said, "I will be leaving again for my base camp, so I

guess this will be goodbye for awhile." I thought Seth said that in a way where there was regret in his voice.

I said, "Well, Seth, I'm really glad to see you. The three of us are all that remains of the old times; it would be a shame if we become enemies. Seth and I embraced. Ishtar hugged and kissed me on the lips, and stuck her tongue in my mouth in the process. Seth and Ishtar walked over to the Jordanian military copter. I yelled at Seth and said, "Maybe I'll take over the job as the hidden Imam."

He shouted back at me over the sound of the helicopter's engines, "Sorry, the job has already been filled. Remember, my brother, the blood of the East and our mother flow through our veins. Remember what our mother used to drum into our heads. She would say, 'Always remember your roots, my sons.'"

They boarded the helicopter and it lifted off. The Jordanian troops left, and soon I was all alone. They had not bothered to take the table and chairs with them. I sat back down and finished my goblet of date wine. I just sat there thinking, and picking up red grapes and crunching them in my mouth. I have found that I think very clearly when I eat grapes or pomegranates. At least our meeting did not end in bloodshed.

There is a secret that I have always withheld from Seth. It is my secret weapon that I have used only once. The day my mother gave birth to Seth she had the foresight to know that someday he might turn on me. She looked deeply into my eyes and said, "Seth is the name that the world will know your brother by. His name will strike fear into the hearts of humans living now and in the distant future. Seth is only his earthly name, my son. It is not his real name. I will tell you, Horus, his real name—remember it always."

I said, "Why does he have a secret name, Mother?"

She said, "We all have a secret name. We each have a secret name, my son, so that no one can put a true curse on us. They

only think they know our real name." I have never forgotten Seth's real name. This practice became the norm for everyone in Egypt for centuries.

When Seth got older—I think he was about 12—I decided to try out the curse. I sat by a fire one night and listened to the Nile as it made its way to the sea. I went to the Nile and filled a pot with water and went back to my campfire. I heated the water over the fire until it was boiling. I then made a small figure of a man out of some firewood and uttered Seth's secret name over it. I put the wood figure half way down into the pot. I left it there and hurried back to our home where I knew Seth was sleeping. I could hear him screaming long before I got to our hut. I found him doubled over holding his gut. Our mother was bent over him trying to find out what was the matter with him. I came in and innocently said, "Is Seth sick, Mother?"

She stood up and slapped me. She said, "What have you done?" Seth was in such agony he was unaware of our conversation. He just kept rolling all over the floor screaming. Our mother shook me and said, "I know what you have done! Did you think for one minute you could deceive me?" She ran out of our hut and ran off into the night. After awhile Seth quit yelling. I thought for a minute maybe he was dead. I looked and he was lying on a bed mat sleeping. Our mother came through the bushes and came up to me and threw my stick man at me. She said, "Do that ever again while I live and you, Horus, will suffer. Remember, I know your secret name. I gave it to you! I will put a curse on you that will last forever if you ever cross me again." She never did, though, even when she died. Since that day I have never cursed Seth again.

After a while a young couple from England walked over to me and said, "Is it okay for us to look around now? It is not off limits any more is it?"

I said, "No, it's not. Look around all you want. In fact, you

can have the place." I held up my goblet of wine and said, "Take the wine, too. It is a present from the people of Petra."

He said, haltingly, "Thanks." I said nothing back. The conversation was over. They walked around taking pictures and ignoring me.

I went back to Ethiopia to the church of Mary of Zion. I found that I had been wasting my time. I knew my trip had been futile when I saw that the place was no longer being guarded. The ark had been moved. Assuming that touching the ark really would have brought instant death, then it must have been moved the same way it had been brought here. Two wooden rods made from an acacia tree were inserted into the slots on each side of the ark. Then it could be safely picked up and transported. My problem was—transported where? I read the minds of everyone there. No one knew where the ark and the old priest had gone. I believed the priest was probably dead, and if I went looking for the ark, it might take months or years to find it. By then Joshua would have already been long dead. I kicked myself for not taking it in the first place when I had the chance.

Chapter XXX

I got home on a cold winter's day. The Christmas season was now long under way. Thelma, staying true to her Jewish faith, had prepared her home for Hanukkah. I thought there were only eight days of life left for Joshua—whatever I do, I better do in a hurry.

I decided to go back to the museum and get my third stone knife. The place was closed for the day and was deathly quiet,

save for the over-head heating system that would run every now and then. I walked up the escalator the hard way to the third floor—because it had been shut down for the night. I kept thinking I might run into a night security guard, but it seemed there were none around. The museum had done a good job of trying to make the place appear like an Egyptian tomb. They had the *Book of the Dead* written on the ceiling, and in the antechamber they had black silhouettes against a white background of Egyptians in various stages of work and everyday life.

I went over to the case to retrieve my long lost property. I didn't open the case because my knife was gone. I just stood there for a minute and looked around. As I did, my gaze froze looking at the white walls. The silhouettes were gone. They were now in ranks on the floor as an army. They were coming after me! I can take on the people of the dark in small numbers, but this was something else. There were thousands of them. I don't know if they were sent by the king of the dark, or maybe they were a rebel band sent by Seth. I did not want to stay to find out. This was a trap that I had never imagined I would fall into. I ran and jumped over the railing down to the second floor. They were everywhere. I pulled my stone knife and slashed my way through perhaps twenty of them or so. Death from my stone knife made them fade away to nothing. I wasn't so worried that I would not be able to hold my own against them. I was worried because I knew one of them had that stone knife—and that knife, which I had made and consecrated, could kill me.

I kept telling myself: "I must think clearly. I can get out of this situation." I made a stand in the doorway of a small closet. As they came at me I would mow them down. Soon they began to lose their nerve. I closed the door to the closet and let them think I would stay in there. I thought to myself: "This is a real mess." My fortress contained cleaning supplies, a mop, and a vacuum cleaner—not much use against an army from another

world. I turned and walked through the back wall of the closet. As I emerged from the wall, I felt a sharp pain in my left arm. The one person of the dark, the one with a knife, had obviously been expecting me. My arm was now bleeding from a gash about four inches long. I was soon surrounded by about forty dark people—only they did not try to attack me. They watched while my adversary with the knife came at me.

The advantage was now mine. I've had a lot more experience fighting with a knife than he had. He lunged at me, confident of victory, thanks to the wound he had already inflicted on me. I threw him to the floor and quickly drew back my knife to finish him off. This time his friends did not watch; they all piled on top of me. It was like trying to fight through a wall of molasses. I thought I was done for. But then a security guard turned on the second floor's main lights. The people on top of me scattered. Now the only one left was the one I was holding down. I didn't kill him. I put my knife away and tore off his hand, holding my other knife. Tearing the flesh off the people of the dark is about the same as pulling apart a chicken wing. I let him go and he went scurrying for the darkness, leaving a trail of grey blood. I picked up my other stone knife and beat a hasty retreat from the museum.

I went home and hunted high and low for a needle and thread. Since I was cut by one of the sacred stone knives, the wound would not instantly heal. This would take a while, just like it would for humans. That little gray son of a bitch had cut me clean down to the bone on my arm. I couldn't find any needle and thread, so I went to one of those all-night drug stores. I wrapped my arm up to stop the bleeding. I got the supplies I needed and went out back of the drug store and sat on their trash dumpster and sewed up my arm. When I was just about done, a police car came down the alley and a policeman asked me what I was doing. He took one look at my arm with the

blood-soaked bandage on it and offered to take me to a hospital. I thanked him and lied and said I had a ride already on the way.

Once home I washed off my arm again and rebandaged it and, as I got ready to go to bed, caught a glimpse out of the corner of my eye. Standing in my living room was the dark man whom I had spared in the basement of the schoolbook supply building. He once more held out his hands in submission to me. I said, "I know the ambush was not your doing. You don't have the courage for it. So what brings you here?"

He told me that there was a split among the people of the dark. The ones who attacked me were a rebel group that wanted revenge for their people that I had killed. I said, "That's interesting, but I think they are a little late on the revenge factor. I have been killing your people for better than 200 centuries."

He said, "Yes, but the king of our people has kept everyone in check for fear of an all-out war. They believed they had a chance when they realized that the stone knife in the museum was the one that could kill immortals."

I said, "With the split in your people, what is the other group doing?"

He said, "It is three groups." He told me his group, the smallest of the three, just tried to live in peace, taking only enough light particles to survive on.

I said, "What about the last group?"

He told me the king of the dark had made a pact with my brother and they were keeping in their own universe thousands of their people in a large pen and letting them slowly starve.

I said, "What is that going to prove?" He told me that on Seth's command they will be released into this world and they will destroy one third of the human race. The humans will disappear all in one night, just like I had seen them do before in Italy. He told me that the rest of the king's people are doing

Seth's bidding, which I knew already. The sun was starting to come up, so I told him he could leave in peace. I said before he left that I would leave his clan alone, but that I wanted a report once a month on what his rebel people were doing. He agreed. I could not sleep with my arm hurting, so I sat up in my living room considering if there was something that I had not tried to save Joshua from certain death.

I turned on the television and watched a Christian musical. The people were very good singers. I waved my arm back and forth because my arm throbbed with pain. The t.v. had a close-up of one of the singers. As she sang a tear ran down her cheek. She was a godly woman. She truly believed the words she was singing. Her tears and Thelma, Sara and Joshua had made up my mind. Seth will have an enemy in me if he does not want to listen to reason. I sat in my living room chair and thought: "Today is the 23rd of December—only eight days left. I will play my last card. I'll persuade Thelma to let me take Joshua to Abu Simbel and lay him on the feet of the statue of Amun and ask for his divine help." Egyptians used to do that. It was believed that if one's faith was strong enough then Amun would intervene and save the one facing death. I have faith in Amun. I truly know he can do anything.

The musical performance went off, so I lay down on the couch. I lay on my back and held my hands up to my face. They blotted out the ceiling light. I looked at them and said to myself: "How many humans have these hands killed for Amun—a lot. The youngest was 14 and the oldest was 87. I can understand the 14-year-old, but Amun should have let the old 87-year-old woman die of old age. She could not possibly have had that many years left. She was, though, the most heartless individual that I have ever met. When was that? Maybe it was in 476 A.D. in a village somewhere in Germany."

I went to sleep, and I dreamed that I went back to the ceme-

tery to put some fresh flowers on Geraldine's casket. I went into the tomb and found her casket was open and empty. The lid was on the floor. I looked and saw that Sophia's coffin was open, too—and also empty. I heard a creaking noise and saw the lid on Emilio's casket was being raised up. Emilio sat up and then climbed out. He stamped his feet on the floor, looked around and walked past me. I thought: "He looks the same as he did when we first met in 1934."

He turned around and said, to me, "Those who were never born are the lucky ones, for they are blameless and blessed. The ones who walk the earth now are cursed. The cancer that has fallen on Zion will spread across the face of the earth. All will be begging for a quart of wheat for a day's wages. No one will be spared, for all will have fallen short of the glory of God." I stood there speechless and watched him tear down the iron gates of their tomb and walk away.

I saw that the sky was becoming black as night, so I ran back home. A hard, cold wind began to blow, making the trees bow to its will. The front door to Thelma's home was open and kept slamming against the wall. I went inside and saw Joshua's empty rock-a-bye chair swinging to and fro. It made a clicking sound with each backward motion of the chair. It began to go even faster, as if being pushed by an invisible hand. I watched in amazement until first the chain on the left side of the chair came loose and started being dragged on the floor. As the chair moved back and forth, the other side of the chair's chain broke, and the chair fell to the floor. The wind came through the door and sent a floor lamp crashing against the wall.

I went into Joshua's room. It was empty. The glass in the frame that contained the plaque that Thelma had made was broken. I picked up the frame, and I got cut by the glass. I looked at my hand and saw blood oozing from the palm of my hand. I was not immortal anymore. I wiped the blood off on Joshua's

blanket and thought I heard a noise in Sara's bedroom, so I went to see. I saw the window in her bedroom was wide open and the wind had blown over the bamboo plant. The vase the plant was in was broken. I reached down to pick it up and turned my head and saw Sara. She was on her knees with a paint brush and a clay pot full of blood. She was painting the cartouche of Amun on the walls. They were everywhere—hundreds of them. She held out the brush to me. The blood on the brush dripped onto the floor. She said, "If you want to help me, I will need more blood. Can you get me some more?"

I saw that one wall did not have any cartouches on it, so I ran through that wall to my freedom. I found myself in a grove of trees. They were crying to God for mercy. They said, "You created us first to be the greatest on the earth. You then caused some of us to be cut down and used for vile purposes, and you blame us! Are we to be destroyed now for crimes that we did not commit?" A large willow tree took hold of me with its branches and begged me to help them. I worked my way free and ran from the forest.

I walked down a street and turned the corner to see a crowd of people cheering at something. I pushed my way to the front of the crowd to find that it was a parade. It was a parade in four sections. Leading the first section was a skeleton wearing the uniform of an army general. He was weighed down with medals and was astride a sickly looking white horse. Behind him marched a unit of young infantry men. They were all marching in step, with their weapons of death slung over their shoulders. The front row held high the guide-ons. Each guide-on carried a pennant of a particular victory, with the number written on it of the casualties and dead who had paid the price for the victory. One fourth of the people watching the parade ran out to march with the soldiers. They were all old men and women who, when they were young, recoiled with fear with the thought of going to

war, but now with old age and the knowledge that the sounds of the guns were far, far away had seen their bravado increase tenfold. As they marched away, the second rider and pale horse came into view.

This skeleton wore only a red brassierre and red panties. The horse had a garland of flowers around its neck. There was a float being pulled by the horse. On the float were people of all ages performing every vile act known to man. A naked whore quit performing oral sex on another woman just long enough to ask the crowd to join them. One fourth of the people watching the parade ran out into the street—eager to join them on the float. They cheered as they watched a pregnant woman aborted and then took turns raping her. Quickly tiring of her, they looked around for someone else who could satisfy their carnal lust. They studied the crowd on the sidewalks and begged them to join them. Once in a while they would get a taker. A young man ran out to join them and was instantly caught up and devoured by their lust. Their sexual god was so all encompassing that when they could not get anyone else to join them, they saw a stray dog and started whistling and saying, "Here, boy; here boy." Soon their float, too, was out of sight.

Next came the third horseman. He wore a tunic of silver with a purple border on it. On his head was a wreath of gold. His horse was covered with a red silk blanket. He had a bridle made of pure silver. A breeze blew his tunic, exposing his legs. Though he and his horse were richly adorned, you could see for a brief moment that only rotting flesh was underneath his royal clothing. He was leading a band of people who were convinced he was the true god of the universe. They ran over to the crowd asking them to join them and worship their god. He spoke lies to the people, and they believed it as the truth. Again, one fourth of the spectators ran to join him. They danced with joy in the street and chanted, "We have found God." He commanded that

his followers should find a human sacrifice from among them and present the dead body to him as an offering of faith. His followers fell upon a young woman and beat her to death. He held his hands up in the air and said, "I am thy God—go and bring me all the gold and silver that you can and then I will love you." They ran into the crowd begging for money and saying they would do anything for gold and silver that they could take back to their king.

Lastly, I saw the fourth rider. He was a plain man, wearing the clothes of a beggar. He was barefoot. His feet were bloody because he was walking the horse, rather than riding it. He held the bridle in his hand. His horse was a plain plow horse that you could find working the fields in poor countries today. He offered charity and kindness to all. His followers, too, worked the crowd, offering glad tidings to all. To the hungry he offered bread, to the down-hearted he offered hope, and to the poor, charity, and to the despised, love. He stopped his portion of the parade and reached down and gently picked up the aborted fetus that had been thrown out of the float of sexual perverts. It was not dead, so he wrapped it up with a piece of his own garment and gave it to his followers to care for. He saw me and walked over to me and held out his hand. I shook it. He said, "Don't you remember me, Horus?"

I said, "I'm sorry, but I've never met you until this very moment."

He smiled a big grin and said, "I'm Joshua."

I said, "No, you're not. Joshua died as a baby of Tay-Sachs disease."

He said, "Well, I'm here now aren't I?" Before I could reply, he said, "I'll prove it to you that I'm Joshua. Remember how you would wind up my rock-a-bye swing, and I would squeal with delight."

I said, "That proves nothing. All babies do that."

Again he spoke and said, "My grandmother asked you if you would watch me for her, and she left a bottle of milk for you to feed me. You kept pulling it out of my mouth so you could watch me get mad over and over."

I said, "Okay, congratulations on being alive. What do you want?" Joshua said, "I want you to join us."

I said, "I don't think so. Besides, it looks to me like you are getting all the takers you want. Look at the people flocking to your cause."

He said, "But I want you, too." He put his hand on my arm and said, "Please, Horus."

I pulled away, and as I turned my back on him, I said, "Joshua, you have your fate and I have mine; we can't change it. May God be with you always."

He replied, "And may God be with you, Horus."

I woke up hearing what sounded like a music box. It was playing "Be Our Guest" from *Beauty and the Beast*. I felt a hand on my arm and thought I still might be dreaming. I opened my eyes and looked right into the eyes of Sara. She rubbed my bandaged arm and said, "Horus, you have a really big owie. Did that bad snake bite you?"

"No," I said.

She said, "I wanted to show you my birthday present. See, you wind it up and the people dance around to the music!"

I said, "Did your grandma give it to you early?"

Sara said, "No."

I replied, "I thought your birthday was December 31—New Year's Eve."

She said, "It is, silly."

I was now awake. I said, "Sara, what is today?"

She said, "My birthday. Well, I have to go, Horus. I'm going to my friend's house." She yelled, "Happy New Year!"

I said, "Same to you, honey."

I felt of my arm and thought: "That wound in my arm has knocked me out for better than a week. I've run out of time for Joshua." I sat on the couch thinking and realized there was nothing I could do.

Dear Diary, this will be my last entry. I'm running out of pages. It is now 11:32 p.m. on December 31, 1999. It has been a very long year. I have done almost everything I can for young Joshua. Nothing has worked. Thelma is sound asleep, thanks to a sleeping pill. Sara is sleeping over at a friend's house. It is pretty cold outside. The new year of a new millennium is making its way across the earth. Thelma has no idea that when she awakes on the morrow that she will find Joshua in an eternal sleep. I have let Sara down. I promised her that Joshua would live, and now in just a few minutes that won't be true. Sara will come home tomorrow prepared to help feed Joshua. She has become protective of her brother. She will be crushed over what she sees. She will never enjoy another birthday in her life. For her it will always be the day her brother died. She will hate me for letting her down. I think I will wrap him up in a warm blanket and he and I will sit out on the porch in the rocking chair. I went into his room. I looked at the plaque on the wall that I had dreamed about. It was made by Thelma for Joshua. It read:

> *Today was born the most*
> *beautiful little boy in all the world:*
> *My grandson, Joshua Alan Bloom*
> *One who is truly blessed by God*

The words touched my heart. I can only hope he was really blessed by God. I saw Joshua was awake, as if he knew the fate that awaited him. He had lost much of his vision, but he had learned to feel with his hands. What he wanted was his cloth duck that when squeezed made a quack sound, hence the name

"Mr. Quack" that Sara had named it. I picked him up and put the blanket around him. His soft baby skin smelled like a combination of baby lotion and sour milk. We went outside into the winter's night. There were already fireworks being set off prematurely. It is interesting how on the same block some people are excited and happy and at the same time just a few hundred feet away there is only sadness. I took a look at the stars, wishing beyond hope that Joshua's death mandate would no longer be there. It was.

I thought somewhere a half a world away Seth has greeted the new year with the renewed hatred for the West. His demon troops, Islamic zealots and the people of the dark were in closed ranks ready to do his bidding. Partygoers, oblivious to what the new millennium would bring, were counting down the minutes. On the television channels celebrations from all over the planet could be seen. Some of those cities would become battlegrounds. A large portion of London will be gone by 2018, and a form of plague (circa 2700 B.C., an ancient deadly disease that wiped out everyone in Sakara before lying dormant until resurrected by Seth) will have turned cities such as Brussels, Berlin and Paris into ghost towns by 2020.

I thought it had now been 26,000 years since Lillith had escaped from the doomed garden. Historians will ask what has the human race learned over all of those centuries? It does not matter any more what the human race has learned—although they did not learn much. What matters, as far as the human race is concerned, is what the Eternal has learned. Maybe he knew all along that the human race is not, and never will be, worthy of his compassion. It could be that he is planning on starting all over again with a new universe and a completely different race of humans—a race that has kindness and mercy inbred in them, and not the hypocrisy and injustice that now drives the human race.

I'm not the same anymore. A little boy's life has changed me. I will no longer do the Eternal's bidding. I used to believe in justice. I don't any more. I used to believe in mercy for the good people of the world. I know there isn't any now—maybe there never was any. Like the old Indian Shaman I met at the north rim of the Grand Canyon who told me that he had lived too long and had seen too much suffering and was now waiting to die, I too have lived too long. Soon, I will go back to Petra and send a message to Seth. I will say, "Can we have a thousand years of peace or will it have to be Gotterdammerung?"

First, though, I will hold Joshua on my lap until the end comes for him. I put his "Mr. Quack" in his hands. It made him happy. It is now 11:50—only eight minutes of life left for Joshua. If it would add a year to his life by my killing everybody on this block, I would gladly do it. The problem is it won't, though. I am now considering the unthinkable. I pulled out my stone knife and closed my left hand around the blade. I squeezed it tighter and tighter until I saw my blood begin to ooze between my fingers. I opened my hand and put my knife away. I can give Joshua immortality. Even the Eternal will withdraw death's embrace from Joshua if I put God's secret name on Joshua's forehead.

I lay Joshua down on my lap and dipped my finger in my blood. I looked up at the night sky and posed a question: "What are you going to do to me? Will you kill me? I'm as good as dead already. Will you make me suffer? Far better people have been made to suffer than me. What did Thelma and Sara do to deserve your wrath? Their ancient heritage claims that they are a part of your chosen people. If that is true, why did you abandon those who worshiped you as Amun? Were the Egyptians not loyal to you? They erected monuments to your glory when the world was still young. They would have loved you forever, but they were cast off to be replaced by the Jews?

"Being Jewish does not seem to be much of a benefit to Thelma, Sara, and Joshua now does it? He is to die tonight. Thelma and Sara will live with that hole in their hearts all of their lives. Both will still speak of Joshua in loving terms, but in past tense. Thelma will tell about the cute things he did in his short life. She will repeat these things over and over since there will be no way to add any new experiences. You let Abraham believe that his descendents would out-number the stars. I guess he was never told that his bloodline would be hated and persecuted forever and that no decade would ever pass without some of his offspring being slaughtered. You have been known to allow the wicked to live and prosper and the good and innocent to die. Is it justice to say you will take the good to your bosom after allowing them only a short life? What about those you take to your bosom that you allowed a long life? Did you love them more? Why create them in the first place only to let them have a fleeting life? You, the King of Mercy, should have reached down with your celestial hand and crushed Joshua while he was still in the womb of that coke-infested whore who would become his mother.

"When you did what you have always done since the time of Adam and took a piece of your own soul to be fashioned into the soul of a human—in this case little Joshua—did you have a second thought and want it back? Was it because you're losing too much of your own self to souls that are cast out to oblivion because they turned evil, never to return to you. When the angel who is your 'keeper of the souls' showed Joshua who his mother and father would be and when he would die, did he say, 'Why me?' When he was told that he would never be any older than an infant, and his grandmother and sister would be grieving over him, what was the reply from Joshua's soul? Did he say, 'Gee, thanks'? Maybe he said, and rightly so: 'What did I do to deserve this?'" I pointed toward the heavens and said, "You

keep death hanging over the heads of your creations. There is not a day that goes by without the fear of death crossing the minds of all who inhabit the earth. Is that because you considered that without death the human race would not need you? You would have been better off destroying your garden and its inhabitants rather than making them live in fear.

"Feeling guilty about this plague of finality that you poured out on the human race, you gave them a gift to soothe their souls: Music, the language of the gods. Perhaps you did not notice it but your first creations were your best work. Of course, they were soulless. You did not think they were worthy of everlasting life. Did you not say to your heavenly lackeys: 'We cannot mix the milk of the gazelle with the honey of the insect and the dung of the baboon to create a man greater than the angels in heaven, so we must try again.' Your heavenly hosts secretly hoped you would abandon the idea altogether. They were not too wild over the thought of being lower than Adam. So you yourself sowed the seeds of evil first in the minds of your archangels and then in the human race. You cast your first humans aside and created your garden as a buttress to keep the two races of humans apart. You then let the one race slowly destroy the other and did not care. The real evil, though, resided in the seed of Adam. He was your pride and joy. You were proud that in each of Adam's seed from generation to generation forevermore was a small part of your own soul. It was your present to your true creation. Otherwise they would be no better than the Neanderthals. Adam let you down. You must have known that was going to happen. After all, you are the King of the Universe aren't you? Maybe this little one on my lap, if given a chance, would be far greater than Adam, but the universe and its living beings will never know." My lamenting has probably sealed my fate.

I started to write God's holy and secret name on Joshua's

forehead, but I hesitated. Do I have the right to make Joshua endure a never-ending life? How happy would he be once he realized that everyone he loves would eventually die and he would continue to live? Would he thank me or curse me? I wiped off the blood on my index finger with my handkerchief. It was now too late. I looked at Joshua's now forever sleeping body. He had a look of contentment on his young and innocent face. I did not look at him anymore. Waves of grief overwhelmed me. I sat there holding his little corpse that just minutes before was a living, breathing baby. I saw several teenagers running around in the street. One came up on our lawn and yelled, "Happy New Year, Grandpa!"

Filled with despair, I leaned my head on the back of the rocking chair, closed my eyes, and rocked back and forth and began to think. Tears ran down my cheeks. Hate began to boil up inside of me. I started running different humans through my mind that I would enjoy killing. I had found through experience that there is nothing in this world that can placate despair as much as killing. No, I should not say killing—I should say slaughtering. I think I will start with Reverend Mel and his wife Eleanor. I'll meet them at their church. I will gut that pregnant bitch and leave their bloody demon fetus on the altar as an offering. On the right side of the altar I will nail up Mel's body, and on the other side Eleanor's. When Sunday rolls around and the true faithful show up in their Sunday clothes, they will be met by the smell of rotting flesh. I'll see to it on the morrow.

I'm still left with one grim task: What will I tell Sara when she comes home? She believed in me! Even if she begins to hate me, I will protect her against all evil—and at all costs. Hell, I don't think I'll kill anyone—not even Seth's demon Christians. I'm sick of death. Sara, too, is of the bloodline of Lillith. It could be that Sara was meant to be the one all along to play a role in the fate of the world. Maybe Seth is aware of Sara's bloodline.

However, he never mentioned it to me—probably because he does not know how I would react.

Dear Diary, maybe Seth thinks his bloodline died out with both of Lot's daughters. I know that there are no others of the bloodline left alive from Seth's union with Lot's other daughter. The bloodline had made it all the way to 620 A.D. to Muhammad's wife Khadija. They had two sons who both died young. Maybe they died from Tay Sachs. They also had four daughters. It was with the last daughter, Fatima, that the bloodline stopped altogether.

I looked up to see one last brilliant fireworks display. As the fireworks and smoke faded away, the stars once more showed through. I stared at the stars in amazement. I saw that Joshua's death mandate was erased from the night sky. In its place were seven stars in such close proximity to one another that they were now appearing as one star. I had seen this formation once before: Two thousand years ago over a small and insignificant town in Judea. The Eternal said he would send a Jewish Messiah as a thief in the night. I guess he just did.

I looked down at Joshua. He was looking at his duck. His blindness was gone. He looked up at me with a big toothless smile. I felt true joy in my heart. Thelma will now awake tomorrow to find a healthy Joshua standing up in his crib and rattling the bars. Thelma will rejoice and get down on her knees and thank God for his mercy.

I took Joshua and put him back in his crib. I put his blanket around him and kissed him on his head. The Eternal had commuted his death sentence at the last moment. Perhaps, though, Joshua's death sentence had never been in effect anyway. I looked again at Thelma's plaque to Joshua on his bedroom wall. Maybe Thelma's words were prophecy. I thought: Who am I to question the ways of the King of the Universe. Maybe God is not through with me just yet.

I thought about something else the old priest at the tomb of Adam and Eve told me. He said Seth would battle to the death against his own bloodline. I assumed that would be me. Maybe not, for in 2032 young Joshua will be 34 years old and he, too, is of our bloodline. Maybe God will forgive my deceit and my blaspheming, which was spoken not out of hatred, but despair. Then again perhaps I was already weighed in the balance and was found wanting. If so, when death for me comes, let the last thought of my life be: God is good; God is great!